*
* *
The
Wizard's
Child

By Helga Sandburg

THE WHEEL OF EARTH

MEASURE MY LOVE

THE OWL'S ROOST

SWEET MUSIC

THE UNICORNS

THE WIZARD'S CHILD

Children's Books

BLUEBERRY

JOEL AND THE WILD GOOSE

GINGERBREAD

BO AND THE OLD DONKEY

*
*
* *The*
Wizard's
Child

by

Helga Sandburg

*

The Dial Press

1967, New York

*
*

Design by Elliot Epstein

© 1967 by Helga Sandburg
All rights reserved
Library of Congress Catalog Card Number: 66-27394

MANUFACTURED IN THE UNITED STATES OF AMERICA

FIRST PRINTING

For
my husband,
BARNEY CRILE,
who gave me
gardens full
of animals
and
birds
*

Foreword

WHILE THE PERSONS in this book and places are largely fictitious, the animals and birds are real, ones that I have known and loved. I was brought up in a house where dogs and cats, baby goats, and a variety of pet birds lived also. It was an isolated countryside in Michigan, beside the lake, and my school companions were the children of farmers and small-town people. Later, in the pastoral country of Illinois, I lived among the farm folk, one of them. Now in mid-life, our barns and yards contain crows, turkey vultures, deer, a pony, a donkey, goats, and cows. In our house are doves and finches, squirrels and robins, blue jays, and thrashers. As I observe the difficulties and pleasures that beset the people upon this planet, I find myself turning to Job, chapter 12, verses 7 to 10: "But ask now the beasts, and they shall teach thee; and the fowls of the air, and they shall tell thee: or speak to the earth and it shall teach thee: and the fishes of the sea shall declare unto thee."

Helga Sandburg
Cleveland, Ohio

Contents

*And
all the people
then shouted and said,
"Great is Truth, and
mighty above
all things."*

—THE FIRST BOOK
OF ESDRAS

*

1
The
Mother-of-Pearl
Mirror

MARN SPOKE TO the mother fox as she pulled the jaws of the trap apart. The animal whined and panted slightly in the misting dawn air of the swamp; its dark, round eyes were fixed on the girl. "Now run," she told it, and it scampered off, its broken fore-leg close to its body, leaping from hummock to hummock, familiar with the territory. Last year Marn had found a fox earth with two cubs and an emaciated mother fox nursing them with a trap attached to her foot that she dragged about with her.

The baying of the sheep-killing dogs had roused Marn early that morning. It was her birthday and she was seventeen. Her parents had not wakened as she went out of the rude frame house that had been their home since the Wizard came here to the Old Mountain country in 1900, at the turn of the century, fifteen years ago, from heaven knows where. He'd brought his wife and baby and settled on the edge of what the farmers and mountain people called Endless Quagmire. In prehistoric days the swamp had been a great salt lick left by a receding ocean, and sometimes the great bones of ancient fauna, mastodon and mammoth, were found. The Old Mountain country was far in the west of North Carolina, Tennessee lying not far off.

It was warm for early September; Marn listened again for the barking of the pack of dogs. She pushed back her flaxen, fine hair, that her father said ought to be put up in a bun by her age. Marn's gray eyes were narrow because she was still angry about the frightened vixen she'd released. All she could hear was the wheeze and bray of Dutchman's little brown jack far over in the valley, across the road that led to Greenfield.

"I'm seventeen," she told herself, "and I wish Henry would ask me now to go to the church and marry him."

She had come out this far in the swamp to see if the wild dogs had got at any of her father's traps. Wizard Coombs got his living by selling the charms and medicines he made from the herbs he gathered out here, and from the animals and birds he trapped. He took the pelts from the foxes and muskrats and beaver over to Greenfield, where they bought them for women's coats and men's hats and gloves. Wizard carried braces of wild ducks there, too, and sold them for rich men's tables. And now and then in the winters he hauled over venison that he'd shot and dressed out, and the white-tail hides that he had a way of tanning into the finest buckskin. Wizard kept the babies of the animals and birds that he caught, and let his two women tame them, to sell at the Fair that came once a year. Marn's mother had the house full all the time with their cages and boxes. Cardinals and thrushes and mourning doves and finches, brown rabbits and raccoons, deer mice and flying squirrels were about. Some birds flew freely in the house, and certain animals too were loosed when they were tame enough. This time of year there were more than usual around because a whole wagonload was to go over to the Greenfield Fair in less than four weeks' time.

Sometimes Wizard took a fancy to a bird he'd got, and kept it for himself—like the baby buzzard he'd found in June, in the twenty-foot-deep hollow of an ancient sycamore. He'd taken only one of the two baby birds so the mother wouldn't worry and maybe leave the countryside; Wizard believed in taking care of the wild where he got his livelihood. The young buzzard couldn't fly yet and was penned at nights in the barn with Wizard's big yellow goat. Wizard owned a crow, too, that he'd had for years; it responded to Wizard's call and never even knew what the wild crows were saying when they barked down at him. The wild birds saw his shape and color and reacted, but the crow knew only the Wizard for parent and mentor. People said Wizard traded souls and flew anywhere he wanted in the body of the shiny black bird. It wasn't allowed in the house. It would kill anything from a dove on down. It couldn't help it, for that was its rapacious nature. The buzzard came in to visit often, because Mrs. Coombs liked her. She went about, pattering on the old wood floor, and when Mrs. Coombs or Marn talked to her or gave her a bone to play with, she ducked her head, excited by the attention. She never even looked at another living bird to harm it because that quality wasn't in her.

On the way back to the barnyard, where she had the milking and feeding to do, Marn circled through the smoky, wet land, passing a muskrat drowned in a trap and setting free a few mourning doves that had been baited with cornmeal and fluttered in Wizard's woven net. It was almost five now, and the sunrise lay scarlet above the silhouette of Bald Mountain in the east. Over to the north, beyond the vague morning light, was Old Mountain, on the other side of Dutchman Willem's farm. The mist lay heavy in the valleys and swamps, wreathing the feet of the tall hills, their summits clear. Marn was meeting someone at the sheep pasture on the top of Bald Mountain later in the morning. No one was going to stop her, either. Today was her birthday, the second of September. She had looked in the Almanac that her father went by, and it said that the wandering planet, Uranus, would be in conjunction with the moon shortly, and that the moon would be at its full that evening.

Along with the books Wizard kept on the mantel on Arts and Remedies and Witchery were a Holy Bible and a Catholic Missal. Marn knew the Wizard's volumes well. "Holy Michael, the Archangel," she said, hurrying, using a prayer for a charm, and knowing that Wizard would punish her in some devious way if he found her footprints by the vixen trap or bird net, "be our safeguard against the wickedness and snares of the devil. Cast into hell Satan and all the evil spirits who wander through the world seeking the ruin of souls."

As she left the circle of drowned dead trees bordering the swamp and approached the barn, a squirrel scampered up, springing to grasp the thin material of her cotton dress, climbing up it to her shoulder to ride there, muttering to himself, hungry, wanting corn grains. A pair of wild turkeys, tamed by Marn when poults, their bronzed feathers iridescent in the rising sun, strutted after her, begging in high voices for their corn. "Queet, quit!" They went in and out of the barnyard at will. So did the mixed crowd of chickens: banties and games and not one like another, who depended mostly upon the countryside for their livelihood. Wizard gave Marn a little grain to keep them all coming back, and she shelled corn now on the ground. The hens sang and the gray game rooster and the tiny speckled one flapped their wings and shouted to the east where the sun hung in the sky.

They were an intelligent lot because, as Wizard said, any of them that couldn't see an owl watching, or a hawk dropping down, or a coon sliding up, soon would be eliminated. The squirrel was on the ground now with the birds, sitting on his tail and holding the corn grains in his paws, eating rapidly.

Marn was calling, "Come now, come!" And from the swamp, quacking and shrieking, their wings rushing upon the air, they flew in low, the wild geese and wood ducks and mallards and widgeons and teal that Wizard had turned over to her. They lit on the ground nearby, to shovel in the grain, bobbing their heads, waddling, strutting, talking each in its own way. The mallard drakes whispered and their mates barked, nasal; the wood ducks lisped. The Canada geese were slim and grave, weaving their necks, following the girl's feet.

In the barn she milked and threw hay down for the four brown cows that Wizard used not only for family milk, but for dragging loads that were too heavy for the yellow goat. And when he went off to Greenfield he would hitch a pair to his wagon; they were stolid and enduring, and he drove them without reins, using a long pole to guide them. They would make the fifteen-mile trip to town in less than three hours, up and down the hills. Sometimes Wizard used them to snake out logs from the swamp when he was building a new shack to house his creatures, and they moved like fate, indomitable and steady. Marn went to where the great buck goat was snoring in his stall, his chain tied to the wall. "Wake up, Odin," she told him, and his amber eyes gazed lazily at the hay and the ears of corn she put out. His knees were bald, his coat was shaggy, and he had long coarse side-whiskers and beard, and twisted horns. Wizard had to chain him at night, because he could open any latch or door hook or knob invented by the hand of man. Wizard had traded a newborn fawn for Odin when he was a weanling kid years ago at the Greenfield Fair, and since then you seldom saw one in the swamp without the other.

Odin was in his prime now. He'd been named after some ancient god or devil that Marn's father had read about somewhere, you could be sure. And Wizard had rigged a harness out of thick ropes and a wide piece of leather that ran across the buck's chest, and he dragged a sled made of a box of green hickory sticks interlaced and dried and set upon two wood runners. Wizard liked Odin and even if he were using a pair of cows that day he'd let him come along for company.

The crow was always with them, too, and he got on with Odin, because he'd bullied the goat when it was a kid, biting its tender ears and legs, and it seemed the buck still thought that some way the bird was his master, for even today the crow would make Odin get up, by pecking the big beast's bare knees until he sighed and rose and moved somewhere else. The bird would fly overhead, from tree to tree, when they were out in the quagmire, and he would duck down and ride the buck's back for a while every now and then, his claws in the shaggy hair. Wizard was planning to take the young buzzard with them soon, too, when she could fly. Now she came out from her corner of Odin's stall, where she slept lying flat on the ground like a person would. She greeted Marn, ducking her head, which was blackening as she lost her white baby down, and spreading her wings. The Wizard called her Venus, after some goddess, probably. All Marn knew was that Venus was at times the Morning Star and then the Evening, and the Almanac told when.

Marn let Venus climb on her wrist and stay there while she went to the house, the pail of milk in her other hand. The vulture's wings, already four feet wide, were spread to balance her. Marn left her sitting on the porch rail while she went to strain the milk into a kitchen pitcher and set it on the table. She lit the fire laid the night before, and set the water to boil for tea, and began to make breakfast. She could hear her parents moving in the other room. Wizard's voice was rather shrill.

"She's been going off there to see him regular!"

"Nonsense, Wizard," her mother said. "And what if she has?"

"I know what's going on, and I've put a spell on him, too."

"What did you do now?"

"And this is a spell that works," Wizard said, "and I'm not telling what it is. If I'm going to hold onto my powers, I've got to keep my secrets, and that's the truth." He stamped into the kitchen and stopped on seeing Marn. "Have you finished your work, girl?"

"I have," she told him, the flush on her cheeks because her nature was as strong as her father's, and though she wouldn't openly war with him, she thought how she'd do as she pleased and sometime have her own home and her own animals, and get away and she hoped soon. "I put Venus on the porch like you said to, Father."

He went out and Marn could hear him talking to the baby

vulture, winning her to him with scraps from last night's supper and attention. The crow joined them, swooping down out of one of the scraggly trees that bordered the road to Greenfield when he saw the man. Wizard said, "Catch," and the black bird snapped in mid-air the bits of bread crust he tossed.

Marn knew the Wizard couldn't wait until Venus accompanied them, dropping out of the sky when called. She whispered to herself, laying the plates and setting the kettle to boil, "Next, he'll claim she's about to change souls with him, too."

The wind, warm and moist, was blowing up. Her mother came from the other room. "There might be a storm by noon."

Marn put the bread in the oven to bake. "That's what the red sunrise was about."

"Happy birthday, too," her mother said, "and I thought I'd make a sugar cake for you and maybe I will. What do you think?" The woman went past the wall candle holders and the mantel shelf, where the finches built nests of this and that and occasionally laid three or four wee eggs and raised their broods upon the food that Mrs. Coombs left about for them: the yolks of duck and goose eggs that she boiled and bread soaked in milk. The tiny birds whirred up now, familiar with the room and their freedom. Canaries and a lame baby robin and a blackbird flew loose, and followed the finches about.

"I'm too grown now for cakes and all that, Mother," Marn said, "and did you hear those sheep-killing dogs early?"

"No, but maybe they were at the traps," the woman said.

"I went out to look," Marn told her, "but they'd already left. I might take the gun later. I heard where they went." She wanted an alibi to be gone.

"Should I make a potato pie, open top, instead? I could put in the morning cream when it's risen." The ringneck doves cooed and a baby squirrel chattered. The woman went back and forth, and while Marn set the breakfast out she filled the seed cups and dishes and pots for the numerous waking birds and the crouching small animals that watched the humans' movements with varying degrees of trust and suspicion.

"The dogs seemed to be after something halfway up Bald Mountain, and were baying as I came in," Marn said, eager. "I'll go look for them. I'll be back to help you by afternoon."

"On your birthday you go where you please," said her mother. "We're not that busy."

"That's not so," Wizard quarreled, coming in, hearing her words, going to the sink to comb down his bushy black hair before the small square mirror. "This is our busiest month. I want her to work on that cageful of parakeets. They'll never sell for anything unless they're finger-tame."

"She's going to hunt those sheep-killing dogs," Mrs. Coombs said, "and she knows where they are."

"That's different," he said, but his eye caught Marn's in the mirror, and she looked away. Wizard's eyes were different from most people's. No one knew their color because they were deep-set, and the irises were as dark as a deer's, which is nocturnal. People said that in firelight Wizard's eyes were like a bear's and didn't shine as other animal's did. Marn felt, though she knew most of her father's outright tricks, that in some ways he *might* be magical and cast spells. He'd always been called Wizard, her mother had told Marn, as far as she knew, because of his innate and picked-up skills. Mrs. Coombs said that might have been the name Wizard's mother gave him at birth. Marn believed in the power of the mirror her father kept in his pants pocket in a small black bag. It worried her a little at times.

"I'll just see if the dogs are denned up there," Marn said. "If I can't find them I'll be back right away."

"If they're bewitched," the man told his family, "it takes a silver bullet to kill them."

"Stop talking fiddle-faddle," his wife mocked, indulgent. Mrs. Coombs didn't believe in much of her husband's witchcraft. The way she felt was that everyone had to make a living, and the tonics Wizard brewed from the herbs he dried and the roots he dug were legitimate enough. If he made extra cash by selling a few charms or casting a spell or raising a ghost now and then, and folks paid for it, there was no harm done. Mrs. Coombs said to her husband's face pretty much what she thought, and it was a trial for him.

"I've heard of more than one bewitched dog," the Wizard stated. "And after you fire that silver bullet in it, the dog'll change back to the person he was, just as he dies."

"Posh," she said. She'd claimed it was a case of happenstance when Wizard predicted and it came true that Dutchman Willem's wife would die last autumn. Dutchman always went around saying a man had to be stronger. than his land and his beasts and manage them. Then Wizard saw one of Dutchman's mules in his mirror, kicking Mrs. Willem in the head. And that was what happened, too. Mrs. Coombs said at the time that any man who let his wife groom the mules because he was too stingy to hire more hands to do the work was asking for trouble. Next, Dutchman would be sending his daughter, Katrin, into the barn! She chaffed Wizard now. "Gracious, why not look in your mirror and tell Marn and me who's going to be the next Mrs. Willem!"

"Hold your tongue, woman," Wizard growled.

"Is he going to marry Sheepman's old daughter, from up on the mountain?" She laughed at him.

"Now let's have some peace around here." And Wizard sat to the table and sipped his hot tea and milk with loud noises.

As soon as breakfast was over and Wizard left, Marn went to her bedroom and changed to a fresh dress, one she didn't wear at chores and that was nicely mended. She got the twelve-gauge shotgun from the wall where it was kept on a mounted pair of white-tail deer antlers. She took some shells from the drawer and put them in her dress pocket. "I'm off," she said at the doorway to her mother.

"I'll have a birthday pie or cake or something baked for you by the time you get back, girl."

Marn didn't answer, preoccupied, hurrying off. She planned to leave the gun in a tree crotch as she went up the mountain to the sheep pasture. The inconstant wind was whining in the high trees, the sound coming and going as if someone approached on wings, passed over, and then returned. She crossed the quagmire, familiar with the paths and ways and which hummocks and stumps were safe to use and where bridges had been made by the Wizard felling trees over quicksand spots. She knew where most of the traps were set and where certain animals and birds lived. The trees she passed were as different from those that grew on the mountain above as night from day. Here most were drowned and gray-barked, and waiting to fall. They weren't trees any longer, but homes for wood ducks and owls and squirrels and raccoons. Where branches had grown, there were only knots now. After a while the trees would be stumps, and then they would rot and join the water and be muck and earth.

The wild countryside at the mountain's foot was full of birds, and as she came out of the marsh and started up, doves rose before her, complaining, their wings whistling in the heated sweet air. It was almost five miles to the top of Bald Mountain. It took a lot longer to go up than to come down, and even if you had lived in that rough Carolina mountain country all your life and were as strong-legged as Marn, it would take over an hour to get there. A startled brown owl darted from an elm when Marn put the gun in a lower branch and hid the shells at the foot. It was known as the corpse bird, and Wizard said it could smell as good as any dog.

Close to the top, breathing hard, she stopped to rest and to drink from an icy stream; the rock walls were steep, and in the deep clear bed moss-covered boulders were visible. About her was the ancient and untouched forest; the girth of some of the hemlocks and spruces was fifteen feet. There were deciduous giant magnolias and buckeyes and tulips, too, and they towered. The underbrush was dense and knotted and the ground spongy. No bird sang. The wind had ceased, and the air was moisture-heavy and still and ten degrees colder than below.

The forest had an eerie quality for Marn, used to the liveliness of her parents' home and the activity of the fauna of Endless Quagmire. When a twig snapped under her knee, she stood up, brushing at her dress. No one ever sighted game here, though there was plenty about: grouse and rabbits, raccoons and skunks, and a herd of flighty white-tail deer that roamed the mountain in this season and came down to feed about the Wizard's swamp in winters, all of them slipping away before a human, faster and shyer than the lowland wildlife. It was said that long ago when hunters came through, they could starve if they didn't find a cabin or if they ran out of cornmeal to make a supper on. Marn felt it was as if everything were larger than life size here and enchanted, that a fox might turn to a ravening wolf, the slinking brown sable into a sharp-toothed tiger, and a hidden baby deer into a gold-horned unicorn. She continued up on her way, nearing the pastures that spread over the top of the mountain and were covered with Sheepman Blackburn's flocks.

At the edge of the forest grew laurels and scrubby blackberry bushes; and then she was in the open, and an island of grass spread before, with outcroppings of stone. Beyond the mountain were distant green-blue swells that continued to the horizon and melted in purple fog. Milling over the pasture were the grazing sheep. She waved to the young man in the distance.

"I was about to give you up," Henry Blackburn shouted, and sprang from the boulder where he had perched. A brown, heavy-coated shepherd dog trotted, barking hoarsely, before him as he ran to Marn.

She met him halfway, and he caught her around the waist familiarly, kissing her. "I'm seventeen today," she said, pushing him away, "and you ought to treat me with more respect." She patted the dog, who whined and knew her. "Hello, Tam."

"Come and see what I've got," Henry cried, running before her, back to the boulder. "And I've been up here all night! My dad sighted those hounds yesterday evening. There are seven of them. And we found the stray lamb they tore up."

"What is it!" She took the package he offered, flat and done up in brown paper and tied with a string.

"And I'm staying out here every night to watch for them. Open it."

It was a small mirror, its handle and back made of mother-of-pearl, the glass wavery but clear. Marn looked at herself in it. Her light-colored hair was around her shoulders; her gray eyes were soft and her mouth was full. She seemed beautiful. Henry came to stand behind her shoulder, and she looked at him in the glass, too. His sandy hair was rough and his face was strong and his grinning mouth stubborn; his eyes, like all his Scotch family's, were hazel, greenish with gold flecks. He kissed her again, on her neck, and she was sober.

"I've never had a mirror of my own, Henry. I like it." But Marn was thinking how a mirror always gave back the reflection, and it wasn't the real thing, and how could she tell if what she saw of herself there was the way she really was. And she didn't want the gift because she'd hoped Henry would give her some small ring to promise themselves soon.

"I don't think you like it at all," he said.

"Oh, but I do," she cried. He had shopped for it in Greenfield sometime, and thought of her.

He pulled her down on the ground beside him, leaning against the boulder, his arm about her, the mirror on her lap. "The Fair is twenty-six days off. I'm counting every day, Marn. This year, my dad's letting me take that Wrestling Ram for an exhibition. I've been working on him. He stands like a rock now and knows every trick."

It was cold, but Henry didn't feel it, his plaid homemade wool shirt open. Marn shivered; she had forgotten to take a sweater because it was so warm below. In the valley the mist was spiraling in the updrafts. Some day, when Wizard's young vulture could fly, Venus would take the tide-winds and circle all the way up here, effortless. Faintly, a sound came to them from Dutchman's farm. It was a racket made now and then by

Dutchman's hired people and his daughter Katrin, as they gathered before one of the beehives in the row and shouted and beat upon pans and kettles to deafen the queen and keep some restless honey drove at home. It was one of the Dutchman's queer ways, and the folk around accepted it, because he had a reputation as a prosperous farmer.

"There he goes, holding on to every bee he's got," Henry laughed.

"Do you believe that bees hum the One Hundredth Psalm every Christmas, Henry, like Father says?"

"No, and why do bees hum, Marn? It's a riddle."

"Who knows?"

"Because they don't know the words. And why are you so gloomy this morning?" Henry ran his hand over her hair, mussing it.

"I don't mean to be."

"Are you hungry? My sister's bringing us some breakfast. I told her you'd be coming."

"Your sister's my best friend."

"I thought Dutchman's Katrin was."

"I like her, too. And I wish they both lived closer to me."

Marn gazed into the mirror while she spoke, watching her lips move and how her even white teeth showed; she blinked her eyes. She thought of Wizard's magical mirror and how when she was a child once Wizard had seen a barn burning in it and that came true, and another time when a man was knifed in Greenfield, Wizard had said he was about to be.

Henry took the mirror from her. "Stop looking into that, and pay attention to me. Kiss me, Sweetheart." He grinned.

"No, Nell's coming."

"Then lean back and go to sleep while we wait for her."

He pulled Marn to him, closing his eyes. The dog settled nearby.

"You don't love me at all," Marn sighed. He didn't answer. She felt his warmth and his careless ease with her. The clouds were collecting themselves in gray heaps that would grow blue-black and lowering as the temper of the storm built itself. For some reason Marn was put in mind of her father and his stiff wrath when he now and then knew that she had turned free an animal he had trapped. She could barely hear the distant coughing of thunder behind some far-off mountain, and the hoarse gabbling like a flock of whistling swans that might be those killer dogs baying. Marn wished she could leave her home and come here to live. All the Blackburns' livelihood was their sheep, and the pattern of their lives was tuned to them. Sheepman Blackburn's first Scottish ancestor had come to Old Mountain country two hundred years ago with the key to weaving and the love of sheep. Nell and Mrs. Blackburn made coverlets and quilts and won prizes at the Fair for them. When Mrs. Blackburn was a girl she'd had to make one hundred quilts before she was allowed to marry anyone. And both Mrs. Blackburn and Nell could shear a sheep right along with the men of their family when the time came. Marn would fit in with the life. She was plenty strong and could learn to shear, and she loved the baby lambs and knew how to save an orphan or a twin when the old ewe rejected it. She'd groom Sheepman Blackburn's two famous red oxen for him, too. He put on a yoke and chain and drove them to town, like Wizard did his brown ones. Only Blackburn's oxen were three times their size, and every year Sheepman won a sack of sugar or flour with them when they pulled off the wagon of stone that no one else could budge. Irish and Brown were each shod with eight little iron half-shoes for their cleft hoofs. Everyone asked Sheepman Blackburn how he grew the ox team to that size, but he wouldn't reveal the secret.

Marn sighed again, wanting the young man Henry to say he loved her and not to treat her lightly and not to call her Sweetheart if he didn't mean it. She saw Nell, a basket in either hand, coming out of the woods that hemmed the far end of the bald. The brown dog galloped to meet her, barking. Marn turned to rouse Henry, pulling on his hand. "Here's Nell."

He stood, stretching, yawning, and pushing his shirt into his trousers. "I guess I need some sleep." He waved to Nell.

Nell called, "Wait till you see what I've got for Marn!" They joined her where she was setting the baskets down beside a flat stone and spreading a cloth. As they came up, she was taking out a little cake and plates and silverware. "I've got a candle in here someplace."

Henry said, "I don't think she likes the mirror you picked out, Nell. She didn't say much."

"Yes, I do. I love it." Marn put her hand on her pocket where the mirror was that Henry hadn't selected for her after all. "And the cake is beautiful, Nell!"

It was frosted with thick-whipped cream in which a red-dark jelly was dribbled to make indistinct flowers and leaves and the name *Marn*. "I had to hurry getting here," Nell said, "before the thing fell to pieces."

Nell struck a match and lit the candle. While it burned, she brought out napkins, and a dark smoked shoulder of mutton, and a pot of heavy soft cheese the Blackburns made of ewes' milk, and their gray homemade bread. She put a spoon in the cheese while Henry cut thick slices of the mutton and bread, and they knelt around the food.

"How did you get away?" Nell asked Marn.

"I said I knew where the killer dogs were denned up. I left my gun down there."

"You'll catch it from your father when you get back," Henry said.

"No, I'll not."

"And I'll bet the Wizard knows you've been coming up here off and on to see me, too."

"I'm seventeen now, and who cares?"

"That's not so old," Henry said. "And when are you going to put your hair up?"

"Don't push her," Nell said. "I can remember when you were seventeen and thought you owned the world."

"I still do," he said. "I'm twenty-one and not any minor." And he laughed. "Marn wants to be treated with respect hereafter, Nell."

"My father says to put my hair in a bun," Marn sighed.

"You'll be doing that soon enough," Nell told her. She was a plain woman, hazel-eyed, straight-browed, with gray strands mingled in her brown hair, made in a long braid and circled around her head. She put her hand on it and straightened the pins. "Well, I wish I were seventeen, and not an old maid of twenty-six."

"You're not old," Marn said.

"Yes, I am, and don't think I don't want to marry and get away, either."

"How could you bear to leave this mountain?" Marn said. "Don't you love it here?"

"I'd like my own house. Our ma's too strong-minded for me."

"Our dad says they're like two hens over the same nest," Henry said. "And they ought to decide who's to do what, like the hunters used to do around here, when a bunch of them killed a bear."

"Eat your breakfast and be still," Nell told her brother.

"They'd skin it and split what they sold it for, and the meat they cut up into as many pieces as there were hunters. And then one man went behind a tree and another laid his hand on one piece of the carcass after another, and said, 'Whose is this? and whose is this?' and the hid one told them off."

"Eat your cheese," Nell said.

"Blow out your candle, Sweetheart," Henry told Marn.

"When are you two getting married?" Nell asked.

"Oh, Nell!" Marn cried.

"How about yourself? When's your wedding with Dutchman Willem?" Henry said, aggressive, as if trapped—restless, standing, done with his meal. "I heard our ma asking you that yesterday."

Nell was angering too, her cheeks flushed. She put her food aside. "I'll tell you the same as I told our ma. Whoever Dutchman weds, he'll work to death. I like to sit out on the porch after supper and rest. I'll find someone else or I'll not marry."

The wind had risen and began whipping the girls' dresses, roughing the hair of the three. It snuffed the candle out. Don't fight," Marn said, tucking her dress around her knees, anxious. "I don't think Mr. Willem's so mean, Nell."

"You can criticize him all you want," Henry said to Nell. "But look how Dutchman lives. His mules are the finest anyone ever had; people come from counties around to buy them and pay his price. And look at that brown pedigreed jack that he studs to everyone's best mares. And those big barns that he fills with harvest."

"You'll notice he's always hiring new hands," Nell said, "because he pushes them too far. I can't bear that manner of man!"

"He's never short of hands, though," Henry said, his voice rough. "Everyone wants to work for him."

"He's grasping," Nell cried. "All he thinks of is a bargain!"

"What about painting that big white mule on his barn? That's spending money," Henry roared.

"It's advertisement," she said. "He does it to pull people in!"

"Well, I, for one, admire Dutchman," Henry growled. "And I can't stand the way our dad sits around the house and polishes that fancy gear he puts on his fat oxen, and fusses around chairmaking, and then sends me out to do all the heavy work with the sheep. Dutchman might be a driver, but you'll find him working just as hard as his hands somewhere on his place. That's the reason he stays ahead."

"I know what I'd do." Nell was scornful. "Why not try to catch Dutchman's fat little daughter, Katrin, for a wife?" Nell's eyes were brittle. "Instead of Marn. Then you could live and work there, since you think it's so grand."

"Maybe I will!" And Henry stalked away. He passed the Wrestling Ram and turned to push at its huge, woolly, lowered head. It stood squarely, wanting to play. But Henry went to the high boulder, climbing up and looking off to the distance where thunder muttered and the cold whipping wind was born.

"Why does he talk that way about your dad?" Marn whispered, folding her arms for warmth.

"Doesn't he say anything ever about the two of you?" Nell was gentle now, cooling.

"I don't think he loves me at all," Marn cried.

"I know he does. Henry gave me the money for that mirror for you a long time ago. He was afraid he'd forget the date."

"Oh, Nell," Marn said. "I am unhappy, though."

"No, it's just always that way when you get to be sixteen or seventeen. Going from a girl to a woman is hard." Nell was packing the food up, tucking it into one basket. She put the cake in the other and covered it with a cloth. "It took me a while to learn how to be strong. Now, you haven't even eaten your birthday cake. I'll leave it for you two. I'm going. The storm's almost here. And it must be noontime. As soon as I'm gone you can make it up to Henry. Give him some of the cake."

Marn put her hand in her pocket and felt the small hard mirror there. "It won't do any good. He's angry."

"It's my fault. But he's got no right to talk like that about Dutchman to me."

"Has Mr. Willem asked you, Nell?"

"Not outright, but that's because before he can say a word, I tell him straight out I've no notion to leave my home for any man ever."

"Henry likes Mr. Willem's ambition," Marn said. "He wants to get ahead in the world."

"You can talk all you want about that to Henry." Nell

laughed and stood up. They looked over at the aggressive fig-ure outlined against the blackened sky. "Tell him I'm sorry I lost my temper, too."

"Thank you for the cake and everything," Marn said, "and you're my best friend, Nell!"

"Everything will come out all right," Nell said. She went off, the wind pulling at the clothes about her staunch form. She waved to Marn before she disappeared into the woods. Marn turned to Henry.

He was grinning, now that his sister was gone, pointing, calling, "There it comes!" Far away, the silvery sheet of water was seen approaching Bald Mountain. Henry leaped down from the rock, shouting for Marn to follow. She ran through the flock of sheep to a shelter at the edge of the pasture, built out of outcropping rocks by Blackburn shepherds two centuries ago, chinked with clay and weatherproof. Inside, the light was dim and the air was still, and since there was no bite of wind it would seem warm. The wooden door swung on leather hinges. Marn ducked her head as she came in, and the door slapped behind her.

"Where are you?" she whispered, hearing his breathing, her eyes unaccustomed to the dark.

"Right here. There is where I slept last night in between rounds." The dog had followed them, and was scratching at the door outside. Henry shouted, "Get away, Tam!"

"No," Marn said. "He'll get wet." And she pushed the door to let the heavy-furred dog slip in.

"Down, then, Tam," Henry said, and the beast dropped at once to the floor, panting, quiet. "And you come here." He spoke from the dark.

"Why did you quarrel with Nell?" Marn held her distance,

petting the dog. The rain had arrived, and beat staccato upon the wood door. A thunderclap roared out from the bordering forest.

"We always fight," Henry said. "It doesn't mean anything. The Blackburns have quick tempers. We shout a lot at each other and then it's over." His voice came low and persuasive upon the husky air. She was beginning to make his form out, stretched on a pile of blankets along the opposite wall. "It's like the storm there," he said. "Come over here, Marn."

She felt the lump in her throat and knew she was going to cry, and didn't know why. "I wish you loved me."

"I do," he said, his voice deep and different. He got up and came to take her hand, and was pulling her down beside him. He put his hand on her cheek. "Are you crying?"

"I don't know."

And she couldn't even protest when he fumbled at the fastening of her dress and slipped it from her. He was telling her there in the dark, over the racket of the outside downpour, how beautiful she was and that he loved her. He did love her!

"And I love you, Henry," Marn wept.

"Then you must let me," he said, his knee upon her.

"No, I won't." She pushed him away.

And on the howling of the gale and the hoarse sounds out there like wild swans passing over on their way southward, Henry spoke clearly. "I'll marry you, then."

And so she relented and experienced the ancient issue, and after a while she lay wakeful, her tears and emotions spent, in his arms, while he slept deeply. She listened to his even breath, and thought of the promise and how she'd hold him by it. She tried to remember if Henry had said the exact word *love* or just agreed when she'd asked him if he loved her.

She thought of the mother-of-pearl mirror in her dress pocket, and of Nell's cake standing in the drenching rain under the napkin, ruined, the cream melting and the name *Marn* disappearing. No one had even had a piece of it. She had promised to be home before now, and it was well into the afternoon. There would be trouble there. The huge brown dog was restless, pacing back and forth, whimpering, snuffling at the door. The raving of the storm lessened, and in a while the rain was stopping. Tam came to stand above the two. Marn moved her hand to stroke his nose and rub his ears.

She said some words with her lips, silently, to the dog; it was Matthew and she supposed it was for consolation. *Behold the fowls of the air: for they sow not, neither do they reap, nor gather into barns; yet your heavenly Father feedeth them. Take therefore no thought for the morrow: for the morrow shall take thought for the things of itself. Sufficient unto the day is the evil thereof.*

"Tam, what is it?" she said, and the man stirred. The shepherd dog licked Henry's face, whining, urgent; he ran to the door and growled.

Henry sat up suddenly. "What's the matter with you, Tam?" He pulled on his clothes in the dimness, hasty, stuffing his unbuttoned shirt in. "I'd better go look. You get your dress on."

Marn felt the stab of fear. He'd left the door ajar, and by the light that came in, she dressed. She ran her fingers through her tangled hair to straighten it and went out. She heard his shouts of dismay. The gabbling, swanlike noises had been the marauding dog pack, and in the cover of the storm, with neither shepherd nor dog to drive them off, they had charged upon the flock. The Wrestling Ram, as the senior leader, had stood his ground in front of the ewes and the younger rams, who closed in behind him. Trained by Henry, even as they leapt upon him, the Wrestling Ram had lowered his head and braced himself. Henry found the ground ploughed up all about his muddied, stained, thick-wooled body, the jugular torn and the eyes staring, the hot life ebbing. Henry relinquished his favorite, kneeling over him. He glanced out over the field, where there were other bodies, mostly the well-grown-out lambs of spring. Tam went from one to another, snuffling. Henry was familiar with the scene. Two or three times in his twenty-one years he'd witnessed it, the scattered gray victims, dying of shock rather than injury, their throats ripped by the cunning predators, who seldom stayed to feed on their prey, their appetites wholly hysterical and nourished by excitement and the taste of blood.

The young man turned on Marn in a fury, as she came over. "It's because of you! I ought to have been at my work. I didn't even hear them."

"You had to get out of the rain," she told him, pale.

"Rain never hurt me," he said, cold, getting up from where he knelt above the beast. "I ought to have been on that rock watching out. The hounds would have stayed below on the mountainside. They're that clever."

She shook her head. "It's not right to blame me."

"And you let Tam come in." He rehearsed it. "The dog would have kept them off. Tam doesn't mind a storm on him, either."

"Why didn't you put him out then?" The red was rising in her cheeks.

"Do you know what our dad's going to call me? And not only because of what the Wrestling Ram was worth to him, but it's the start of the breeding season, and this was our lead ram and always got the best spring lambs this herd ever had."

The young man looked away to where the dog barked, tracing the wild ones' scent to the distant woods' edge. Henry whistled, piercing, and the dog turned back, galloping.

The wet wind blew, the chill temper of autumn in it. Tam came to the man's side, settling by his knee at his gesture. Marn looked at Henry's strong frame, the shock of sandy hair, the eyes that turned angrily to her, greenish, the gold flecks dancing in the irises.

"Go on home, then, Marn."

She shivered in the light dress, her hands clasping her arms, her long damp hair framing her face. Her eyes narrowed, their color like the gray clouds rushing about overhead. "You said that back there."

"What now?" He was impatient, wanting to get to his bitter tasks and be rid of her.

"You promised it in the hut to me," she told him. "Marrying."

"I never will," he declared. "Not any woman ever." And he went to salvage what he could of hides and flesh, leaving her standing there.

Marn slipped, hurrying over the slick surface of the forest floor, where the hemlock and pine needles over the centuries had fallen and made a thick bed. As she finally neared the mountain's foot, the sunlight came shafting down through the last of the big trees. There was no wind to speak of, and it was warmer here. As she reached up into the elm to get the gun, the little owl, startled, pitched down nearly to the ground, and fluttered away, low and half-blinded, along the alder bushes that crowded the path toward Endless Quagmire. "Father Son and Holy Ghost." Marn whispered the way

Wizard did for protection, because who knew really for sure that the brown bird was just a bird.

The sun was blooming and the swamp's trees stood stark and drenched ahead. Her shoes were muddied and her dress wet. She hadn't heard her father and suddenly saw him at a little distance at the swamp's edge. He stood in a spreading patch of thistles.

"Come on here, girl!"

Unable to retreat, she masked her guilt and approached. "I will, then!"

The crow, his feet fastened in the long hair of Odin's back, shouted a welcome, nasal and brash. Odin was behind the Wizard, his hoofs muddy, and his shaggy legs and beard and the great strap that went across his chest. In the box of the drag-sled were damp, just-digged roots of sassafras and dogwood and wild cherry and black alder, and fresh strips of the bark. And there were spicebush twigs tied in bundles with withes of willow. Upon the load, her front legs bound together with the same supple willow twigs, was a doe fawn, newly born, with large, dark, nocturnal, hesitant eyes.

"Now, look," Wizard said, straightening his back, holding a thistle in his hands that he'd pulled for its seeds and roots. He gazed at his daughter, despising Sheepman Blackburn and his no-good son up on the mountain, observant of Marn's tangled hair and her soiled dress. He saw how her eyes were dark and how she was unprepared for the bitterness of the world. Young Blackburn was ungentle and unfaithful and unworthy! "What was that about coming back right away this morning? It's close on three o'clock."

"Well, I don't know, Father." Marn leaned over the fawn to stroke it.

"And what was that about finger-taming that lot of

parakeets your mother's got. You're to get to work on that!"
His voice was high-pitched, complaining.

She shrugged. "All right."

"And you can leave the gun with me and bring this baby
doe back to the house. You're to take care of her. I can make
seven dollars on her at the Fair. I want her to wear a collar
and learn to lead, too."

Marn untied the fastenings and lifted the fawn out, tiny,
warm-bodied. "It's late for one to be born."

"I know where the flock's been feeding and where the old
one lays up. Next year I'll let her raise what she drops. I knew
her fawn was coming any time. And I'll tell you something
else I know. I found another dove nest loosed this morning,
and a trap sprung. Now who do you think would come on my
land and do that?" And he turned to grasp a thistle with a
firm hand, because if one grasped it lightly, one got stung,
but if taken hold of hardly, the soft thorns bent to the grip
and there was no pricking. Wizard pulled off the seeds, while
the girl stood ready to go and waiting for him to finish. "And
I could have used that fox or a cage of doves to pay for a dress
or a pair of shoes or a sack of flour."

"Well, I know."

He broke off the root of the plant and looked over at her.
Marn wouldn't meet his eyes. "As you know, I cast a spell
because I'm not going to have you running off and marrying
anybody. You're our only child, and your mother and I want
you to stay with us for a good many years yet, till we think
you're ready to be on your own."

Marn glanced at him and felt the fear in her voice. "What
do you mean, a spell?"

"And like I told your mother this morning, this is one that

works, too. And I've got one more thing to say."

"I know why you want me at home!" she cried.

"No, it's not what you think, girl. I can always hire some woman to play a ghost for me, like I did before you got grown."

"I'll run away, Father."

"I want to say, too, that you don't have to play games and carry that shotgun. I can spot sham a mile away. I heard those dogs come by after you went off this morning, and I heard them running up the mountain and heading for that lazy Sheepman's flock, too. And I'll let you know someone was shooting at them as they came on down from there. I was hoping the dogs would get away again."

"What do you mean, shooting? I never heard a thing."

"That's because you were listening to your own mind telling you what lies you'd said today to your own folks and brewed yourself a kettle of trouble. Now you get that fawn home. And tomorrow see if you can get a little milk goat from Dutchman Willem. That fawn sucked at the old deer, and you'll never coax her to eat a thing tonight. You trade Dutchman something for the goat. Don't give him money. Ask your mother what." He turned back to his work and Marn knew she'd never hear another word out of him that afternoon.

She made her way through the boggy land, more treacherous than usual because of the heavy rain. When she came into the house, her mother was mild. "I figured because it was your birthday you'd be late. There's cake for you there, fresh-baked. I had company. He gave me some honey to help out on the cake."

"Thank you for it, Mother." Marn went to put the tiny doe in a box, where she lay dozing, waiting for the mother deer's return.

"Where'd you go? Did you hear about that new School-master shooting the dogs?" The woman was moving about the room, busy. "He stopped by to tell me, riding his mare and leading another and a spaniel following. He said he'd been tracking them for over a day. He got under a ledge when the storm hit and then he saw them coming down, and there was blood from some work they'd been at. He shot five of them before they could get off. His little dog held them at bay. He said now the pack would break up; the other two or three would leave the country." Mrs. Coombs looked at her silent daughter, wishing her well. "Where'd you go, anyway?"

"Father thinks he can get seven dollars for a fawn, and do you think he can?" Marn asked. "He's taking her to the Green-field Fair, and I'm to break her to lead."

"Did you go up to Blackburn's? Because Wizard doesn't want you going there. Did you visit with any of the women? Did they have anything new to say?"

"What can I trade to Dutchman for a milk goat?" Marn asked.

"Well," the woman considered. "Katrin Willem would like a cage of cardinals for her kitchen. You could take that lot over there. Now sit down and have a piece of cake and some tea, girl. You haven't had a bite to eat all day."

"I'm not hungry, Mother. Can't I have it for supper?"

"Come along. It's your birthday. I'll pour the tea."

But the gorge was in her, and Marn could scarcely eat, sitting before the plain, dark, honey cake, feeling the slight weight of the hidden mirror in her pocket, thinking of the ruined basket of Nell's little fancy cake topped with cream and jam up there by that rock where the angry young man stalked about. She paid little heed to her mother's chattering on about the Schoolmaster, and how he was a bachelor and was going to live alone up on Old Mountain, that was north of the valley where Dutchman lived.

"His name is Randall Grim, too," Mrs. Coombs said, "and he teaches school, and he thinks he might like this Old Mountain country, here in the Carolinas, and he has a reputation for the honey he makes from his bees, he said. What he gave me for the cake was nice and clear. I told him I hoped he wasn't the kind of teacher that thinks men are descended from long-tail apes." She gave Marn a steaming cup. "And I wish he was here now so I could give him another cup of tea and he could see how the cake turned out. Can you fancy a man living all by himself and doing for himself? He says he likes it and it gives him time for all he wants to do in the world. He's got no mind to marry ever. And he knows how to knit a sweater or a pair of socks. He says his object in life is to overcome the wickedness of the world and to foster good. That's why he picked being a teacher. I asked him why not a minister. And he said all a preacher does is talk to older folks that are set in their ways already and never listen. He'd like to catch them young, before they know what they think, and tell them about what's good and what's evil."

"Who knows?" Marn sighed.

"And he has curly brown hair and a soft voice and I hope he comes back soon. If there's one thing gives me pleasure, it's company on hand."

But Marn wasn't hearing the stream of words. She went to get the fawn and hold her on her lap, comforted by the soft, warm breathing. The doe settled down, the long lashes shutting over the dark eyes. Marn went out after a little while to feed and tend and move about the creatures and birds. Obedient, she coaxed the cageful of parakeets. And later, in the dusk of evening, she went to her room, to lie on her cot, waiting for the sleep that would not come. Dark arrived and the moon rose slowly, first appearing slightly squashed at the bottom as it hung suspended in a tree for a while, and then sailing free, white and huge. Just into its full, it blazoned its reflective light through the small-paned window onto the bed and the girl.

The objects about the room, the chair and stool and chest of drawers, were now colorless, their shapes magnified or their contours unclear, so they assumed a character slightly threatening or sinister. The moonlight was strong and constant and would return for seven or eight more nights; those of the countryside, like Dutchman Willem, who had immense harvests to gather in before the frosts, would have sent their men out into the fields. Those with flocks on a mountain would watch from a high boulder the animals that got up to graze, thinking it might be day, their foreshortened shadows preceding them everywhere. And the night animals that walked about in Endless Quagmire would be snuffling in the blue-white light about the lures that Wizard baited with, from corn and old bread, to a fresh-killed pigeon or one tied by its leg in the back reaches of a trap, or again to the musk or some secret scent of a female fox or beaver or shiny, brown-furred muskrat, that Wizard knew of, to coax the creatures into his nets.

Sometimes, out on the road to Greenfield, the hollow sound of hooves of a horse or mule would clatter by—someone on their way to one of the farms about, a late-returning lover or husband. Occasionally, one or more would turn into Wizard Coombs' lane and tie up outside, the beat of their hearts heavy and quickened as they came in and sat at the table where Wizard poured out little glasses of lightning or his wife brought cups of hot tea, and business was transacted. Wizard relied on the fast-beating pulse, signaling a desire to believe in whatever he promised, first customers almost always returning, ready to try a stronger or a different remedy, if the first happened to fail.

Marn could hear one arriving out there now, the Stableman from Dutchman Willem's place, stolen away from the job his master had given him to finish that night, lured by tales he'd heard of Wizard's powers, needing help on his wandering-wife trouble. Wizard's sharp, reasoning whisper came, as he counseled like some father confessor on an oldtime business.

Marn sighed and considered how she felt about Sheepman's son. She was cured of love, that was for sure. She hated Henry now because of what he had promised and done and then denied after. She knew the Bible words in Proverbs: *when the desire cometh, it is a tree of life.* After a long while she drowsed into sleep, feeling the man again pulling her to the pile of blankets in the dusky light of the shepherd hut.

*

*

2

*

The Master's Chair

"ONE THING I'll give credit to a hen for," Wizard was railing at his wife, as Marn came from the barn in the morning to make breakfast, "is you don't hear her cackling till after she's laid the egg." Wizard was fussing because his wife kept talking while he was studying over one of the books he kept on the mantel.

"Well," she told him, unable to cease talking ever, and if Wizard or Marn or company weren't there, she'd go on and on to her birds and little beasts, "it's a good thing humans aren't like animals or we'd go broke, for sure. Men love to have the unknown mixed into their cures and remedies. An animal never thought of that. Now take a bear: if he gets an open cut, he just goes and rolls in mullen leaves."

"Be still then," Wizard said, while Marn laid the plate and cup of tea beside his book. He looked at his daughter. "Did you groom those little cows like I told you to?"

"I always do, Father."

"But a human doesn't have the sense to do that," Mrs. Coombs went on, "and he'll pay you cash for a fancy bottle of mullen leaves laid down in Spanish oil to bandage on the hurt!" Mrs. Coombs was repairing a tear in the reed cage that would hold the cardinals Marn was to take over to Willem's farm that morning for Katrin, crested, the two males bright red and the female brownish. "And you see if you can't get a ham off Dutchman, girl. Cheap. Get one from a hind quarter too. And, Wizard, you give her the money. And take that smallest brown cow to carry everything," she told Marn, "because you'll have the bird cage and the fawn both, and it's too little to follow. And if you see anything else you want to trade for, go ahead."

"I've got no money," Wizard said, without looking up.

"Well, get some from out of that bowl on the top shelf," Mrs. Coombs sighed to Marn. "You ever hear of a man so close with what he makes?"

"I wouldn't talk about close," Wizard growled, his finger on the line to hold his place, "with all the free spenders around this shack." He looked up. "And Proverbs says here that *a bargain well made is like apples of gold in baskets of silver.*"

"You made that over to suit you, Father," Marn said. "I know the Bible, and it's *a word fitly spoken* that's like that." And she cut him a piece of the corn bread and put out a pitcher of the freshly drawn cow's milk. He poured it in his tea.

"You don't know all the Bible," Wizard told Marn. "Nobody ever lived that knew all the Bible."

"One thing I'll say about you, Wizard," his wife told him, affectionate, "is you keep life entertaining, anyway."

Marn left them, the woman still gabbing, the man getting ready to go out to his two black birds waiting on the porch and the great goat in the barn, all of whom kept their peace while he went his rounds. Wizard wondered what harm Marn had done his trap line that morning. There was a need in the young to rebel, but Wizard thought his daughter's opposition went further than the ordinary. He felt the anger down in him because of her secret recalcitrance. He wished Marn conformed to his image and were docile and helpful. *I have nourished and brought up children, and they have rebelled against me,* said Isaiah in the book on the table before the Wizard. He had examined the mother-of-pearl mirror under Marn's pillow when he'd heard her going out into the swamp early that morning. It had taken him half a minute to find it, for her possessions were few and he kept track of them. Wizard had wondered if it signified the Sheepman's son's intent or was an idle gift. He got up now and put the Bible back on the mantel. He patted his wife's shoulder and stalked out.

In the bedroom Marn was pulling off the old dress she wore when she went about her work in the barnyard and on her trips out to the quagmire. She'd sprung another trap that morning. It was a woodchuck, cowering, thick-set, almost two feet long, grizzly-furred with a short, bushy tail. It didn't make a sound when it saw her coming. Sometimes there were animals that died just from fear. They were so used to running to avoid harm that when they couldn't do that, they went mad and leaped about in one place till they died. Marn had maneuvered the gate of the trap with skill, using a branch and keeping a little way off, to conceal her footprints from her father's clever eyes. The animal didn't notice the opening for a while, and then finally it walked through and ambled away as if it had all the time in the world. It still didn't know what had happened, she felt, and would stray right back in for the corn bait, maybe tomorrow.

She took the mother-of-pearl mirror from its hiding place while she combed her hair out. She'd put on a blue smock, and its bright color made her eyes in the wavering glass a paler gray than they were. And the beauty she'd seen yesterday when she first received the mirror wasn't there now. How plain and common she was, really! She wondered if there were some apparent change in herself since yesterday, and looked for it. Would everyone see her as unmarred? Her mother, joking and chattering, surely thought she was the same. Did her father know? Wizard could have taken his own small mirror from its black bag in his pocket and seen all that went on during the storm yesterday. Was it true that only one person besides Marn herself knew that she had had a new experience? She thrust Henry's gift back into its hiding place and went to get the money from her mother's bowl in the cupboard shelf and the fawn from the box. The small animal, no more than ten pounds, hung helpless in the girl's arms, soundless, waiting for what those around her would do for her.

Mrs. Coombs followed Marn to the barn, carrying the cage of three cardinals, clinging silent to their perches, still surprised at their capture not too long ago in one of Wizard Coombs' nets. The small cow, Hebe, had no horns and couldn't be led by a head chain or strap like the other three, who pushed her around authoritatively with their pointed sharp spikes. Hebe wore a collar made out of an old piece of horse harness breeching the Wizard had picked up somewhere. A small bell was fastened to it. She was an amiable animal and stood quietly while the women tied a lead rope to her collar and hung a double sack over her bony back, stuffing the reed cage in one side and in the other the fawn, limp and sleepy, hungry.

"Katrin Willem likes things fancy," Mrs. Coombs said, "and she's been after me for a cageful of birds just like these. It's a fair trade for a little goat. Don't let Dutchman say it's not."

Marn started down the path. "Come along, Hebe." It was almost three miles from Wizard's door to Dutchman's, across the pike and the valley.

"Don't hurry back, girl. Get some news, if you don't mind," her mother called, vigorous, her iron-gray hair loosened from the tight bun she started every day with.

Her voice followed, faint, as Marn disappeared, crossing the road that went to Greenfield and then passing a gray clapboard church. Mrs. Coombs was shouting further directions and advice, but Marn couldn't make out the words by now. The sunlight plunged ahead, and Hebe's bell sounded on the sweet-scented, cool air. Beyond the church was an unfenced graveyard; one of the slabs had been set there less than a year ago. Dutchman had sent an order for twenty-seven dollars and fifty cents to Sears Roebuck when he ordered it. That was just after the Fair, and Dutchman had sold his yearling mules and extra harvest and had plenty of money. At the top of the stone were two carved hearts, and there were flowers at the bottom, and in between it said: *Bertha Willem, 1855–1904. Beloved Wife and Mother. Farewell, Vain World.* The valley ahead was higher land than Wizard's; it was rich and well cared for. Dutchman's grandfather had broken it in with a metal-tipped plow about a century ago. Marn went through the orchard that had been planted around then, too; greedy bees and butterflies were sucking at scattered fallen fruit, half-hidden in the grass and unnoticed by Willem's hired men, who were this week beginning to get the harvest in. Dutchman's favorite apple was the Rambo, its flesh white and firm and perfumed; and there were Vandevers and Russets and Greenings. Farther along, Marn passed pear trees and quinces and scrubby peaches, and then a long vineyard from which Bertha had made a good red wine. Dutchman had hoped for a while that his daughter Katrin would take hold and follow in her thrifty mother's ways. But he was beginning to think that would never happen, which was one reason he was so anxious to get Nell Blackburn down to the valley to be his wife. Dutchman was fed up with the slovenly ways of the hired women among his people. As a matter of fact, he'd sent his daughter this very morning on her long-legged, shod pony up to the top of Bald Mountain, with a gift and a note, as a part of his program of breaking down the resistance of Sheepman Blackburn's daughter.

When Marn came out of the orchards and vineyard, the walking was easier. She skirted cabbages, huge-headed, and patches of turnips that would be sliced and fed in the winter to the mules and the jack, for which the farm was famous. Ahead, cornfields stretched, along their rows sometimes yellow-green pumpkins about the stalks, waiting for frost, and threaded on a thin, browning vine. Marn stopped to pull an ear of corn for the small cow following her, the rope dangling. Over the next rise, far enough away so the vined plants wouldn't interbreed and spoil the pumpkins, were crookneck squash or else cucumbers that were put down in brine all through the summer in the farm's kitchen and seasoned with dill seeds and apple vinegar or dark sugar and the spices got in Greenfield.

Further along, in a pasture, a black-and-white spotted bull lifted his head to watch the progress of the girl and the jingling-belled beast. And then she came to hay meadows. In one, a last crop of mixed clover and meadow grass was being made. An old man and woman stood on the wagon, drawn by a span of heavy mules wearing nose bags, and packed the hay back. A heavy-set, tow-haired man tossed it up to them; he had a great red kerchief tied about his neck to pick up the sweat. He waved his fork at Marn, his white teeth flashing. "Hey! Are you bringing that cow for a visit, little girl?"

Marn pulled at Hebe to hurry her pace, wanting to get over the next roll of the land. The bell clattered. Marn hated all men and their ribald character, and how they were self-loving and didn't mind how they used a girl! She wished Mrs. Willem were still alive, because the woman had always brought Marn into the big kitchen when she came there on an errand. She'd given her a chair and not bargained hardly with her. And she hadn't been cross or unpredictable, as Dutchman was, but talked with Marn the same as Katrin, who was about five years older and the Willems' only child. Marn was eager to get to the Willem farm; she needed to unburden herself about Henry to Katrin. It crossed her mind fleetingly about the possibility of a baby, and she thought she might mention that. But mainly she just wanted to speak about the quarrel and get her friend's advice and comfort. They would gossip about the Fair in a few weeks and how Marn had gone with Henry last year; maybe this year that would be the time they would make up this quarrel!

It was mid-morning by now, and the brown jack of Willem's was starting to bray ahead in the rambling barnyard, which had fences and lots for the variety of pigs, fowl, cows, and mules. The jack shut his eyes, dug his feet into the earth, and wheezed and squeaked like iron being rubbed on iron. Finally he was honking, "Hee-hee-honk-whizzz!" his mouth gaping, eyes slanting. His braying was prolonged, and he had just finished and was breathing stentorian, as Marn came by the cabin where Willem's Stableman lived. A hoarse, angry shouting and a woman's high protest within were audible as the jackass' call ceased.

Marn didn't want to interrupt the noisy family dispute to ask the Stableman if Dutchman were about. She continued to the great barn, the entire side of which was painted with a giant white mule, caparisoned with an elaborate red bridle and britching. Marn stepped in the doorway and called, "Mr. Willem!" Her answer was a muffled stamping of hoofs and a munching of hay. The barn's air, heavy with the scent of the animals' breath and bedding, was overlaid with the honeyed odor of new hay crammed into every corner available. Dutchman had his own ways, and claimed he liked to use roofs and walls; underneath the barn in wintertime he would keep a whole herd of pigs. Now they were out in one of the pastures, and when the corn and pumpkins and apples and pears were gathered and picked and put in a safe place, they would be turned loose to find and eat whatever was missed or damaged and couldn't be sold in Greenfield or used on the farm.

Marn left the barn and went around the corner and toward the house. Past the row of beehives, two horses unfamiliar to her were tied to the fence of the dovecote. Below the gray birds, brown rabbits hopped and banties clucked about the variety of greens and kitchen debris thrown to them after meals. The lead strap of a shaggy bay was knotted to the saddle of a tall black mare. Marn spoke to them as she tied Hebe's rope to one of the big iron rings fastened on the fence. She got the bird cage out and lifted the fawn from her place and went up the graveled, unkept walkway, that in the day of Mrs. Willem had been raked every morning in an orderly curved pattern.

The door to the big kitchen was ajar, and a faint crackle came from the big black stove, where a whole young pig was slowly roasting in a great iron pan. The breakfast plates, used at dawn, had then been hurriedly wiped clean and set back on the long table, where half-cut loaves of bread and pots of fresh-made jam and a dish of pickles and a plate of dark sausages were scattered. Benches lined the table, and at its head was an imposing high-back armchair. Dutchman's custom was to feed his hired men the first two meals of the day in this kitchen. Dutchman's father had done the same, saying that in that way the men always got started on time, and he knew they were eating well and so would work properly. The workers' wives had their own stoves in their cabins and could take care of themselves and the children during the day, and at suppertime feed their men, too. Marn set the cage on a sideboard where two ornate, tall, silver candlesticks stood; she went to sit on a corner bench, keeping the fawn on her lap. The creature nibbled at the cloth of her blue smock, and then at her fingers, and began to suck on one. The sun poured through the windowpanes and upon the unscrubbed wood floor, where bits of breakfast food had been spilled and ignored. The cardinals rustled in their cage, plucking at the seeds put there by Mrs. Coombs, glad to be freed of the jostle and the dark sack.

Marn stared at the shadows unmoving on the floor. Some people were poor and came from nowhere and had to scrabble to get a living from the wild. Others had substantial lives, and the dignity of forebears, and barns the size of that giant one out there. Ecclesiastes had said *the race wasn't to the swift, nor the battle to the strong, neither yet bread to the wise, nor yet riches to men of understanding, nor yet favour to men of skill.* He'd said, *But time and chance happeneth to them all, as the fishes that are taken in an evil net, and as the birds that are caught in the snare.* Marn looked over at the jam and spiced fat meat and smelled the roasting pig. She was hungry and wondered if she dared take some of the bread and preserves. It was getting on into the morning and the workers would come in at noon. She thought she might sweep up the floor, and then she could make herself a cup of tea. But she was hesitant, and wondered where Katrin was. Dutchman told his daughter to cook and put out the meals as her mother had done. But she never satisfied him, being untidy and as different from his departed wife, Bertha, as red from black. Willem ordered the hired women to clean up the kitchen and to look after the house, but then he shouted in wrath and reproach at them, so they always worked too. hastily and wanted to be back in their own cabins.

One of the mares out in front whinnied now. There was a muffled clatter of shod hooves, and Marn heard Katrin's voice in laughter and a man's call and a dog's bark. She went to the door, the fawn in her arms. Katrin was dismounting from her pony, and a stranger was leading it away to the barn; a spaniel, golden-colored, was at his boots. Katrin called after him, "I never heard that one!" And she came running to the house, heavy-footed, gay.

"Where have you been?" Marn cried. "And I heard you people keeping your father's bees at home yesterday."

"That swarm nearly got away." Katrin laughed, kissing Marn's cheek, holding her hands; then she was pulling off the heavy sweater she wore and hanging it on a hook behind the door.

"I want to talk with you, Katrin!"

"Have you met Randall Grim yet, Marn? The new Schoolmaster?"

"I heard about him," Marn said. "My mother's met him."

"Where did you get the fawn?" Katrin ran to the reed bird cage. "Are these mine? Your mother remembered! How much money does she want for them, so Papa can give it to you. And did you know Schoolmaster's the one who shot those sheep-killing dogs on the mountain yesterday?"

"Yes, but now sit down and listen to me, Katrin." Marn strove against the girl's ebullience and her noise.

Katrin leaned over the new cage, delighted. With reddish-gold hair in two heavy braids, and with deep blue eyes and bright pink cheeks, she was heavy-boned, her breasts and hips full.

"Schoolmaster Grim likes jokes and stories. He just told about the lady in the Greenfield Courthouse, and she said to the judge, 'Well, I probably don't have my facts right, but everything else I'm saying is true.'" Katrin's rush of words scarcely halted, and she was eager. "How long has your mother had the birds, because they're quite tame, aren't they? And I have to say something quick, Marn, before Mr. Grim comes! We're having a fight here this fall, and it's exciting!

The wife of the Stableman got caught last week out in the woods behind the hayfield with Papa's new Farmer. She's too good-looking, Papa says, and that's why she's so troublesome. And Papa won't let either Stableman or Farmer go because he needs them both and they're his best hands. So now everyone's quarreling and fighting. And I want to tell you that he kissed me, too."

"Who?" Marn said.

"That Farmer who's making all the trouble. He's been with us all summer, and he knows where every crop is, and he's got next year's planned. He's ugly and tow-headed and the hardest worker Papa ever saw. He doesn't have a wife yet, and I know two girls on this place that he's kissed and I don't know what else. Besides me. And I never told Papa about me, either."

"Aren't you afraid of him?" Marn said. "He waved at me from the field when I was coming here. I didn't like his way at all. And your father wouldn't want you to wed a hired man."

Katrin giggled. "I know. Papa's picked out someone else for me to try to get to marry me. He's that rich man's son from Greenfield, Sam Trail. He's bringing a string of his father's mares here this afternoon. But I don't like Sam. Every time he comes he tries to court me, and he stands around like a dummy. I'd rather have Farmer chase me in the barn and catch me any day." Katrin flung her braids back.

"I need to tell you something, Katrin!" Marn urged.

"All right. But help me with the dinner while you're telling it. I'm late getting started. Papa'll be angry again if the men have to wait on me to eat. It happens all the time. And who's the fawn for? I don't like a fawn for a pet. Did you bring it to trade, Marn? Where did you get it?"

Steps were outside, down the gravel walk. Marn cried,

holding the baby doe tightly, "Oh, Katrin! I need to talk to you. I have to say something alone to you. About what's happened to me. You and Nell Blackburn are my only friends."

"Why, that's where I've just come from, Marn! I've been to see Nell. Papa sent me up there. And I talked with her brother Henry for the longest time. He made me get off my pony while he fixed the saddle properly, and then he pulled my braids and tried to hold my hand. And he asked me to go to the Greenfield Fair with him, too! Didn't he go last year with you? And next week he's going to bring his father's big ox team down here to get shod. Stableman knows how to shoe oxen properly, and he's got a sling he hangs them in between the barn door. Sheepman Blackburn wants them to be ready for the Fair." Katrin was hanging the bird cage before the corner window, away from the stove's heat. "I love an exciting year like this, Marn. Stableman's too little a man to beat up Farmer, and what if he tries to shoot him! Stableman yells at his wife all the time nowadays. And she told me that since she doesn't have a child yet to hold her to him, she might just run away from her husband and never come back!"

Katrin turned to the door where the man stood, taking off his homeknit round cap, the spaniel behind him. "How do you do, ladies."

"Come in, Mr. Grim," Katrin ran to welcome him. "You haven't met Marn Coombs yet, have you? She's the daughter of that Wizard I was telling you about."

"I met your mother yesterday, Miss Coombs," School-master said, "and it's nice to meet you today. Do you always carry a baby deer wherever you go? I didn't see it in your house yesterday, though I saw a lot of other little beasts." He laughed, shifting on his slender, strong form, running his hands through his brown curls to flatten them, his eyes remaining sober.

"Tell Marn one of your jokes, Mr. Grim," Katrin urged, while Marn nodded in greeting.

"Why not let that fawn alone in the forest where you found it, Miss Coombs?" Schoolmaster asked.

"No," she said.

"People are always thinking a fawn's lost when it's staying where its mother put it. Take it back where you got it."

"No. My father's going to sell her at the Fair the last of this month."

"That's against the law as I know it." Randall Grim shrugged. He thought how he had come upon a primitive enemy of all the justice and logic he believed in, when he found there was an actual wizard here, right after the turn into the twentieth century. Schoolmaster had sized up the Wizard's wife yesterday afternoon and accepted her as an average, lonely, gossipy, countryside woman. She was the one to carry the seed for Wizard, and Schoolmaster wondered if the potential for making magic had been transmitted to the Wizard's daughter. He wanted to unravel the mystery. Was she naturally a witch, then? And did her father verse her in his craft? Randall Grim felt the challenge, and how all his poring over the books and listening to the professors in the college he'd attended stood behind him. He twisted the wool cap in his hand, stirred.

Katrin laughed. "The law never bothers Marn's father, Mr. Grim! Wizard knows every judge there is, and they get together on the law. Papa says they do. And won't you tell us some jokes, Mr. Grim? I've told Marn it's your way. And we have to get dinner started, too! Put that fawn down, Marn.

You make up the pies. We'll need six. Use those blackberries in that hamper. They were picked last evening."

"I'll help you two with the meal, Miss Willem, if you don't mind," Schoolmaster said persuasively. "Cooking's one of my accomplishments."

"Well, peel the potatoes, then," Katrin said. "There's a bushel of them over in that corner. Take this pan for the peels, and put them in that kettle, and stay out of our way!"

"Why peel them?" Schoolmaster asked. "The skins taste good." He looked down at the dog crouched at his feet. "Take this," he said, offering the spaniel his cap, "and go lie down somewhere." The animal took the object to the far wall and settled there with it, head on silky forepaws, honey-colored eyes on his master.

"Because Papa likes potatoes that way." Katrin began opening cabinets and drawers. "And then core the apples over there. And you leave their skins on, for Papa likes *them that* way."

"Well, let's see . . . there was this man died and got buried, and they put up a gravestone." Schoolmaster unsnapped his knife, and the peelings curled thinly into the pan on his lap. "And on the marker they carved his name, and below it, *Devoted father and loyal son.*"

Marn whispered to Katrin, "Are you really going to the Fair with Henry Blackburn!"

"Listen to the story, Marn."

"And one of his friends came by to pay his respects, and saw the stone, and said, 'My stars, they buried two other people along with him!' "

"I'm glad you're the new Schoolmaster!" Katrin took the roasted pig in its iron pan from the oven and put it on a folded cloth on the table. With a long iron fork she filled a bowl with the new white sauerkraut that was aging in brine in a crock. "And Papa's got six children on this farm to turn over to you to learn their ABC's, Mr. Grim."

"I know. I've got close on forty from this Old Mountain country by now and I'm all ready to get started. The oldest's eighteen and the youngest is four, and the first thing I'm teaching them all, with a stick in one hand and a sugardrop in the other, is the Golden Rule."

"I doubt my Papa will let you have these six from here till he's got the fruit in, at least."

"He has to send them, Miss Willem," Randall Grim said.

"Next, you'll say it's the law," the Dutchman's daughter teased him, "and I don't mind if you want to call me by my first name, either: Katrin."

"You can call me Randall if it suits you, Miss Willem, but I've got to call you by the long way for respectable reasons. I must say, I'm beginning to feel at home in this countryside, although I haven't been settled in that cabin on Old Mountain for two weeks yet. I've got a good reliable school building, and the roads to it cleared, so the young people are going to have to do a lot of thinking to find an excuse for not coming." He laughed, although his eyes stayed stern. He was watching Marn at the sideboard, mixing flour and butter and water for pie dough, and rolling it out for the waiting tin pans. "What's your opinion of the Golden Rule, Miss Coombs? And I liked your mother. I gave her a pot of my honey. She said she was mixing your birthday cake."

"Was it your birthday, Marn?" Katrin cried. "I wish I had something to give you."

"I see you're not a bit like your mother, Miss Coombs,"

Schoolmaster said. "I haven't met your father yet. And how old are you, for such a quiet one?" He watched Marn closely, sensing that she was disturbed and wondering at the reason. Her hair, straight and fine and pale yellow, hung about her oval face. She was working in the shadow, so her eyes were darkened and he couldn't see their gray color.

"You're about eighteen now, aren't you, Marn?" Katrin asked.

Marn frowned, glancing at the Schoolmaster and wishing he weren't there, anxious to know everything that had happened in Katrin's visit to Sheepman Blackburn's that morning. "How old do you think me, Mr. Grim?"

"You're not near eighteen," he said. "Have you finished with school? You seem a child in some way."

Katrin passed by Schoolmaster, moving about the room. She swayed her plump hips the way she'd seen Stableman's beautiful wife do to raise a comment from one of the men when her husband wasn't about. "What's my age, Randall?" Katrin dared him.

But Schoolmaster didn't heed her, waiting for Marn's sharp reply. "I'm five years younger than Katrin Willem, Mr. Grim. And if you can figure her age, you'll know mine. I finished school two years ago." Marn placed a rounded sheet of rolled pastry in one of the pans.

"Marn was the top pupil," Katrin said, "and she skipped some of the grades. Why, I only left school a year before she did. That's because Wizard made Marn do numbers and read ever since she was a baby, and my Papa doesn't own a book besides the Bible and the Almanac. I'm twenty-two this year." She straightened the plates about the table. "And you needn't think you're so terribly clever, Schoolmaster, just because you shot those killer dogs yesterday. I happen to know someone else that nearly got them." She turned to Marn. "Henry told me he almost cornered the whole pack. He'd been there all the night before and just stepped into a shelter for a wink of sleep while the storm came on. And as luck would have it, it was that moment the dogs got into Sheepman's flock. They ran down the top ram and a bunch of young ones before he scared them off."

"Why did the young man get out of the way at the moment the storm came on?" Schoolmaster asked. "Then's the time to be on the lookout for them; that's when that kind of dog likes to be at work. I was right in the middle of it, and the thunder and lightning all round me. He sounds like a lazy fellow!"

"You're wrong," Marn said coldly. "He's as ambitious as anyone you ever saw."

"Anyway," Katrin told them, "Henry left his dog in charge, and that was his mistake. For Tam's getting old and Henry wants a new dog."

"Is Henry your beau?" Schoolmaster asked Katrin, "since you seem to know so much about what goes on?"

"No," Katrin giggled, "but all of Sheepman's family are glad you shot the killer pack, and they wondered how you managed to get five out of seven, Randall."

"For one thing, I've got two double-barrelled guns," Grim said. "And then, my dog over there isn't like that one of Blackburn's." He looked over at his spaniel, whose long-haired tail moved slightly in acknowledgment. Schoolmaster felt he was talking about himself and another human when he said, "My dog's clever at keeping whatever he wants to in a corner at bay. He's willing, if you tell him, to hold a fighting badger or a hurt lamb or a bear or a yellow dog."

"Well, when you did that deed," Katrin said, "you made a lot of friends around here, Schoolmaster. Didn't he, Marn?"

"That was the idea, Miss Willem." Grim got up to put the kettle of peeled potatoes on the stove. "I've got to plan what I'm doing if I'm going to change this countryside."

"Why do you want to change us?" Katrin asked. "Don't you like the way we are?" And she smiled at him as she gave him a dish to put the apples in as he cut them up.

"I don't think Henry should get rid of Tam," Marn said. "And why did your father send you to see Nell Blackburn?" Marn leaned over the pies as she put in the purple berries and dusted on sugar and flour. She kept her face hid from the other two, feeling the constriction in her throat and the tears that came suddenly in her eyes, because life lately seemed a series of betrayals. She carried the pans two at a time to the oven for the sweet food to bake.

"I took Nell a present and a letter," Katrin told Marn. "And I don't think Randall knows yet that my Mama died last year. I miss her every day. I dream about her at night. My Papa doesn't. He says he never dreams about anybody that's died. But I do. I can see Mama polishing those silver candlesticks over there, because that's one thing she loved to do. You've watched her cleaning them, haven't you, Marn? And going down the paths with a rake and making the gravel in a waving design."

"I know about your loss," Schoolmaster said. "Mrs. Coombs spoke of it when we visited yesterday, and I asked her to tell me about my new neighbors." Grim had seen Marn's tears and studied her to see if his words affected her. "I know your father predicted the death, Miss Coombs." His voice was low and gentle. "Do you believe in his wizardry? Do you ever help him in it?"

"Everyone had to believe in the Wizard that time," Katrin told Grim, "because Marn's father was on his way over here to warn Papa of what he'd seen in his mirror, and he talked about it to one of our hired hands before he ever reached our house and found it had come true." Katrin drained the water from the potatoes, and tossed them in a bowl, and put a great chunk of yellow butter on top to melt, and a dipper of sour cream.

"Will you go to the Fair with Henry, Katrin?" Marn asked, urgent.

"I don't know. Papa might not let me. He doesn't like Henry. But the thing is, Randall, we need a woman here to run things, and I'm tired of working so hard. And Papa admires Nell and how she can shear sheep just as fast as the Blackburn men, and then she can weave and cook, too."

"I should think the Sheepman's daughter would be glad to come down off that poor mountain and live on this big farm," Schoolmaster said. "What's wrong?"

"And the letter I took Nell from Papa said he wanted to take her to the Greenfield Fair in a month, and he sent her a little clock he'd ordered by mail that chimes the hours, to remember him. But Nell said she didn't care for it. She loves me, she says, but as a friend, and she won't be my stepmother. She said I must take back the clock to Papa. And it was only because Sheepman and Mrs. Blackburn spoke up and said Nell had to accept Papa's invitation if she liked it or not that

Nell finally said yes. And they made her keep the clock, too, and Mrs. Blackburn put it up on their mantel."

"What did Henry say about it all?" Marn mourned. "Does he want Nell to be your mother?" And she thought how she'd dreamed up on the mountain yesterday, hoping to have Nell for a sister, if she could only marry Henry and live up there.

"Henry claims he doesn't care who does what," Katrin said. "He says he's twenty-two and one way or the other means nothing to him and his life."

"If your father decides to turn you down on going to the Greenfield Fair with that Sheepman's son," Schoolmaster laughed from his corner, "how about asking him if you can come with me!"

"Are you going to take your honey there, Mr. Grim?" Marn said, defensive.

"Well, I might, Miss Coombs," he told her. "I'll get a prize for it, that's sure. And do they have any contests for strength? I can both box and wrestle."

"They have a Wrestling Match, and Henry Blackburn won the medal last year," Katrin said. "And he trained that ram of his to wrestle, too, the one that the killer dogs just got."

"That's a shame now," Randall Grim said. "I'd have liked to work on a Wrestling Ram instead of men all the time."

Katrin said, "Sheepman's going to look around for some fine new breed of ram at the Fair this year, for Henry to teach to wrestle like that old one." And she went to the open door and hauled on the rope that rang the black bell mounted in the roof of the dormer window overhead. There were shouts of reply from the barnyard and the lots, where the mules were getting their noon hay and the hands were splashing water on their faces from the troughs outside the milk house or barn, drying themselves with the red or blue huge hand-kerchiefs they pulled out of their overall pockets. They came clumping in, nodding at the girls and the new Schoolmaster, sliding in on the benches that lined the table, the Stableman holding his distance from the hulking Farmer who disturbed his domestic peace. Dutchman Willem came last, his feet heavy in his tall boots, a square-cut, powerful man. He washed at the sink, using the brush and the strong yellow soap to clean his broad hands and stubby wide fingers. He dried on the rag that hung nearby.

"This is the new Schoolmaster, Papa," Katrin told him.

"Well, so I see, and what's that Wizard's daughter doing in here? And did she bring those birds? Eh? And who let that spaniel into the kitchen? And is that a baby deer?" Sharp-eyed, domineering, expecting no reply, the sleeves of his gray homespun shirt rolled on his work-hardened arms, Dutchman came to the table, swaggering before his family and hired people. "And why not slice the pig before you set it out on the table, daughter, like your Mama always did!" His blue eyes were round and bright like Katrin's, and his hair had some gray in the red-blond that was almost the color of her braids.

"You slice it, Papa. I can't."

He took the fork and speared it into the crackling skin; the hot fat ran down into the iron pan below. He pointed his knife at Marn, standing at the wall by her fawn. "Did you bring that bird cage?"

"I came to get a milking goat to raise this fawn on," Marn said, frowning, "and those birds are in trade for one, Mr.

Willem. And I'm to ask you for a ham quarter, too, for my mother, and I've got the money to pay for that."

The odor of the baking berry pies was on the air, as Dutchman turned his attention to the roast before him, ignoring Marn's request. Schoolmaster moved suddenly, light-footed, quick, and came to the table. "Why don't you sit here by me, Miss Coombs, and you can do your business with Mr. Willem later."

"I asked Mrs. Coombs for the cardinals, Papa," Katrin said. "I want them."

"And I've come to tell you school opens next week, Mr. Willem," Randall Grim said, "and while those six children you have here ought to come for a whole day, they can come just mornings if you like, until your harvest's in. I can see you're pretty busy." He made a place for Marn, who put the wobbly-legged fawn on the floor and came to sit next to the Schoolmaster.

Dutchman sliced the meat and helped himself. He reached for the kraut, and then sat in the Master's heavy armchair, brought over from the other country by Dutchman's grandfather a good hundred years ago. The piece had been well-used even when it made the trip across in the ship; already it had passed through generations, now a new leg, now a new round, a new back or seat, but the shape remaining always the same. The chair was high-backed, thick-legged, the seat generous. All its parts were well-polished and smooth as silk to the touch. And as a human body during its lifetime changes all its cells, so the wood of the chair was not the same as what had been there at first.

"Why not pass me those potatoes sometime today?" Dutchman said.

That was the signal, and everyone reached and dipped, tearing chunks from the bread loaves, spooning the gravy and apples, forking the dripping hot meat onto their plates, clattering their utensils, smacking as they chewed. Conversation ceased for a while, until the first edge of appetites became satisfied. Then tongues were again loosed.

"What sort of books did your father make you read as a child?" Randall Grim whispered to Marn.

She shrugged. "Why did you back down and say Mr. Willem didn't have to send the children for a full day?"

"I didn't know he was so strong-minded," Schoolmaster told her. "Give me time and I'll have him in my pocket. I like to play a foxy game. Now tell me, did you ever read the Bible, Miss Coombs? Does your father know the Word at all?"

But Marn wouldn't answer that, and she worried, "I'm afraid Mr. Willem won't give me a goat at all and my fawn hasn't eaten for a whole day now."

The old man whom Marn had seen earlier on the wagon as she came past the hayfield inquired of the master of the place, "Are we going to work on getting in the rest of that field of hay tonight, Mr. Willem? This full moon'll last just about four more days."

"That's good, old fellow," Dutchman told him. "And you and your wife keep up on the wagon bed and Farmer'll pitch the hay to you. Isn't that right, Farmer? Can you handle it alone on the ground?"

The big tow-head grinned. "I can easy. But have you walked through the apple orchards yet, Mr. Willem? There's a lot left in the grass, and the bees are busy. That fruit's too good for the pigs, I think."

Willem leaned back in his chair. "I want them picked up.

Old man, you put those two big daughters of yours on that, and then tell them to get up here to the kitchen and they can make up apple butter for all the hands this winter. This is a good fruit year."

"Isn't the orchard where Stableman was supposed to be working last night?" Farmer asked. "I looked but I never saw him out there in the moonlight. Where were you, Stableman?" And the two men glared along the length of the table at each other.

"I won't have war around here, either." Dutchman pounded on the table with his fist. "You can every one work on your woman problems outside of my sight. I've got too many of my own." He turned to Katrin, somewhere down the length of the table, calling, "Now what did that woman say when she read that letter of mine?"

"She says she'll go and be glad to, Papa," Katrin told him. "And thanked you for the package you sent, too."

Dutchman nodded, flushed. "All you've got to do is give a woman time to think, and they'll see sense. Remember that, you men. They're like a heifer, and they don't consider anything. They get carried away in every direction. You mind what I'm telling you," he threatened the big Farmer, "and leave the easygoing wives around here alone. You'll never find a place where they treat you better than me, and come Christmas you're one of the few that's getting their pay raised. And Stableman's another. Farmer, you go and find yourself one of the young ones on this place and get properly fixed. Eh?"

"I can't seem to find any young one that I want yet that beats the older ones," Farmer grinned.

Stableman turned red and kicked back his bench and stumbled up from the table. He stamped from the room, feeling a cuckold, heading for his handsome and desirable wife, wondering if the charm he'd got from Marn Coombs' father last night had done any good so far. He felt the need to give his woman another tongue-lashing, the only way he'd been able to find peace ever since he'd caught her on the floor of the woods in the arms of that roughneck! Muffled laughter from the table followed his steps as he went down the walkway.

Dutchman, beneficent because of Nell Blackburn's new acquiescence, turned to Marn. "Wizard's girl, my daughter can keep those birds if she's so set on them, I guess. And you can have a goat in trade. How about it, Farmer? Have we got one for her?"

The big man spoke, his mouth full, his voice muffled. "There's five or six out there, milking fair."

"As soon as you're done eating, you show her. And she can have a ham, too, if she wants it. Make her pay for it proper. And then get back at that hay!" He slapped the table. "And isn't there any end to the meals around here! Where's the dessert?"

"Let's get the pies," Katrin said to Marn, and the girls brought them from the oven. They were cut and passed around, the blackberries swimming out in their hot syrup, and topped with thick cream by those that wanted it. Katrin poured coffee in the mugs, steaming, and the men stirred spoonfuls of sugar or honey in and drank, sipping loudly.

"Can you tell everyone a joke?" Katrin asked School-master.

"How about the relatives gathered around to hear the lawyer read the will, Miss Willem? And it saying, 'Being of sound mind and body, I spent every cent!' "

"I like Randall, Papa!" Katrin cried.

"You call him Mr. Grim," Dutchman told her, watchful, from the table's head, "and behave yourself and mind all those manners your Mama tried to teach you but it didn't do much good."

"Has the Schoolmaster been in Old Mountain country long enough to hear about our ghost girl?" one of the hands asked.

"There's always a ghost about," Grim said. "If people haven't got one from their forebears, they'll make one up the first chance they get."

"This one's brought up by the Wizard," one told him.

"Have you met Wizard yet, Schoolmaster?" cackled the old man. "Do you know he can change himself into a crow when he wants, and that's the truth!"

"The Wizard can call down any bird from any tree, or any animal from its hiding, too," said another.

"That's only because he knows their language and how to make his voice like theirs," one of the younger hands said. "That isn't a charm."

"You didn't see Stableman around your house last night, little girl, by any chance?" Farmer called over to Marn.

"What's your father's ghost that they're talking about, Miss Coombs?" Schoolmaster said softly to Marn.

"Who knows?" she said and got up, taking her plate and his and gathering others, scraping the leavings on the dishes into a pail for the doves and rabbits in the cote outside, wanting to be gone.

Farmer laughed. "This isn't a free ghost either, Schoolmaster, that just anybody that wants can see. You've got to pay plenty. How much does he charge, little girl?"

Marn glanced at the head of the table, where Dutchman

now was lighting a long white clay pipe that he would smoke before he went out. "Mr. Willem, can I feed this pail of scraps to your doves?"

"Go on, Wizard's daughter," Dutchman said roughly. "Then you wait for the Farmer to come out." He spoke absently, not involved in the chatter of the men at the table, his mind on where he would send who to do what chore next.

Marn went to get the fawn, and with her under an arm and the pail in her hand, she hurried past the table of joshing, well-fed men, some smoking a cigarette they rolled and some a pipe, for Dutchman didn't permit a match to be struck in barns or fields for fear of fire, and this was the time he assigned his permission for the pleasure.

Outside on the steps Marn whispered to the hungry deer that nuzzled her hand, how she hated every one of them in there. She heard the talk going on and on. Schoolmaster asked if any present knew that in the Bible it was written in Exodus, *Thou shalt not suffer a witch to live,* and he wondered if the Bible mentioned wizards anywhere. No one laughed, and Grim told them that was a joke. And then they began to recount to the newcomer in the community how in Endless Quagmire during the nights a whispering was heard continually as the dark-loving animals and birds moved about on lush paths and hummocks under drowned trees. And there, for a prepaid sum, if you stood where you were instructed, by incantation the Wizard would struggle with underworld elements until he brought back from the dead a young woman who had been lost in the swamp once and had slipped into quicksand and gone down into the earth's bowels. Her spirit was strong, and she longed to return to life and walk about unclothed on the meadow beside the marsh. A unicorn with a long gold horn would trail after her. The pair would fade away before your eyes if they knew you were spying on them.

"Talk, talk, talk," whispered Marn, fierce, dumping the bucket of scraps in the dovecote yard. Hebe, tied by her rope to the fencing, mooed low at her; the Schoolmaster's two mares tossed their heads and their bridles jingled. Marn sat on a stump to wait for the Farmer, holding the fawn, wanting her fed soon.

The gold spaniel came racing down the path, and after came Randall Grim, pulling the knitted cap over his curly brown hair, whistling. He stopped the tune on seeing Marn and called, "That's one country fable I just might like to have come true!" He laughed, coming over. "Have you ever seen the ghost girl and her horned beast that your father raises, Miss Coombs? I'm trying to keep true and false apart. Do you ever have that trouble?"

Marn's arms about the fawn tightened. "You go and mind your lessons, Mr. Grim. You've been trying to make me say what I don't want to since you walked into Mr. Willem's kitchen."

"No." He was mild. "I just came to get my mares and be on my way. You can give your mother my regards if you want."

"You talk about true and false and what it says in the Bible. I don't know the difference in the words right and wrong," Marn said, thinking how Henry Blackburn had told Katrin that the shepherd dog, Tam, was no good and was responsible for all the deaths that had happened in Sheepman's flock yesterday, "and that's how I feel, Mr. Grim."

"Well, I've read the philosophers and the poets and the preachers," Schoolmaster said, fired by his desire to ferret out if this Wizard's daughter that he felt so lucky to have come upon, were or were not as ignorant and simple-minded as she appeared, "and I can tell you that truth is truth every time, Miss Coombs."

Marn wouldn't listen. "Mr. Grim, my father says it's true that if the white mule that's painted on that barn over there had a real animal for a model and bore its name, you could fire a gun at that barn side and it'd kill the real mule."

Randall Grim walked away from her to his mares, untying the lead strap of the small one, and putting his hand on the pommel of the other and mounting lightly. He rode to where the girl sat, looking down at her fawn.

"Do your father's spells work?" the man asked.

She gazed up, baited. "Some might, Mr. Grim."

"I presume he sends you to church once a week. Maybe you've heard where the Word says, *as for the truth, it endureth and is always strong: it liveth and conquereth for evermore. She is the strength, kingdom, power, and majesty, of all ages.*"

Everyone was leaving the house, and the women were coming from their shacks to clean the kitchen. Farmer was striding over to get a ham for Marn, and show her the goats. Dutchman was bellowing because the rich man's son, Sam Trail, whom Katrin disliked and whom Dutchman was hopeful she'd marry, was coming up the lane from Greenfield Pike, riding a sweat-flecked chestnut sorrel gelding and leading a string of eight mares to be bred to the little jackass, from whose lot now came a sudden wheezing and squeaking.

"What's the matter?" Schoolmaster's voice was persuasive, as he leaned down from his horse to her. "Why are you sad, Marn Coombs? Tell me."

But she turned away, the fawn in her arms, and went to follow the Farmer. She heard the hooves of the Schoolmaster's horses trotting off. The tow-haired man led her to the smoke-shack first, and in the dark interior pulled down a ham from a hook.

"I want a bigger one, from a hind quarter," she told him.

He grasped her arm and Marn pulled away. "Give me a kiss, little girl, and I'll take another down." She smelled the tobacco scent on his breath.

"This one's all right." Hasty, she backed out into the sun-light. "How much is it?"

"You can just take it," he laughed, "as long as you don't forget who gave it to you!"

"No." And she shoved some money at the Farmer. "And where are Mr. Willem's goats?"

"Come on." He preceded Marn into the barn and to the door of the goat pen. He brushed her breast with his heavy elbow. "Take any one of them you want, little girl. And I'll put the ham in the sack on your cow. I thought you were a pretty one when I saw you coming by this morning. Don't stay away too long." Farmer was gone, humming a song.

A late wasp was buzzing at the high, cobwebbed pane of the stall. Marn went in and closed the gate behind her. She picked out a young white goat with little horns. The baby deer was difficult and while she wanted to nibble at Marn's finger, she couldn't make up her mind to suck from the tiny brown teat. Marn was half an hour coaxing her, until she stood waver-ing at the side of the goat and nursing earnestly. Marn heard voices approaching outside the high window where the wasp still bumbled about.

It was Dutchman Willem and the young fellow, Sam Trail. Dutchman was accepting a cigar, and the two leaned in the September sun against a painted foreleg of the gigantic mule on the barn side. "That café's not hard to find," Trail was saying, "and all the clothes those girls wear you couldn't cover a chicken with."

"You write down the address for me on this paper," Dutchman told him.

"Did you ever hear about a queen bee at one house," Trail asked, "who said she was quitting, and the Madame couldn't understand, and told her, 'But you're our best girl and I saw you go up and down those stairs twenty-two times last night.' And the queen bee said, 'That's right and my feet hurt and that's the reason I'm leaving.' "

Dutchman bumped the barn side with his fist, pleased. "Now, tell me, boy, what do you think of my daughter? Eh? Did you ask her to go to the Greenfield Fair like I told you to?"

"I did just now, and Katrin said everyone else wanted to take her, too, and she'd have to think about it. I figure I'm good with horses and mules, but not much with women, Mr. Willem."

"Women don't ever know what they want, boy. She'll go with you as soon as she stops and thinks. I'll tell her to. You can count on it. Eh? I had the same trouble for a while with the woman I'm setting out to get for a new wife."

"Well, all right, Mr. Willem. I like Katrin a lot. I thought maybe if I spent some money on her at the Fair, she'd come around to liking me."

"You're big on money, Trail. Someone was telling me about you getting a five-dollar fine for riding your gelding up the steps and through the courthouse doors in Greenfield, and then giving them a ten-dollar bill and turning down the change. Now you ought to be careful with your father's money. Eh?"

"My old man doesn't care. He's a faster spender than I am."

"Well, it's not in my Dutch blood, boy. I take pleasure in saving."

"Would you like to know what I'm paying fifty dollars in cash for one of these days, Mr. Willem? Coming up here with those nags, I stopped in to see the Wizard, just off the road from Greenfield. He's going to arrange to let me watch a ghost girl without a stitch on, I swear. Who do you think that is, Mr. Willem? Does he hire someone from Greenfield?"

"Could be," said Dutchman, and ground his cigar stub out carefully with his boot. "But I call it free spending. Put out that fire you've got in your hand and let's go turn those mares in with the jack. As I said, that café address is enough for me. If I can see a few girls like that while I'm paying for the food I have to eat anyway, it's a different matter. Eh?"

Marn waited until they would move away, their voices fading. She found a string to tie about the white goat's neck and led her out of the barn and into the yard. Marn saw that the ham was in one side of the sack, and she put the satisfied fawn in the other. She took Hebe's collar, and the goat trailed baaing after as they set out, winding back through field and orchard.

Marn thought of how she was seventeen years now, and ought not to be pushed around any more. And she remembered the winning voice saying, "Tell me why you're sad, Marn Coombs?" And she recalled the words in her father's Bible, *thou knowest not what is the way of the wind; thou knowest not which shall prosper, whether this or that, or whether they both shall be alike good.*

*

   *

3
*
The
Ruby
Ring IT WAS the day of the

Greenfield Fair. Wizard's largest pair of brown cows stood
yoked to the four-wheeled cart outside the weather-beaten
frame house; their sharp horns glistened in the bright rising
sun. There had been no frosts yet, but a few cold rains had
fallen during the month of September and leaves were beginning to turn; bright spots of red and amber touched the trees
around the swamp. Flocks of birds moved through the countryside in restless migration. Many were unnoticed, the tiny
sparrows, wrens, and kinglets, who traveled mainly in the dark
hours, needing to feed during the daylight. The big birds,
mallards and wood ducks, Canada geese and swans, hurled
themselves in formation during either night or day, depending
on their mood and sense of urgency. Just a few hours ago, by
the light of a three-quarters moon, a flock of whistling swans,
following in the wake of some geese, had approached and
then settled on Endless Quagmire to feed. They had wing-

spreads of seven or eight feet and had gone along in the sky with a beat more slow than the wild geese, their big black feet trailing behind. They had cried as they came down, in varied voices, from a deep bass to a shriek that carried for miles, so that not only the Coombs heard them, but the Blackburns up on Bald Mountain, and Dutchman, and Schoolmaster in his cabin on the mountain beyond Willem's farm. Two of them had been netted, and Wizard was pleased now because he could take them to Greenfield. They lay side by side and hissed now and then, in the straw of the bed of the cart, legs bound with withes, and a strip of sacking tied about their powerful wings. Wizard had had ready wide gilded collars he'd made just in case; now he slipped them over the long white necks to decorate the birds, hoping to sell them quickly, for, as a matter of fact, their capture wasn't within the law.

Next to the swans were reed hampers tied shut and holding half a dozen wild ducks each, and behind them were open baskets of large rabbits that town women bought for food or pets, the animals never trying to leap out. Piled in an orderly way in back were various home-fashioned small cages containing woodchucks, squirrels, deer mice with long golden upper fur and underparts whiter than ermine, pairs of mourning doves, and finger-tame parakeets and thrushes and wrens and tanagers. Many of the animals and birds had been raised in the household since babies in spring and felt quite at home in their baskets.

"There's just that much room and no more in the cart," Mrs. Coombs called to Wizard, when she saw he was going to let Venus come along, too. He was bringing the buzzard from the barn; she rode his wrist, flapping her black wings strongly in the crisp air to stretch them.

"I know why Father's doing that," Marn said. "He wants to get more stories going about him. He likes to make a mystery, and he wants people to be uncertain of him and what he'll do next."

"It's a fact," her mother agreed.

The doe fawn followed Marn everywhere the girl went nowadays. She wore a leather collar, and Marn was braiding flowers about it now. "And I hope nobody'll want to buy this fawn!" She broke off the lower stalks of the goldenrod and groundsel, and twisted the upper stems into each other. She'd already strung the yellow blossoms about the horns of the brown cattle, after grooming them longer than usual so their coats shone. They were chewing their cuds, the wood frame across their necks fastened to the tongue of the cart by a heavy chain.

Wizard was worried about that chain and intended to re-replace it with a stouter one at the Fair. He examined the links at the point of stress and decided that they would make it. He went to get his sacks of herbs and pelts, and a small box of frogs and salamanders and the like that he had a use for sometimes, and which he'd left in the kitchen by his chair. "Let's get a move on!" Wizard was in a good temper, and felt the day would be fortuitous. He sat down for his tea and milk before going.

The women were pleased, too. The Fair was the big yearly holiday for the community, and the country people all had put on their best attire and had decked out their animals. The Blackburns were already down from their mountain and going along the road to Greenfield, hauled in their wagon by the span of giant oxen, red tassels on their horns and the shining mahogany yoke across their shoulders. Behind Sheepman and Henry and Mrs. Blackburn were huge bundles of combed wool from the August shearing, and there were stacks of Blackburn's whittled and woven chairs, and also neat piles of his women's quilts. Dutchman Willem's hired men were on their way, too, leading his mules and hauling his wagons of harvest. Willem himself, driving his crack team of matched black mules that he never would sell, was going clear to the top of Bald Mountain to pick up Nell Blackburn waiting there for him as her parents had commanded her.

Marn hadn't seen Henry Blackburn all that month, and the only news she'd had of him was that Henry had brought his father's red oxen down to Dutchman's farm to be shod by Stableman, and that Dutchman had presented Katrin with a new dress for the Fair as a bribe, pink and lacy, and that Katrin had consented to go with Sam Trail instead of Henry Blackburn. Marn was hoping to talk with Henry today. She hadn't confided to anyone the small edge of worry that she'd had the past week. Her birthday, when she'd gone up on the mountain to see him, was on the second of the month, and now it was the twenty-eighth, and her term past due. She patted the fawn beside her, nuzzling her hand for its bread crusts.

"I wish that girl had a new dress this year," Mrs. Coombs said to Wizard, as Marn went to fix her hair at the mirror one more time. Marn had pinned it up and thought it rather unbecoming. Wizard had made a scene earlier about her hair hanging long and told her to act her age on a public occasion and be respectable, for his sake if not for her own.

"Good looks or fine clothes never made kettle boil," Wizard told his wife now, "and we're not putting our daughter up for sale, either. That dress is plenty pretty."

"She's been wearing it for two years and it's about done,"

Mrs. Coombs said, "and I'll say the same for this rag I've got on. I might buy a new one for myself, too. I'll see." The woman was putting the dishes away, pleased with the prospect of visiting and gathering gossip and pocketing the money paid into her hand. Mrs. Coombs felt their daughter looked fine, really, in the yellow gown with the embroidered collar and full skirt; she only complained to make conversation. She thought it fitted a little tightly at the waist and breast, of course, since Marn was still growing, but nevertheless it would do very well this year.

The fawn, as they left the house, sprang into the air, bounding about, wanting Marn to play with her. The white foster-mother goat had had to be tied in the barn by the cow, Hebe. She'd grown so fond of the fawn, she wanted to follow, and bleated now from the distance, as the little deer consented to come and lie in the straw by Marn in the light-weight wagon, and the Coombs started on their way. There were blankets and old coats for anyone who got chilly, and Mrs. Coombs sat up on the seat with Wizard, who drove with a long pole to guide the cows, Venus on the wagon edge in front of him.

"If we're lucky, that chain's going to last, but fifteen miles is a long way," the man said, "and I've got a feeling." He scowled, his black, bushy hair mussed.

A mile up the road, where the two streams flowing down the mountains met and started a river, there was a bridge. As the old cart creaked across it, the weakest link snapped. The oxen, freed of their load, continued to move. Wizard shouted at them to, in the name of all perdition, stop where they were. They slowed and halted, mild, and turned to graze on the high grass and pokeberries at the wayside. Wizard got down to survey his latest trouble. He glanced up at his wife, and his voice was shrill and warning.

"I said I had a feeling, woman!"

"Don't lose your temper," she told him. "And look who's coming there."

It was Randall Grim, ambling along on his black mare and holding the lead strap to the long-haired bay loaded with honeypots and various supply sacks. Schoolmaster was sporting a blue turtleneck sweater he'd knit recently for himself, and wore close-fitted store-bought pants, and had on his little round cap. His spaniel stayed at his mare's heels as Schoolmaster reined up alongside Wizard. "I passed Mr. Willem's Stableman with a load of grain sacks back there, and he'll be along in a minute. He'll have an extra chain or some wire with him."

Mrs. Coombs said, "This is the new Schoolmaster, Wizard."

Her husband looked up at the newcomer. "Get down off your horse and I'll ride back and see what that Stableman's got. I don't like waiting."

"Well, all right," Grim said, shrugging and dismounting, letting Wizard have his mare's reins.

"I'm glad to see you again, Schoolmaster," Mrs. Coombs said. "And why don't you ride alongside us to the Fair, if Wizard ever gets us on our way? Are you in a hurry?"

"I'd like that." Grim nodded at Marn and the flower-decked fawn in the straw. "Because I don't know my way around Greenfield." As Wizard cantered off, Schoolmaster took a bundle from his pack horse. "I was going to stop at this bridge anyway. I've got a few melons here and I'm going to leave them to cool. I'll have them for supper on the way home."

He was sliding down the embankment by the bridge, his spaniel ahead of him, and tying the sack to the base of an alder shrub, and letting it sink into the confluence.

He scrambled back, and looked over at the young turkey vulture perched on the wagon before Mrs. Coombs. "Is that bird for sale at the Fair?"

"That's Venus," Mrs. Coombs told him, "and she's one of the family."

"Are those members of the family, too?" Grim looked in the wagon bed at the pair of swans behind Marn, their long necks decorated with the broad gilded rings, their black bills resting on the sacking that held their wings to their sides. "Are they tamed?"

"Actually, they're not. They only came down from the sky last night," Mrs. Coombs told him.

"Are they out of that flock? I heard those whistling swans calling and wondered if they settled. But you can't trap swans any more than you can that fawn your daughter's got there." Schoolmaster frowned.

"They used to get after Wizard," Mrs. Coombs said. "Long ago. But then he got acquainted with the law and how to pacify it in different ways. If he has to, Wizard can work out an answer for just about any problem anyone can think up."

"Have the rest of you got any like talents? I always thought the world was filled with situations even Solomon couldn't handle." Grim looked over at Marn, who kept her eyes down and stroked the fawn's head in her lap. He went to lead back the team of beflowered horned cows and return them to their position before the cart.

And then the mare was galloping back, and Wizard was pleased. He hurled the chain down at the brown cows' feet.

"That Stableman had a sackful of this and that to lend!" Wizard fastened the chain to the tongue and yoke. He spoke aggressively. "The wife of Stableman's going to be in a piece of trouble before many days are out." He patted the pocket where his secret mirror stayed.

"Posh," said Mrs. Coombs, "I don't need any magic to tell me the same thing, Wizard."

"It's because she's comely as the Queen of Sheba," Wizard said. "You've got to watch about vanity of vanities all the time." And he glared at his daughter Marn in her yellow dress that was almost worn out.

"I was remarking upon these swans and deer you caught, and that load of ducks," Schoolmaster said, mounting his mare. "Now I used to make wine once to sell, and I had to file a form with the Assistant Regional Commissioner before I could even get started, and that's a fact. It's the same with trapping birds. I was telling your wife that. Law is law; and there's one, not two ways of following it."

Wizard climbed up on the wagon seat, unperturbed. "It's my livelihood. Some gain theirs one way and some another. I pull mine from the swamp and the sky. No one's going to lock me up in jail, either. Did you ever know a man could squeeze into the body of a little crow? And just wait till this other black bird here gets a little bigger." He looked at Schoolmaster and winked, his expression gauged to seem malevolent. He clucked to the oxen, his deep-set eyes half shut.

"Well, I'm figuring on doing some wrestling this afternoon that I've heard about," Grim said. "And have you got any extra sight that can tell if I'll win the prize or not?"

"If I pleased," Wizard told them all, "I could stop that

quarrel going on between Stableman and his gadabout woman."

Marn spoke up. "Mr. Grim, have you ever seen a Wrestling Ram?" And she thought of the great one dying up there on the mountain near a month ago.

"I never did, Miss Coombs, but I'd like to take one on any time."

"Here comes somebody," Mrs. Coombs said.

Dutchman's mules were clattering up at an easy trot, a dozen or more of them strung together, and the big tow-headed Farmer riding the lead one. Their black polished halters glistened, and they wore blue and orange rosettes on their brow bands to attract the notice of the auction bidders. Their hoofs pounded upon the roadway, passing Coombs' cart, each of the powerful sleek bodies weighing three-quarters of a ton. Their tails were braided and bound up into knots, and their manes roached. In the Fair stalls, at the last minute before the sale, Farmer would put neatsfoot oil on their hoofs and run a damp cloth over their coats and collect plenty for Mr. Willem that day. He shouted at Marn from his saddle, impudent, over the racket. "Hey! Come and watch me wrestle, little girl!"

Wizard called back some retort, which was lost in the noise. When the cavalcade had gone by and was disappearing in a dust screen up ahead, Randall Grim said, restless, "I wouldn't mind to pit myself against that fellow. I've had schoolboys his size I had to handle and set back in their seats."

"He's too big for you," Mrs. Coombs told him. "You can't tell because he was up on that mule."

"Oh, I've seen him on the ground, too," Grim said, "when I've stopped in at Willem's to collect some of those lazy pupils he doesn't want to send me. And I met Sheepman Blackburn's son there, too, and I intend to wrestle him, if he's not afraid."

Marn bridled. "Henry won the Fair medal last year, Mr. Grim. He's a strong one." And she flushed when Schoolmaster glanced sharply at her. "I went to the Fair with Henry," she said.

"What happened this year that you're going alone?"

But Marn didn't have to answer because there was a quick sound of hoofs and wheels speeding to overtake them. It was Sam Trail's yellow, high-wheeled racing buggy, the young man in a natty suit and fancy white shirt beside Katrin, wearing pink ruffles and waving at Randall Grim and the Wizard's two women. Trail held high the reins to his sorrel gelding and grinned. When they had disappeared ahead, Wizard turned to Schoolmaster, as if riled.

"And take that pair there. That girl's not going to have that young man for a husband, in case she thinks she is, because I'm turning her thoughts upon another for my own purposes."

"Is that so?" Grim said softly, feeling his scorn for the small man on the wagon with the pole in his hand that he used to tell the horned cows which way to go. Wizard's black jacket was patched, and his dark, soiled tie had been handed to him from someone else who had worn it nearly out; his boots still had swamp mud on them from his trip out to the traps where he'd found the swans that morning early. Schoolmaster himself had pride in his neat clothes and his shined boots, and in his trim body, too, that he kept in top shape, swimming in the stream behind his cabin every morning, and intending to continue that practice even when he would have to break the winter ice. He exercised daily in his solitary cabin. *Mens sana in corpore sano.* And he felt that now, at thirty years, he had even gained dominion over his sexual desires. His powerful upper-arm muscles were outlined by the rough-wooled, clinging, blue sweater, and he rode his saddle as if a part of the mare. Grim had observed how Marn blushed when she defended the Blackburn boy. He slowed his mares to ride close to her in the wagon, trying to see her father's features in her oval face that appeared childish and might hide wickedness or innocence, because who could tell from an exterior what was hid inside?

"What does your father mean when he says he's turning Miss Willem's thoughts where he pleases?" Randall Grim kept his voice soft and from her parents' ears.

"You're a curious man," Marn told him, sharp and clear. "Why don't you talk with my mother and tell her stories? She likes that, and I like being left alone."

Mrs. Coombs turned about on her seat, pleased. "Now do that, Schoolmaster!"

"Well," he said, riding up, "did you ever hear of the church deacon who left a message for his signmaker in his office with the motto and dimensions of what he wanted? His wife came in and saw it and nearly fainted. It said, *Unto Us A Child Is Born. Six feet long and two feet wide!*"

Marn didn't listen to them, worrying upon the spell her father had cast upon Henry Blackburn. Had Wizard done it by making Katrin go to visit Henry, with the clock and message? He had known that Henry, angry with Marn because his sheep had been killed, would turn to Katrin easily. It was a sure thing Marn never dared go up to see Henry on the mountain top any more, as she had done all the past summer long. Sometimes Marn had trouble disbelieving in her father's powers. She'd always heard her mother rail at Wizard, and she

tried to guard herself from accepting what she knew was
quackery, but Marn had been under the influence of the
Wizard since a baby and a growing child. She was dependent
in the same way that the fawn was and the caged creatures in
the cart with her, who had, since birth or before they left their
nests, depended upon Marn and Mrs. Coombs. It was so with
the pair of turkeys back at home, and the squirrel, and the
Wizard's crow. Even Venus on the wagon edge, emotional,
ducking her head whenever any of the Coombs family spoke
to her, didn't behave like the wild buzzards or have their odor
or habits. The swans, now, taken mature from the sky, depended only on each other, and would hiss and battle all
human-kind always, untamable. It was what you got used to
when you were young that made up your nature and interests,
and Marn had watched her father make magic always and she
half believed in it.

Randall Grim's spaniel barked, and in the wake of Trail's
buggy Dutchman's cart was approaching, drawn by a handsome team of mules. Dutchman, his red-blond hair restrained
by a bearskin cap, and a stained meerschaum pipe in his hand,
was telling Nell Blackburn, severe beside him, one of his
favorite sayings: *The eye of the master sees more than ten
eyes of his servants!* And he was relating, too, how he'd just
fired another hand for putting apples and potatoes in a store-
house together, which would ruin them all. Nell's straight
brows were in a frown, because she felt the same as ever and
always would about Dutchman, and didn't want to be with
him now. She wished she were far down the road and almost
in Greenfield, where her early-starting parents were with
Henry. She wanted to be helping her mother at setting up
their displays and waiting to see who would buy Nell's favorite

quilt, *The Ten Commandments*. Nell waved her hand in despair at Marn, who understood her feelings, while Dutchman gazed ahead, disdaining the whole poor lot of them, including the new Schoolmaster, who was of no earthly use and who disturbed Dutchman's hired men by stirring up discontent and false desires in their children.

Marn Coombs had missed Nell as well as Henry lately, because when she'd gone up there on the sheep bald in the summertime, Nell had used to come and talk with them now and then. Marn felt again suddenly that same edge of concern which had bothered her earlier in the morning. She thought how there might be trouble ahead, and she was like the creatures in the cart that would be served up their lives shortly, some headed for petting and contentment, and others for destruction.

Schoolmaster Grim saw the girl's indrawn look and spoke in the settling dust of the road, conciliatory. "I imagine your daughter is pretty when she smiles, Mrs. Coombs!"

"Beauty is as beauty does," Wizard told them all, watchful of his offspring, "and it's a fact that thorns will remain on a bush for its life, while the roses fall."

"Tell me something, Wizard," Mrs. Coombs joshed him, and put her hand out to stroke the black bird balanced before them on the wagon edge, "is Venus a beauty or not? And it's a good thing they don't have a class at the Fair for the best singing bird, Mr. Grim. Because our Venus would take the booby prize."

It was mid-morning when they arrived at the Fair. All was commotion: the whinnying of horses and mules, the bawling of cattle, the crying of sheep and pigs, the calling of men, and the shrieking of women, and the laughter and wailing of

children. A chanting blind gypsy with dark Portuguese features begged, a china plate held out, as the Coombs' creaking
wagon, dragged by the brown cows that Wizard guided with
his long pole and followed by Randall Grim and his horses
and dog, moved by. Schoolmaster tossed a coin that missed the
plate, and the gypsy spit after him and bent, murmuring softly,
"Estúpido! Fantástico!" Traders and peddlers were setting up;
some sold wooden seeds to the farmers, some true ones. A
horse dealer called to his son, "Come ride this horse for me.
I want to see his paces." And the boy returned, "Do I ride him
to buy or to sell, Daddy?"

"I wonder where your honey tent is?" Mrs. Coombs cried
to Schoolmaster above the din.

"I'd better find out."

"You come hunt us up later," she told him.

"I'll do that," he said. "Maybe your daughter will let me
show her the tallest dwarf and the smallest giant in history!"
And he left them, and drifted away through the confusion.

The Coombs headed for the same spot they'd used last
year and most of the years before that; it was near the carnival
section, where Wizard could pull in people pleasure-bound
and with money still unspent. The family began unloading
and debating where to place their wares to the best advantage,
tying the brown cows to the back of the wagon, where they
would stand munching the straw in its bed all day long, the
flowers about their horns falling off little by little; and before
them, on the seat of the wagon, the perched turkey vulture,
her wings outspread in her habit, turning a little now and
then to catch the sun rays on each one of the black and
glossy feathers. Wizard set out the heavy whistling swans and
the crates of ducks, while Marn handed down to her mother

the many small cages and hampers of chirping, fluttering birds and curious small animals, who sensed the change as they were taken from the wagon, where they had been jolted and disturbed for the past three hours, and were set upon the sunlit and dusty grass. Marn jumped to the ground, and the fawn leapt after her, delighted to run again.

Wizard told the women, "You both finish up now, and I'll go see what I can drum up. And I want you to push that fawn," he said to Marn.

But when people came by, Marn didn't; and Mrs. Coombs held her tongue, knowing how her daughter fancied the little animal. Half of the cages had been sold and someone was interested in one of the swans when Wizard finally returned. Sam Trail and Katrin were close behind him. The young man wanted to talk with Wizard, and as soon as Katrin saw Marn and ran to her in her gay and effusive way, the two men withdrew and, staying out of Mrs. Coombs' earshot, discussed their business.

Katrin cried to Marn, "Please come and see the side shows with us! I hate being alone with Sam. He didn't say a word during the whole trip here, except would I kiss him when there was no one on the road, and when I said no he didn't even *try*."

"That's a nice young man, Katrin Willem," Mrs. Coombs said. "And how's that cage of cardinals I sent over doing?"

"They're fine," Katrin giggled. "And Sam Trail wants to spend everything in his pockets on me, Mrs. Coombs. You come with us, Marn, and help me do it," she coaxed.

"Get him to buy you a diamond ring, Miss Willem," advised Mrs. Coombs. "Wizard says a diamond outlasts any promise made."

"When does the wrestling start?" Marn wanted to know, for that was where Henry would be sure to be found.

"They don't start on that or the judging or the ox-pulling, either, until afternoon," Katrin said, "and so there's plenty of time to look around. I want to see the Sultan's Harem, don't you, Marn? And the man who swallows mice?"

"Don't forget the strong woman," said Mrs. Coombs. "I go to see her every year, Miss Willem!"

Wizard and Trail were finishing their business and were lighting the cigars Trail produced. Wizard stashed the cash bills he'd received in his breast pocket, affable because of them and the fact that more were forthcoming from the young man shortly. "I'll put four dozen of these game ducks back under the wagon for your father's men to pick up, Mr. Trail. That's the last of them and I'm cleaned out. And you tell him I promise to haul him in two full-grown venison in November when they're prime for his table the way I know he likes."

"All right," Sam Trail said. "Now Katrin wants your daughter to come with us."

Wizard told him crankily, "She can't because she's to sell that little deer of hers first."

"I see," Trail said, convinced by the Wizard for the time being that the woman he used for his ghost girl trick was someone hired from Greenfield. He'd confronted Wizard and been assured that it wasn't Marn. Trail straightened his dark tie and fastened the button on the pocket where he kept his wallet. Sam Trail felt that courting required an incredibly complex and indirect approach. As he'd grown up, Trail had acquired a reputation for daring adventures involving midnight gallops through the town of Greenfield and sorties upon red-light district houses elbow-to-elbow with his friends. But those es-

86

capades were forthright; Trail felt he could out-think any animal in the county and many a man. But he glanced with desperation at the buxom and flirtatious, pink-garbed Dutchman's daughter. He got his comb from his pocket and smoothed down his blond hair, parted in the middle. "Come on, Katrin."

"We'll come back later, Marn, and maybe you'll be free," Katrin said, and the two were going away.

"What kind of bargaining were you doing with that rich Mr. Trail before I could hear?" Mrs. Coombs said. But then the swan customer was returning, and she got no reply from her husband.

By noon, Wizard's mood was excellent. The swan had been bought for five dollars, the women had disposed of many of the little birds and beasts, and Wizard's sacks of herbs and charms and skins and good-luck frogs from the quagmire were dwindling satisfactorily. Mrs. Coombs decided to leave Marn in charge for a while and go off to look around, and maybe get a new dress, and check up on who was there among those that she'd known other years. Dutchman's Stableman came by to complain about the talisman Wizard had sold him which hadn't succeeded in keeping his comely wife's mind on him alone. He wanted to try another. Wizard told Stableman that his problem was that he was a cheapskate. If he could see his way to spending a little more, he might get a charm that would do some good. Stableman said he was ready to give Wizard his last cent, but if it wasn't a success he guaranteed he'd be around to wring Wizard's neck sometime. Right on Stableman's heels came the Farmer, who winked at Marn, and then told Wizard that what he was after was something to keep the Willem chicken-house rats down.

"They're after our eggs, too. One rat'll lie on his back and hold the egg in his feet, while the other tows him off by the tail." Farmer took the poison done up in little packets doubtfully. "I'm willing to try. I've even thought of shooting firecrackers in the holes to confuse the mother rats so they'll forget to feed their young." He grinned at Marn. "Let's go see the cat-crossed-on-a-rabbit's child, Wizard's daughter."

"I don't care to," Marn said, positive.

"And I won't spare her, either, Farmer," Wizard told him. "Now go on!"

But when Schoolmaster Grim arrived, his spaniel at his side, having entered his honey in the competition and won a money prize besides blue ribbons, and having staked his horses somewhere in a lot for the day, Marn felt differently. Wizard was standing over by the wagon, stroking Venus, who nibbled with her curved bill between his fingers, while Coombs talked a group of Greenfield men into certain herbs that were illness preventatives, and were done up in fragrant cloth bundles, or else stuffed in jars and covered with special oils or lotions.

Grim told Marn, "The Blackburns just bought a big English ram with curling horns. I saw it. Young Blackburn's going to wrestle it for the public before the main contest starts."

"I want to watch that," she said, eager.

"Why not come with me, then?" Schoolmaster ran his hands through his brown curls, laughing.

"No," she said.

"Why not?" He was persuasive. "There's time to look around and get a bite to eat, and then we'll go over to the ring for the main event. Wrestling's my favorite sport."

She wanted to come, but she told him, "Father won't let me leave until I sell the fawn here, Mr. Grim. And I don't want to." Marn nodded at her father, haggling with the men, and at the fawn wandering about, never straying too far.

"What's his price on it?"

"Seven. But I don't want to part with her."

"Well, I just bought her, Miss Coombs," he said, "and that's that. I wanted to spend the prize I got for my honey."

"What will you do with her?" Marn frowned.

"She can stay in my schoolyard and be a pet for the smallest ones. You can come to visit her if you want. Now tie her up so she won't follow, while I pay your father. I'll be back to pick her up later."

He beckoned the man over from his customers while Marn fastened the fawn with a rope to a heavy hamper and put a handful of crusts and hay on the ground to keep her busy. She could hear the two talking while she tended the deer. She knew Wizard had brought up the same subject to him as to Trail. Her father was red-faced, his bushy hair rumpled. "Take it or leave it, Schoolmaster. I don't care about your notions of real and unreal. What I propose is legitimate. Forget I mentioned it."

Grim pacified him, "I don't want to argue. How about a charm to keep my bees quiet when I'm moving them to a new hive?"

"That's easy enough," Wizard said grudging. "All you have to do is pick the right day. You pick the wrong day and the best-behaved hive will riot. Now, for fifty cents I've got a list here of the particular days that are unlucky in every month. You can use the list also to apply on when not to travel or to bargain or to marry."

"What about getting born?" Schoolmaster asked.

"Don't laugh," Wizard told him, "because if your birthday

did fall on one of these days, you'd be bad off. And that's the truth."

"All right, give me one, and here's the money. But I hope you've heard about doing unto others as you'd have them do to you, Wizard Coombs, because you're in a pretty nefarious business, it seems to me."

"Stop thinking everyone's got the same needs as everyone else." Wizard pointed his finger at Grim, put out with the man because he'd circumvented Wizard's hope to keep Marn under his eye all that day, not wanting her exposed to temptations and hurts that would surely occur if she went wandering about. "Did you ever try feeding grass to a ferret or new-cut hay to that dog at your feet there? And how about giving meat to that cage of doves or swan?"

"Speaking of the swan, Mr. Coombs," Grim said gently, "why not release it? If you were an innocent prisoner, wouldn't you want to be free? Turn it loose."

"You sound like the preacher in the church where my daughter goes," Coombs told him. "All the wars in the Bible that he's always reciting from are because of the Golden Rule. Now you bring my girl back by three o'clock on the dot. We've got to make it home by nightfall." And Wizard turned back to the waiting men.

Grim shrugged, crumpling and throwing away the list he'd just bought. "Come on, Miss Coombs. Are you hungry yet? I know where the food stands are."

They went down the dusty way, past the variety of displays and shows, the golden spaniel tagging their feet. Marn strode beside the man swiftly; her yellow dress accented her breasts; her hair piled up made her seem taller to Grim than when he'd seen her in Dutchman Willem's kitchen a few weeks before.

She spoke resentfully. "If I'd found that swan in the snare before my father got there, Mr. Grim, I'd have set it free, I can tell you!"

"He's wrong about those Bible wars," Schoolmaster said. "There are times when the only thing to do is go to battle because by so doing you're preventing a worse one."

"And he thinks he owns every animal and bird there is!" Marn was glad to speak out her feelings to someone, and she added, "All he cares about are his crow and his goat and Venus."

"I wondered if you understood what he was like," Schoolmaster said. "Or if you were cast of the same mold as he."

"Some day I'm afraid I'll be in trouble with Father," Marn said. "He knows I go into the quagmire to unset his traps, and he's not caught me at it yet."

Randall Grim was elated at finding that the girl fought with the Wizard. He felt he was coming upon the truth hid behind her soft face: that she was innocent and was being used by her father and wasn't in collusion with him in his fakery. "If you ever need help, you let me know," he told Marn.

She was still stirred by what Grim had said about the swan being an innocent prisoner. Marn had watched the white bird's large eyes on the journey to the Fair and how they watered and seemed to weep. It was different with the hand-reared creatures that wouldn't leave the Coombs' house and, if turned outside, came to stand at doors and look in windows, involved with those inside, and seldom able to start a different life in the wild. "Mr. Grim, if you want to know one book my father gave me to read when I first learned how, it was the Bible. And it seems to me it is about him when God forgave

Noah and his sons and sent them from the ark and told them that the fear and dread of man was to be on all the beasts and fowl and all that moved on the earth and all the fishes of the sea, and said, *into your hand are they delivered.*" And Marn sighed.

They were approaching a stall where apples dipped in a sticky, burned-sugar confection were sold. "Do you want one of those, Miss Coombs?"

She nodded, and he bought one for each of them; and further on they had lemonade from a rusty bucket, and then stopped at another stall where Grim ordered three baked potatoes. The vendor slit their skins and put butter in their hot middles and pushed the shaker of salt along the counter toward the couple. Grim tossed one potato on the grass for the spaniel's lunch. While they stood there, Marn saw Nell Blackburn walking by and called her over. "This is Randall Grim, the new teacher. This is the Sheepman's daughter, Nell Blackburn."

"You want to come along with us?" Grim asked. "We're seeing the sights and heading for the wrestling."

"I don't mind," Nell said. "I'm here alone."

"Where's Mr. Willem, Nell?" Marn asked. "What'll your father say?"

Nell looked over at Schoolmaster, feeling his attractiveness, and how he looked just enough older than her to suit her. She laughed, her Scotch eyes frank. "I told Dutchman I preferred my father's sheep to him for company and he was the most conceited man I ever met. He said he was going off to eat at some café in town that he hoped would be more entertaining than I was!"

"I wish I could be that way with my father," Marn said, "and disobey him outright and not be afraid."

"There's Dutchman's daughter over there." Schoolmaster pointed. On the outskirts of the crowd gathered before a flimsy canvas tent, advertised as *The Sultan's Harem,* were Katrin and Trail.

"Let's go over to join them," Marn said.

As they came up, Katrin cried, "Listen to what the man's saying about the dancer. It's about where he found her and rescued her and brought her over to America, and here she is in North Carolina and who'd have thought it possible!"

The spieler had a ring made of a twisted horseshoe nail on his left hand; his thumb was hooked in his vest. He wore a yellow flat-top hat, and his words were smooth. "Lulu was the favorite dancer of the Sultan, and we saved her from the horrors of his harem so that red-blooded American men might see the secrets of that barbaric land. She's danced for kings and potentates. And when she does that, the old become young, the blind see, and cripples throw away their crutches. No ladies are allowed. Only strong men." The dancing woman, heavily painted to darken her skin and accent her features, rose slowly. Her midriff was bare, and she wore loose-fitting trousers tied low on her belly. She undulated her hips and, turning her back on her audience, walked slowly toward the curtains that hid the interior. She turned around just before going in.

"Come on, Mr. Grim," Sam Trail said. "Let's look just for a minute. These girls'll wait for us."

"Not me, Sam," Katrin said. "If they won't let me in, I won't wait."

"I will," Nell said. "I've got nothing better to do."

"No," Grim told Trail. "I'm just not interested. You go ahead if you must."

"We'll meet you at the ring later, Mr. Trail," Nell said, feeling that she liked Randall Grim about as much, having known him half an hour, as she despised Dutchman Willem, whom she'd known most of her life.

"Sam doesn't want to watch the wrestling contest," Katrin laughed. "He's afraid he'll be tackled by Henry Blackburn and get thrown!"

"I know what," Trail told them. "I'll just buy a picture of the dancer. I'll be right back." He was torn between his fear of losing Katrin and his curiosity. He wound his way through the people to purchase the souvenir.

The hawker was talking: "And for those who are real sports, Lulu has just whispered to me that she might put on a special show. She's never seen so many handsome men before—and she's seen many a good-looking man, I'll guarantee." Trail stood looking up at the weaving body. "Lulu quivers and shakes like an aspen leaf in a summer wind. And for an extra thin silver dollar apiece, Lulu, who is now going back inside, informs me that she might dance without you know what!"

And Marn and Schoolmaster and Nell and Katrin watched as Trail, entranced, became one of the crowd of men pushing their way through the flap of the canvas door.

"I don't blame him," Katrin said. "If I were a man, I'd go in with him. I don't understand you, Randall. Wouldn't you, Marn?"

But Marn shook her head and turned away, starting down the road. She felt affronted slightly and didn't know why. She thought it had to do with the ways of men and her present worry that had been forgot for a while. Grim followed her, thinking the girl, innocent, was disturbed because of modesty. Nell came after Grim, intrigued, and delighted that the man had found them attractive enough to remain with them and not follow the dancing girl. And Katrin was still wishing to go into the tent with Sam Trail and see the show, too.

She asked Nell, "Why aren't you with Papa?" And she sounded petulant. "Why don't you like my Papa, Nell?"

"He's somewhere selling his mules." Nell made up an excuse.

"I can't see why you don't like my Papa!" Katrin cried. "I wish you did."

"Can you hear our Irish and Brown, Mr. Grim," Nell asked, to change the subject, "getting set to pull off the loaded stoneboat up there?"

A yelling came from ahead, where the meadow was roped into various rings. In the largest one, where the people now cheered, Sheepman Blackburn's oxen, their red-tasseled horns lowered and massive shoulders braced, were considering the signal they'd got from Sheepman, who tapped their rumps lightly with his buggy whip and encouraged them. "Gee-whup, you two babies!"

Schoolmaster said, "Miss Blackburn, they say it's a secret how your father got those oxen of his so big."

"That's true," she said. "And his family's bound not to reveal it to anybody but relatives, too," Nell laughed. "Don't ask me."

"I'll wait till you tell me," Schoolmaster said. "Sometime you will." He felt the woman admired him, and it fed his vanity.

They watched the two animals, broad of back and beam and five feet high, slowly start and tow the four-and-a-half-ton load of weighed and stacked stone on the large wooden sled. The shod hoofs dug in the turf and the tails flicked. Sheepman Blackburn had a time stopping them at the prescribed twenty feet, because they thought they were headed for their barn and some afternoon feed. Bets were collected and paid off among the ringside people, who waited for the day when the pair and their master would be defeated. The hundred-pound prize sack of sugar was awarded by the judges, who announced that Mr. Blackburn was renewing his yearly challenge to match his span against anything that wore hoofs or horns. Now bets were beginning to be wagered on the wrestling contests to be held after the exhibition of Sheepman's English Wrestling Ram, just acquired. That exhibition would be held at a quarter of three o'clock, as soon as the ring had been cleaned and raked. The judges said that Blackburn's son, Henry, had been persuaded to show off the ram's style, and it would be worthwhile to see, man pitted against beast.

Schoolmaster said to Marn, "Now, right after that exhibition I'm taking you back to your parents, Miss Coombs. Your father said three o'clock on the dot."

"Here's Sam," Katrin said, as the young man came up, straightening his tie and shrugging. "Tell us, did Lulu dance the way she was going to?"

"If you mean *without you know what,*" Trail spoke drily, "that turned out to be her dancing in those same pants while we were *without our hats on.* And not only that, but after five minutes they dropped the tent walls, so we were standing out in the open and had to scatter." Trail was disgusted. "Do you want her picture, Katrin? I don't."

"All right." Katrin took the card and then said, "Nell, look, there's Papa!"

"So it is," Nell said.

The oxen were moving out of the ring, the sugar sack laid across the back of one, and Dutchman Willem was striding over to Sheepman Blackburn to protest the unmannerly ways of his daughter, Nell. Dutchman puffed at his unlit pipe, stocky, angry. "Go to him, Nell!" Katrin pleaded.

Nell sighed, "Well, it was nice meeting you, Mr. Grim."

Schoolmaster took off his little round cap. "I hope you aren't leaving before the wrestling, Miss Blackburn."

"It depends on what Mr. Willem wants," Nell said. "If he stays, I must. That's what my parents said to do." Her eyes were forthright and her straight brows in a line, and she decided to go further, since heaven only knew when she'd see the nice young man again, who was only a few years more than her twenty-six, whereas Dutchman Willem was an old man of fifty. "And if you ever need any help at cleaning that schoolhouse or your cabin, Mr. Grim, as I know you live alone, don't hesitate to send word and I'd be glad to come."

"Thank you, Miss Blackburn. I'll remember." Grim put his cap on again, and she went away.

The ring cleaners were almost finished. The spaniel whimpered, and Marn said, "Here comes Henry now."

"That's a powerful ram he's leading," Trail said.

"Where have you been so long, Henry?" Katrin called.

"Looking for you, Sweetheart!" he shouted as he approached, controlling the lurching movements of the ram. "And bargaining for this fellow."

"How are you, Henry?" Marn said.

"Busy," he told her, glancing over, grinning. He wore a red

plaid wool shirt; his sandy hair was upright. He led the ram by a chain about the great ridged horns, each of which spiraled out a foot and made three great circles before ending in a forward-pointing, polished, sharpened metal tip. His face and legs weren't heavy-wooled like his body; the elongated pupils of his eyes were dark amber and his hoofs were black; his bag hung low and heavy. He baaed in a baritone, and Henry praised him.

"He's a Dorset, and I always wanted one of them. And the ewes he throws will be heavy milkers, too."

"He's beautiful, Henry," Marn said, urgent.

He felt the emotion in her voice and turned to her, reaching out to muss her hair, lively. "That's a pretty yellow dress, Marn. Say, I thought about you in the middle of last night."

"Why'd you think about her?" Katrin mocked Henry.

"When I heard some whistling swans settling down to the quagmire below the mountain, I wondered how many were in the crowd."

"Father caught two," she told him.

"You didn't get there in time." He laughed, turning to Schoolmaster and Trail. "Did you fellows know this girl's going to send her father to the poorhouse some day? She's always turning loose what he catches!" Henry stripped off his shirt and handed it to Katrin. "Why don't you keep that for me?" His undershirt was of undyed wool and sleeveless; he rubbed his biceps.

Katrin hung the shirt over her arm. "Maybe I will."

The ram baaed, restless, and Henry patted the thick-wooled back. Randall Grim didn't like the brash young man a bit, and he said, "I'll take up or make any challenge as to wrestling, Mr. Blackburn, when it comes to it."

"How about you, Sam?" Katrin teased. "I want to see you wrestle with Henry!"

Trail ignored her. "How come he's got those metal tips? And how long's he been wrestling, Henry?"

"He came from some other district," Henry said, "and has been trained at this sport. He beats that old ram of mine that I lost, both in his breeding and for a fighter."

"Did you get rid of Tam yet?" Marn asked, flushing. "For Katrin said you told her the dog wasn't worth much."

"I'm giving him another chance," Henry said briefly, and went away, leading his ram into the ring where one of the judges was shouting through a megaphone.

"Ladies and gentlemen, now to the event of the moment: Henry Blackburn and the Wrestling Ram! But first let me state that this is a respectable Fair here in Greenfield, and between each of these performances, let us warn you to beware of pickpockets, who rely upon your interest in the spectacles to prey upon you. And here is the show!"

The ram stood his ground and the man played to him carefully, so the beast sometimes rose on his hind legs and plunged in a strong butting movement. He would paw like a bull and call hoarsely, his nose to the ground, horn tips touching a little and digging at it. Then Henry would dodge and catch his horns, and the two would sway there until the ram at last fell and they rolled on the ground together. The man stood back while the beast scrambled up and reared again to try to strike the man. Henry gauged his actions, stepped aside at the last moment, so the pointed metal just creased his shoulder, and then turning and moving in to take hold of the horns again with his vice-grip and wrestle with the ram until he went suddenly to his knees and then to his side,

Henry on top. At length Henry quieted the excited ram by speaking to him and catching the wool at his neck. He slipped the chain back about the horns, and the animal, baaing in bass tones, followed Henry from the ring, while the crowd applauded.

"The first wrestling match will now begin," the ringmaster yelled, "and to be decided by a drawing of straws of everybody willing. Long straws stay in the ring. Thereafter, winner will accept first challenge from the sidelines. Judges' opinions final. Kindly step forward. And as I said before, Ladies and Gentlemen, keep a guard on purses and pockets!"

There were six who came to draw on the straws the judge held out: Dutchman's Farmer, Schoolmaster Grim, Henry Blackburn, and three men from Greenfield. Two of the latter pulled the long straws. Schoolmaster hurried out of the ring and to Marn.

"I'm glad I'm not in this match, Miss Coombs. I want to get you back to the Wizard. It's just three o'clock. Now, I'd like to hurry so I don't miss anything." He spoke softly.

"I don't want to leave now," Marn said, her eyes on Henry, going over to the ringside to wait his chance.

"Come along," Schoolmaster said sharply, as the first contestants locked arms and staggered against each other.

"I want to stay, Mr. Grim." Marn looked at him, pale.

Katrin laughed, Henry's bright plaid shirt in her arms. "Let her alone, Randall. It's a holiday for all of us Old Mountain people. And this is exciting." Katrin's cheeks were pink, and she was beginning to like Henry Blackburn more than she'd ever expected.

"I know my responsibilities, Wizard's daughter," Grim said roughly.

Marn shook her head. "No."

Katrin looked at them and giggled. "Marn wants to stay around to see Sam Trail wrestle, don't you, Marn?"

"Now, I haven't made up my mind yet about that, Katrin," Trail said. "If I will or if I won't."

Marn walked off, crossing to where Henry was at the rope barrier. The young man wouldn't notice her and chafed his arms, beating them to keep the blood hot, his gray clinging undershirt sweated. He grinned at the men who called to him, wanting to know if he would challenge next or wait. They measured their bets by Henry's replies and arrogance, remembering how skillfully he'd handled the new ram.

Grim followed Marn and stopped behind and whispered, "Is that young man the reason you won't go back to your father? Can't you see he's busy at men's business? You come along with me."

She flared at him. "Everything's men's business, so it seems." But she returned with Grim to the others. The winner in the ring was being proclaimed, and the judges were saying that Henry Blackburn had just spoken up in challenge.

"I wanted to get into the ring before him." Schoolmaster spoke aggressively.

"Don't worry about Marn getting home," Katrin said to him. "If her folks go off without her, we'll give her a ride back. Won't we, Sam?"

"Anything you say, Katrin." Trail clapped a hand on his coat pocket. "And I think I've been robbed."

"What I want is to see you wrestle, Sam." Katrin laughed. "Randall, promise me you'll let him go in next, before you do. Otherwise, I'm afraid he'll lose what courage he has and never wrestle today."

"Well, I don't mind." Schoolmaster shrugged, watching Henry enter the ring and stand up to his opponent. People began saying that young Blackburn wrestled a man as neatly as a ram. And that he was light on his feet, dodged well, and was as strong as one of his father's oxen!

Trail turned to his would-be beloved. "Katrin, I have a reputation for breaking in my father's horses and mules that you won't deny. But what am I going to do with a brute man like that!" He sighed and pulled off his dark suit coat and turned it over to the plump and rosy girl, who laid it on her arm over Henry's red plaid shirt. Trail knew Katrin was making game of him. Yet he was afraid she might be serious and decided to sacrifice himself. When Henry was shortly declared a victor, and Katrin put her hand on Trail's arm, and Schoolmaster nodded that he would wait for him, Trail stepped forward, calling, "I make a challenge."

"You there!" cried the judge. "Come in, my friend."

Henry made quick work of Sam Trail, enclosing him in his viselike arms, bending him grunting to a knee, and shoving both of Trail's shoulders before long into the turf, soiling the spanking white shirt with ring dirt. Over the crowd noise, Henry shouted at Katrin, "Wait for me, Sweetheart. And I won't hug you that hard! You don't want to go home with a loser. Come with me."

Katrin called back, her hand on her hip, "Maybe I will!" and everyone roared. But when Trail returned to her side, she helped the young man into his coat and wiped his tie clean with her pink handkerchief and told him, "I don't mind losers a bit, Sam."

"I'm looking for a man to wrestle me today," Henry was

boasting, loud, strutting up and down. "Not just a schoolboy, but some man!"

"How about a schoolmaster?" Grim called softly, pulling off his cap and tossing it to his spaniel. "Would that do, Mr. Blackburn?" He took off his blue sweater and folded and dropped it on the grass. He told the golden-haired dog, "And don't move from it." The animal lay down and put a shaggy paw upon the material, his honey-brown eyes watching every motion of his master, unblinking. Schoolmaster was naked to the waist in the cool air, the dark hairs of his chest thick; he had thirty years to the husky Henry's twenty-two. His physique differed from the Sheepman's son's, being slender and supple, slighter, not so striking. Schoolmaster ran his hands nervously through his hair and spoke to Marn in his gentle voice, "I hope you don't mind to see that fellow whipped for once, Miss Coombs."

"I'll watch you try," she told him coldly, unmoved.

Henry was waiting for the match, feet spread, tucking his gray sleeveless undershirt in his pants, putting his hands out in an invitation to enter his bear hold. And his mocking voice was as noisy as the bellowing ram's had been. "What are you teaching the children nowadays, Schoolmaster? I heard some-one say the other day that the Bible, the hymnal, and the Almanac are all anyone needs to use."

"What about the Sears Roebuck catalog?" some rube shouted out. "Doesn't Mr. Grim teach that yet?"

"Why so silent?" Henry railed. "Tell the folks about your school!"

"I wish they wouldn't do that," Marn said to Katrin and Trail, frowning, "when everyone knows who'll win."

"Give the teacher a lesson, Sheepman's son," someone said.

"Put him on the dunce stool in the corner!" called another.

"How do you think I handle those big farm-boy pupils, folks?" Grim smiled at the crowd, his eyes hard, "when they first come into my schoolhouse?"

He appeared the lesser of the two, but when Henry put out his arms for his usual bear grip, Schoolmaster, in a quick movement and by a twist of his arm, tossed the young man on his side in one motion. Henry's bewilderment was on his face as he got hastily to a knee. The crowd quieted. Schoolmaster stood back, while Henry rose in an awkward plunge, wheeling upon him. They locked and were swaying back and forth, Henry's breathing heavy. Schoolmaster found a place in the small of the back of his opponent that he dug into with his left fist; when Henry responded, twisting, Grim reached his right hand to catch Henry's chin, his fingers bruising his cheek.

"I can't believe my eyes, Sam," Katrin said, hugging Henry's coat.

"The fellow's a professional," Trail told her.

"I don't like Schoolmaster at all," Marn whispered.

Grim was bending Henry's head back. Thrusting his knee into the young man's groin, he brought him down again. He stepped back to allow Henry to gain his feet. The young man staggered up, livid-faced, uncertain.

A judge called over, "You know the rules, friend. Pin both of Blackburn's shoulders down if you're going to. Looks like you're winning, so finish it up if you can."

"Who says so?" Henry cried, his undershirt pulled out from his trousers now, his bruised cheek red.

He half-fell upon Schoolmaster, who took hold of Henry's

bare upper arms and, pulling him off balance, fixed a hip and leg behind Henry and took the young man down as easily as a baby. Grim followed the movement to the ground, on top of Henry, so that there was a thud, and the judge shouted out that he could see that Blackburn's shoulders were both of them touching.

The crowd, unsure of the quick victory and startled to be cheated of a rousting fight, murmured. Those who had lost what seemed a sure bet began grumbling and saying that the stranger had used tricks.

"You call that a fair fight?" someone called over to the judges.

"Fair and square," was the answer. "And judges' verdict final, besides!"

Schoolmaster had folded his arms upon his bare chest after leaving the prone Henry and turned his back on him. Henry got to his feet and made his way in the silence of the ringside over to where Katrin and Trail and Marn were. The judge was calling through his speaker again.

"Next challenger, Ladies and Gentlemen! And I beg of you, let's all remember that in a couple of hours the setting sun will kiss the meadows surrounding this fair town with its ruby rays. Which means we have to keep this contest moving right along. Whom do I hear in challenge?"

"I don't mind to have a try at him!" It was the huge Farmer. The other Greenfield man, the last of those who'd entered the ring to draw straws, had by now melted into the bystanders. Farmer, having sold every mule he'd brought to the Fair and having turned over the cash to his boss, was on his own for the rest of the day. He was looking for a girl friend, because

Stableman wouldn't let his wife out of his sight today. Farmer had knotted the corners of his big red handkerchief and put it on his head and his best wide hat on top of that, for style. He called over to the Wizard's daughter, whom he fancied in her yellow dress. "Hey! Take a look at me."

Marn wouldn't glance up, and bent over the Schoolmaster's spaniel to pet it. She wouldn't look at Farmer as he threw his hat to the ground and walked heavily into the ring, and she wouldn't look either at the blonde and blue-eyed Katrin Willem chattering away and making Henry slip into his red plaid shirt that she held for him.

"I'll button it for you, too," Katrin said to Henry. "I like a loser as much as a winner. And I want you to ride home tonight in Sam's buggy with us, Henry. You won't mind, will you, Sam?"

"Anything you say, Katrin," Trail sighed, as the tow-headed Farmer was closing with Schoolmaster and, growling in protest, would shortly topple to the ground.

"Come on with us if you want," Katrin invited Marn, who shook her head. "Remember, I'm going to make Sam spend everything he's got in his pockets on me." And she linked arms with Trail and Henry.

"You forget I was robbed, Katrin," Trail said. "However, it just so happens that I always distribute my money about me, and I'm standing on plenty in my left shoe. Are you coming, Miss Coombs?"

"No, thanks," Marn said, her eyes on the dog that gazed at its master standing over Farmer in the ring.

"Well, don't forget that if you need a ride home, you can come in Trail's buggy with us. If there's room for three, there's room for four," Katrin called back, gay, as the trio set out arm-in-arm, to look over what they still had time for before the sun went down.

Marn was thinking how her parents might have left the grounds by now, and she would not go in Trail's yellow buggy and be near Henry Blackburn, and how she would walk the long way home first. Schoolmaster came to join her, because no one else wanted to take him on and all the people were turning away from the ringside. The golden spaniel ran to leap upon him, delighted, whining. Grim rubbed his bare, wet arms and chest in the fall air to dry them. "Haven't you gone back to your father yet, Miss Coombs? And do you like the way I wrestle?"

"You have to collect your prize medal," she said.

"Where do I get it? Do you want to show me?" Grim put on the knitted blue sweater and small cap that the dog turned over to him. His hot crusading blood was cooling now, and he noted the curious eyes of passers-by, who had a new respect. "Do you think your father's left you stranded, Miss Coombs?"

"Then I'll walk," she told him, defiant.

"There's no need for that." Schoolmaster sensed his power as the girl led him to the judges' tent. He felt an awakening of his quelled desire, and put it from his mind.

When they came to the edge of the amusement area, where the Wizard's cart had stood and the brown horned oxen, they were gone. The small deer that now belonged to Schoolmaster Grim was tied to a stake by her collar. She rose quickly from the grass on seeing Marn and squeaked in welcome. Out of reach of her hungry nibbling was a small bundle, and on top of it one of the Coombs' tattered coats, handed down from somebody somewhere. Pinned to the latter was a paper addressed to Marn:

> Here is some supper, girl. You will have to come home with someone from our way. Maybe you can hitch a ride on the wagon with Mr. Willem's Stableman or the like. Wizard says we can wait no longer. The wagon is already loaded. I bought a washboiler, second-hand and newly riveted, and a dress, not second-hand. We sold all but the swan and the sheriff came by and declared he would impound it, but Wizard swore to him to turn it loose and will not trap any more. Wizard is packing up the food for you while I am writing this letter. It is only barbeque that he bought at a stall and bread, but there is plenty. He was grousing for a while about you not coming back after giving your word, but he stopped. I don't know why and he won't answer me. Your father moves in mysterious ways his miracles to perform. Ha. Ha. And goodnight. Your mother.

Marn gave it to the man to read, and he said, "What are you going to do?" And the blood beat quickly up in him again, because the young girl was helpless, standing there beside him, considering.

"I'll go see who's around from Old Mountain country," she told him, and then added directly, looking at him, "unless you'd let me ride that pack horse of yours, Mr. Grim."

"I was going to offer it," Schoolmaster said, thinking how he'd planned to stop at the bridge along the Greenfield Road to eat a couple of the chilled melons he'd left there just in case. Now he looked forward to the meal with a different mind, that he wouldn't even acknowledge to himself. He went to untie the fawn and get the supper bundle. "Bring your coat, Miss Coombs," he said in his soft way.

"And thank you," she told him, grateful not to have to beg about for a ride, and glad, too, that the quarrel she'd expected Wizard to start as soon as he saw her was at least delayed.

They walked to where the two mares grazed. Schoolmaster strapped the saddle upon the shaggy bay and shortened the stirrups. "You can ride her sidesaddle because of your dress," he said, holding her hand while she mounted. "I'll go bareback."

The yellow folds of the loose skirt covered Marn's knees. She didn't feel the man's roused emotion, only a certain peace at having her immediate problem solved. She draped the heavy coat about her shoulders, while Schoolmaster strapped the packet of food to his tall mare and set the fawn across her withers and sprang up saddleless behind. They set out at a moderate rate because Marn wasn't used to riding and was awkward in the side position. Grim turned around to see how she was getting on, and Marn smiled at him, thankful.

He responded at once, his eyes bright. "I told your mother that I thought you'd be pretty when you smiled, Miss Coombs, and I was right!"

"How long will it take until we're home?" she asked.

"We ought to be at your house in less than two hours. It'll just be getting dark then. I thought we might stop at the river where I left those melons, and we might share your supper, too, of that barbeque and bread."

She was pleased to contribute something, and said, "I'd like that."

Grim felt how the girl was mistreated by her parents and alone in the world, really. Miss Coombs strove, it seemed to Schoolmaster, to behave as if she were older than her seventeen innocent years, her hair put up with long pins in a bun like her mother's; one would have taken her for over twenty, especially in contrast to that rambunctious Katrin Willem. Randall Grim felt the weight of his thirty years, which seemed in this instant to have been lonely ones, and devoted perhaps to quixotic and unrewarding causes.

The twilight was almost there, as they reached the bridge. The wind of late September was blowing up, strong but with no great chill, reminiscent yet of the August past. Grim let his mare lead the way down off the road to where trees lined the water's bank. He turned the fawn loose to roam and tied his horse to a sapling elm. He took the reins to Marn's shaggy bay and looped them over a branch and reached up to help Marn dismount. Then Grim flushed, feeling he must command himself now, if ever he did, and that he was testing himself. All his imagination and his bones and muscles ached. He hurried to the place where the melons were tied, and Marn followed.

"Hand them up to me," she said, "and I'll cut them."

He gave her two of the cold, wet fruit, and she took them to the place she had selected where they would eat. As she knelt, he reached over impulsively and pulled the pins from her hair so it fell about her face, yellow and long and smooth. "Do you mind, Miss Coombs?"

Marn didn't move, not even looking up. "Why did you do that, Mr. Grim?" And she felt a piece of fear.

"I don't know, and why don't you call me Randall, Marn?" His usual measured and soft voice was higher-pitched.

Marn thought of how when one wanted to lead a balky and fearful beast of some sort to a stable or through a gate which it shied at, one never looked the animal in the eye. It was in their nature to respond actively and willfully when eye met eye. But with a human, Marn thought, it might be different: they had so many thoughts in their heads and were guided by so many prejudices, and she wondered now what to do. She got to her feet and said, "I'd rather just call you Mr. Grim always, if you don't mind."

"I was only going to ask you," he said, "what was worrying you today when you ran off at the wrestling ring to speak with that young Blackburn. What's on your mind?"

As Marn hesitated, swift wheels were heard on the road above the bank, and there was Katrin's voice hailing them. She sat between Henry and Trail in the latter's high-wheeled racing buggy. She wore Henry's red plaid shirt over her pink lace dress. Henry was in his sleeveless gray wool undershirt, laughing, the dark cheek bruise got from Schoolmaster Grim in the Fair ring covering half his face by now.

"Won't you come and have supper with us?" Marn called at once up to them.

Grim echoed her words, relieved at the interruption. "Come on. We've got barbeque and melons!"

Henry held Katrin's hand as they came down the bank, while Sam Trail tied up the sorrel gelding. Katrin giggled. "Now, I want everyone to shake hands. I told these two that it's just the same as if they'd won their matches, Randall, because you were trick-wrestling, and it wasn't really fair!"

"She made that up, Schoolmaster," Henry said. "We keep telling Katrin that anything's fair in love and wrestling."

"And they've both been begging for a kiss all the way," Katrin whispered to Marn and hugged the red shirt to her in the wind. She bent down by Marn. "Look here." Katrin had a golden ring on her left hand, and set with a red glass stone.

"I remember what my mother told you," Marn said, "that you should make Sam Trail buy you a diamond ring!"

"Only it wasn't Sam," Katrin cried. "Henry got it for me at the stall by the place where you swing the hammer and ring the bell. And I'm going to change the ring to my right hand when I get home, too, because of Papa. Or hide it."

"There's some supper here." Abruptly Marn went to get the bundle and put it where she had knelt with Randall Grim's melons. She said loudly, "Is anybody hungry?"

"I am," Katrin said.

"Me too, Sweetheart," said Trail, coming over.

"Watch your language, Sam," Henry told him. "One at a time, if you don't mind." And Henry grinned because he was getting on so well with the Dutchman's daughter.

They sat in the dry grass in the darkening dusk, and Schoolmaster passed out the cut melon slices. Marn opened the bundle and took out the two portions of food that Wizard had fixed for her to eat on the way home in Stableman's wagon or however she might manage: thick slices of gray farmer's bread with the mixture of soft pork pieces and chili that made the barbeque in between.

"Here," she told Henry coolly, keeping bitterness from her voice and giving one of the pieces to him. "This is for Katrin and you." She handed the other portion to Sam Trail. "And divide this between yourself and Mr. Grim."

"Thank you, Miss Coombs," Trail said.

Schoolmaster spoke softly, feeling a tenderness almost for the Wizard's daughter, her hair hanging long, that he'd released, tempted to lust but now safe. "Where's yours, Marn Coombs?"

She shook her head. "I'm not hungry." And her eyes kept

turning unwilled back to the ruby-colored jewel on her friend's plump hand.

"Well, all right," Schoolmaster said, as Trail started to break the food in two the way Henry was doing.

Marn felt the stillness, and she heard Katrin's exclamation. She looked to where the men stared at what they held. In the soft mixture in Henry's hands a slow green frog, suffocating, stirred wetly. And in Trail's food was a tiny coiled snake that slipped from the red-brown sauce and along his palm and fell into the drying autumn grass and away from view. Trail tossed the bread and meat into the bushes.

Henry hurled the frog and what it lay in toward the river. "Where'd you make up that supper, Mr. Grim? I notice you haven't any for yourself, and neither does Marn!" He went down to the stream to wash his hands, and Trail followed.

"I don't think it's funny at all, Marn!" Katrin looked as if she would cry.

Schoolmaster said, "Her father made that supper up, Miss Willem. The Wizard did it."

"I don't care, and everything's spoiled, and I'm going to wait in the buggy for them." Katrin sniffled and started up the bank to the road.

The two men came hurrying back, and Henry said, bridling, his light hair standing up, the green-yellow color of his eyes lost in the near darkness, wiping his washed hands on his pants, "Maybe you're a witch, Marn!" He looked at Schoolmaster. "She came up on the mountain the day my Wrestling Ram got killed by dogs, and I lay it to her. Like father, like daughter, they say. Maybe that's true."

Trail shrugged. "I'm going to the buggy where Katrin is. Take it easy, Blackburn. Watch that Scotch temper you're so famous for. You had some melon, and if you don't like frogs, that's your problem. I didn't mind the little snake." And he was gone.

Henry turned to Schoolmaster, hot. "Maybe you've got fifty dollars cash somewhere to spare. If you have, why don't you go with Sam next Friday to see Marn's father raise the ghost girl this year. He likes to bring her back from that other place right after the Greenfield Fair always, when everybody around's got cash on them. He's been reminding people today. I wish I had a father with money, the way Sam Trail has!"

Grim said, low-voiced, "What's the matter with your powers of reason, Blackburn? Miss Coombs had nothing to do with that food. She's been with me all afternoon. The Wizard prepared it."

Henry looked at Marn, the heavy, torn coat over her shoulders, her face pale. "Maybe so. But I guess I'll bring it up once more that you doled it out so that everyone would have some of that barbeque but yourself, Marn."

And Henry was leaping up the embankment; and then Trail's voice came from the dark, speaking to the gelding, and the buggy was clattering off, the sound becoming nothing but the silent evening and the wind going through it. The fawn, who had lain at the edge of the woods, got to her feet and came with hesitant, springing steps to Marn. Schoolmaster, gazing at them, said finally, "I think I understand everything, Miss Coombs, except why you said you weren't hungry and didn't plan a portion of the food for yourself. Did you suspect or know, somehow? Why?"

The baby deer nuzzled Marn's hand, familiar. She thought of how she'd have to give up the fawn shortly to Randall Grim and seldom ever see her again. And her mind roamed continually back upon the ruby ring Katrin wore, and the sickness it made in Marn to have seen it, sensing, hopeless, that she'd lost Henry to her flighty friend. "I can't explain it to you, Mr. Grim."

Grim threw the split melons and rinds into the bushes and went to untie his mare. Now when he held the stirrup for Marn and helped her to the saddle, his spirit was cold and quelled. He told her, "I've got a private war going on against the evils of the world. I understood you to be the true and your father the false. Now I'm having trouble trying to keep that straight."

They went down the road in the falling darkness. As they came to the lane before the Coombs' small house, Marn dismounted. She looked up at the man with the baby deer across the withers of his tall mare and gave him the reins to her shaggy one. She shivered because of the cold and put her hands in the pockets of the old coat. She thanked Schoolmaster for the ride, and said, "I hope you have a cow or a neighbor with one, because that fawn still needs some milk."

He told Marn, "I figured you knew I had no use for her, Wizard's daughter. I've intended from the first to give her back to you. Remember, she's your property and not your father's. I paid cash."

Marn took the small animal he handed down. "Thank you, Mr. Grim. I'll repay you some way."

"I don't want payment," Grim said, resentful because of the turn of things. "And do you know that you're a riddle to me? I have no use for witchcraft, and I recollect the Word where Matthew says, *Do men gather grapes of thorns, or figs of thistles? Even so every good tree bringeth forth good fruit; but a corrupt tree bringeth forth evil fruit.* It may be that under your innocent face, as they say, you harbor some strangeness. I'm new to this Old Mountain country and I'm easily dazzled. And I wonder, too, does your father hire some woman or are you that ghost that everybody harps upon, Miss Coombs?"

She shook her head, looking up at him. And the uncertain light of night swallowed the tapping of his horses' hoofs before Marn went to put the fawn with the foster-mother goat again. Then she went to the ramshackle house to face whatever lay in life before her.

*

*

4

*

The
Unicorn's
Horn

THE WHEELS of the great machine of fate moved, and the people, through no fault of theirs, but because of happenstance and the way they were made, were caught in it. None of the people were completely good or completely wicked. None were all wrong or all right. Because of his nature, each behaved as he did. If the Wizard had had another daughter to bring up, she might not have warred with him in Marn's silent way, but fought him in the open. Marn's disposition was firm and inclined like her father to dark moody convictions. Another girl born of the same parents might have been like Mrs. Coombs, flexible and open-spoken.

In the cold mornings of the week following the Fair, before she went into the barn to milk and feed, Marn, as usual, was out in the mists of Endless Quagmire. The squirrel followed her part of the way, muttering and chattering, and finally giving her up and returning to his spot overlooking the barn, where he would wait for her return. Marn watched a flock of close-packed ducks, tiny teals, as they whipped up fleet into the sky from the hand-woven net she tugged away from them, their wings whistling.

She felt she ought to have the courage to go back to breakfast and dare her father and say that she had turned them loose. But she couldn't overcome the illusion that persisted that although she was as tall as he now, because Wizard was a small man, there was as much difference in their heights as when she was three and he slapped Marn's hand when she freed a cage of robins. If she went now and said that she'd drawn away the net from the teal, her father would reply shrilly how she was busy saving the Biblical one stray, while he worried continually over the ninety-nine. And it was true that Wizard fostered swampy areas and made brush spots and trapped predators so the teal nested safely and raised their yearly crops of young, out of which Wizard snared what he wanted.

Marn had an image of her father in her mind that was not a duplicate of the reality. She was intimidated by him because of past experiences which had no relation to the present. Wizard's great goat was the same with the crow, who still persecuted Odin now and then; and the goat reacted, feeling in his mind that the crow was the great pecking bully he'd been when Odin had been a helpless baby kid. When Wizard put that toad and snake in the supper he'd prepared for Marn the other night coming home from the Fair, she didn't feel any bizarre quality in the incident as the others present had. Rather, she'd understood perfectly that it was to convey his displeasure in her disobedience, as well as his warning against future trouble with his daughter. Wizard knew his power over Marn.

The wild never intimidated or frightened the girl that way. Although Marn half-trusted in certain superstitions, she felt no evil ghosts behind the leafless drowned trees of the swamp that lay under the mountains, or anything there that might do her harm. When the tiger-among-birds, the Horned Owl, yellow-eyed, his feathers fluffed, nearly two feet tall, with great ear tufts, gave his piercing scream like a strangling woman, she only thought how he was one of the few birds that, even if captured as a baby, wanted to stay a savage. Sometimes one of those owls would come down upon a trap Wizard set up in a dead tree, tying a pigeon or rabbit by a leg underneath to lure the predator. Occasionally, it would break the chain that nailed the trap down and carry it off, the rusty links dangling. And again, Wizard would find it flapping, hanging by a claw from the trap, and he'd wring the short, tough neck and nail the bird by its great-clawed feet to some tree, hoping its fellows might profit by the lesson. Back in the quagmire even now the Horned Owl was spreading its wings and moving through the rising fog with no more sound than the shadow of a cloud. Following its nature, it was lighting in a tree beside a sleeping blue jay and edging it off its branch, snatching it as it fell; then beheading it and taking the trophy to store in a tree notch. It would do the same in the dark of night to a great Canada goose or even a turkey vulture, killing it and then taking only the head and neck, wasteful, depraved, leaving the heavy carcass for whoever would follow. Now it was snatching up some loping wood varmint in its feathered talons that were almost as large as

Dutchman's Farmer's hands and as powerful as the jaws of a new steel trap.

In Scriptures, it said, *And owls shall dwell there, and satyrs shall dance there. And dragons in their pleasant palaces.* Marn knew Isaiah, and wondered sometimes what her faith was and what she believed in. She could say many of her father's incantations; one, the cure for snakebite, went: *God has created all things and they are good. Thou only, serpent, art damned above all cattle and above every beast of the field and must go upon thy belly and eat dust all the days of thy life. Cursed be thee and thy sting. Zing, zing, zing!* And she could as easily say a Catholic prayer from the missal: *Hail, Holy Queen, Mother of Mercy, our life, our sweetness, and our hope! To thee do we cry, poor banished children of Eve!*

Wizard never went to the country church, though he had sent Marn to the children's classes when she was little; and often nowadays she and her mother would go, if it were Christmas or Easter or some other religious festival or local occasion for meeting. She listened to the sermons and was seldom satisfied, her mind being inquiring and in that way like Wizard's. She read his old books and any new one that he came by. She felt her father was a pagan, really, though he knew the Bible far better than Dutchman, who had a vague concept of a god who looked rather like Martin Luther and ruled Heaven in the same way that Willem ruled his farm and house. Wizard, making his living directly from the flora and fauna about him, respected them, and, over his wife's protest that he continually misinterpreted the Bible for his own aims, he had read Ecclesiastes to Marn as soon as he thought her old enough to understand the words: *Man hath no pre-eminence above the beasts: for all is vanity. All go unto*

*one place; all are of the dust, and all turn to dust again. Who
knoweth the spirit of man whether it goeth upward, and the
spirit of the beast whether it goeth downward to the earth?*

Back near the barnyard she stopped to feed the whistling
swan, kept in a concealed marshy pen just in case the sheriff
came by to check on whether Wizard had kept his word to free
it and stopped his practice of trapping the wild birds. Wizard
had built a pen so small the bird had no room to flail its wings
and build up enough momentum to get off the ground. Wizard
figured on using the swan in some way, and had named it
Jupiter. He'd told Mrs. Coombs some ancient rigmarole about
a god called that turning into a swan, who'd bred a woman,
and she'd laid an egg afterwards. Out of it in time came twins,
called Castor and Pollux, and those were stars you could barely
see in the northeast now. Mrs. Coombs made game of the
story, and asked, "Who sat on the egg?" And the Wizard
growled, and said, "The book doesn't say that. Don't ask so
many questions." But Marn thought perhaps there had been
a reason for part of the story in the first place. Because Jupiter,
though he beat savagely at Wizard always, standing on his
black legs and hissing and screaming, never struck at Marn.
She brought him a bowl of bread crusts soaked in the milk
she got from Hebe, and Jupiter let her stroke his long silky
muscled neck while he gulped it, his great yellow eye upon
her.

When she went into breakfast, Wizard glowered. "How
come you've been out there so long? You're the slowest I ever
knew at doing chores."

"I had to feed the swan," she said.

"And that wasn't all, I expect," Wizard complained. "Why
don't you take a walk up to the schoolhouse sometime and turn

Mr. Grim's pupils loose? I trap animals and he traps those children. Both of us change the lives of what's in our hands, and make our living at it. The next time he joshes at me about my business, I'm going to tell that teacher that."

Mrs. Coombs couldn't help but laugh. "I doubt anybody can reason about things the way you can, Wizard." But the man ignored her and asked Marn what had been in his mind and he hadn't mentioned since the Greenfield Fair a few days past. "How'd you like that barbeque I fixed for your supper, girl, as a warning to behave and act as you've been brought up to, and come back when your mother and I look for you?"

Marn shrugged, stubborn, and wouldn't say a thing. She got up to scrape food into a dish for Venus, who was waiting by the door. The bird came hurrying over, wings raised and head to the ground in delight. With her strong curved bill she nibbled at the strips of fatback and pieces of boiled potato and fried eggs. Mrs. Coombs carried a saucer to the crow waiting on the porch rail. It shouted and then took everything it could hold in its bill and throat and rushed off to store it in a tree hollow somewhere, and then came dashing back for more.

"Did you find that pair of horns I told you women to hunt for?" Wizard asked.

"They were on the top shelf in the closet," his wife told him. "I remembered where I put them as soon as I found them."

The pair of horns were almost straight. Wizard had had them in his possession for the past twenty years. Once he'd trained a growing steer's horns that way with bands and wires, just in case, and when the animal was butchered and the meat hauled off to some town to sell, he'd cut off the horns and gilded them and stored them away. A dozen years ago, Wizard first started the ghost girl idea, hiring a Greenfield waitress who was willing. He'd had to give her half the fee each time to insure her secrecy, while he waited for his daughter to grow. Two years ago, when she turned fifteen, he'd first informed Marn that she was to play the part. It hadn't occurred to Marn to object, since it had to do with the family's living; but from then on she'd begun to hope for the day when she'd escape her parent's bidding and go her own way.

"I've been trying to think," Wizard said, "which animal to use this year. That white goat from Willem's is out; she's the right size but her horns make her useless for this."

"How about the fawn," Mrs. Coombs suggested, "that Schoolmaster gave Marn?"

"She's too little." Wizard frowned. "And the horn's too long for her size."

"Saw one down to fit," Mrs. Coombs said, and she looked at their daughter. "What do you say, now?"

Marn glanced at them. "I wish it would rain or storm and everything had to be called off."

"Money's money," Mrs. Coombs said. "My land."

Wizard clattered his cup in the saucer and rose. "Give me the horn and I'll get it ready. I'll need to fasten some straps on it, too, and fit it to that deer." He was anticipating the event and knew just what use he was going to put Sam Trail's fifty-dollar fee to. "And I want a few bushels of those walnuts and shagbark nuts not only gathered, girl, but spread on the barn loft before the afternoon's over." He was gone, quick-footed, slamming the door, the buzzard and crow accompanying him.

The woman looked at her daughter. "There's no use mooning about in life. There's plenty have it worse than us." Mrs. Coombs hummed, moving about the room. The cages of the birds she liked, sold at the Fair, were emptied now; but there were still pairs of parent doves, ringneck and mourning, that she never let go, who kept their nests full of pairs of eggs or growing young at all times. They cooed now, busy. Nothing discouraged them; and if she found a wild dove nest, she just gave those eggs to the doves to raise and they never knew the difference. There was a thick-furred, newly caught raccoon cub in the corner; its paw had been bruised by the trap, and she bent to pet it. Mrs. Coombs accepted her husband's ways and viewed the hurting of the cub or his use of Marn in the same way as the blowing of the wind or the glowing of the sun. If the cub held its foot up, or if Marn protested, her reaction was the same. "Gracious, give it a week and it'll be well." She clucked over the little animal and poured it some milk and handled it a piece of fatback to gnaw, sitting up like a diminutive bear.

The day went by without incident until late in the afternoon, when Wizard discovered he was out of coal oil for his lanterns and lamps and the kitchen stove. He shouted for Marn to come down from the barn loft. "Go to the store and get me some right away!" He clanked the can down on the path. He called out to Mrs. Coombs, who had come to the house door on hearing the ruckus. "Why didn't you say something when you poured the last up!"

"She'll be back in an hour," his wife shouted back. "And aren't we lucky the weather's staying clear, and it's not turning cold yet?"

He ignored her, grumbling, bent over the railroad lanterns he'd got in Greenfield, with red glass so they glowed but dimly.

He trimmed the wicks. Wizard liked things to go right every year. He'd already gathered the damp wood for the fire he'd make at the edge of the clearing by the swamp. He wanted a dense smoke screen to mask the clarity of things and create a certain atmosphere. He figured he might use some incense this year, too, that he'd got off a Portuguese gypsy at the Fair. He tried the shortened steer's horn on the fawn and knocked on wood that it wouldn't slip off, because the baby deer was so tiny. He'd considered not even using a unicorn at all, but ruled that out. A legend was a legend; and since he'd made up the tale, Wizard felt it ought to be accurately presented. The first time he'd made Marn the ghost girl, he'd advised his wife to drape some flimsy cheesecloth around her face, which he'd not even considered with the waitress; for neither of the parents wanted their daughter recognized and customers getting wrong ideas. Mrs. Coombs suggested making a thin gown for Marn, and brought it up this year again. But Wizard said no. Bargains were made to be kept, and he'd like to think if Sam Trail were satisfied maybe he'd spread the news to his old man's rich friends.

While Marn waited at the store for the kerosene can to be filled, she heard the talk going on about the corn and pumpkin crops Dutchman was making, and the size of the fields he was plowing and planting to autumn wheat. And how, since the moon was full again, he was pushing his men into the fields every night. The Almanac predicted *Local Frosts* to start on Sunday and run into next week. The storekeeper gave Marn a message for Wizard, too, that he wanted a dozen more jars of the cough syrup her father concocted from mulberries and honey and the inner bark of slippery elm or black cherry. Marn paid the man and hurried back down the Greenfield Road.

When she reached the path which led to the Coombs' house, instead of turning down it, she went the other way, off the road and into the churchyard. Beyond was the unfenced cemetery where Dutchman's wife, Bertha, lay, under her Sears Roebuck stone. Marn knew Wizard would be furious if he knew of her delay, and so she stayed only a few minutes inside the small clapboard church.

Marn felt she was behaving in a way that would cause Henry Blackburn to say again, "Like Father, like child!" For she was there on what he might term wizardry. The interior was bare, and there was no human about. Marn stood inside the door and gazed at the wooden crucifix up in front where the preacher read and talked. She used words from Exodus, saying them aloud, not like a prayer, but as witches would to make a magic: *"And if a man entice a maid that is not betrothed, and lie with her, he shall surely endow her to be his wife!"* Marn laid a curse then and there on the young man from the sheep pastures on top of Bald Mountain, visible from the church door.

Then she added, whispering, "And let him come to harm if I am in trouble. And let me think about him no more! I'll find some other one to marry and be its father." As she started to leave, she heard hoofbeats, and waited until Sam Trail's chestnut sorrel had gone cantering past the burial place and down the beaten mule path and over the fields to Willem's. The young man intended to court Katrin until it was near midnight and time to meet the Wizard.

Marn went home quickly, and as she set the coal oil can down inside the barn door, she could hear the faraway, almost inaudible hee-hawing of the jackass over in the valley, announcing Trail's approach to Dutchman's house in the coming dark. Wizard came out of the barn shadows from where he was tending the yellow buck, Odin. She started on seeing him, as if she were guilty of something. Wizard began filling the lanterns to light the dark barn inside. He complained, "Let's get the feeding done while the creatures can still see what's thrown before them, girl!"

Marn wondered at her quick reaction that the sudden sight of her father, his eyes hidden and dark, had instigated. The small songbirds of the meadows and swamp always ducked for cover when there came across the ground the shadow of a short-necked bird. If it were long-necked, signifying a duck or swan or goose, none minded or stirred. Only that specific shadow which was of a predator evoked instant, inborn fright. Marn sighed, moving about at her chores, while the man lectured her upon all he had to do in life single-handed. Tomorrow he was bound to get his brown cows out at dawn and begin snaking trees to fill in some of the watery quagmire close to home, so he could coax the ducks in nearer to nest. That way it was easier for him to trap or shoot the predators that bothered them, the owls and certain small hawks and the coons and skunks and foxes.

"I just want to mention," he said, withering, his voice shrill, "that while I trap in this swamp, which it seems you've been praying the Lord this afternoon to keep me from, I also protect what's here the best I can. I know what I'm doing because I intend to spend the rest of my life here. Now you can go off and waste my time kneeling in that church, if you want to. But stop judging everybody's thinking by your own, and stay out of my trap lines!" And he was stamping away.

The day darkened and became night. A cold mist settled, wreathing the wet lowlands. Any heat that had been had risen into the moonlit sky above the mountains, where the radiant constellations wheeled in their patterned ways. Wizard was glad about the fog and was having his late tea at the table, his books before him. The coal-oil lamp cast a wavery light, and the shadows of the people were thrown vaguely upon the walls. Wizard wanted to impress and was boning up on the right words and phrases. Although tonight the ghosts would be manufactured from living stuff to please a curious man, there were times when Wizard was called upon to bring earthly people into communication with the other world. Then he used the same incantations that he studied tonight. One of the books he referred to had been published openly by a gypsy, another sold secretly long ago to him in some town before he ever arrived in the Old Mountain country.

Mrs. Coombs was knitting, pushing her rocker back and forth, trying to hold her tongue so he could concentrate. Marn was at the table across from her father with a cup of sweetened hot tea and milk, and fiddling with the mother-of-pearl mirror Henry had given her, that she kept out on the corner table in her bedroom nowadays, having no reason to hide it, because who could care where she got it or why?

The gelding could be heard approaching, and Wizard instructed Marn to stay in her chair because he'd like Mr. Trail to see her in the room and get no ideas, when he met the young man at the door. Marn didn't mind, if that was what he wanted. She nodded over at Sam, half-dreaming, as he came in. That rich man's son isn't ugly. And he's bold enough, that cigar half-smoked, back from Willem's, wooing Katrin. What if this were my own house and Mr. Trail were my husband come in for the night? It seemed a dream of paradise, and Marn turned again to gaze at her pale image in the lamp-light.

"It's just possible," Trail said to Wizard, "that someone else might be coming, too."

"If someone does," Wizard told Marn, to strengthen the illusion that the girl wouldn't leave the house, "you direct him out there where I'll be."

"We will," Mrs. Coombs said, "and you think Mr. Trail wants some hot tea?"

"My wife's always talking," Wizard said and scratched a match to light the red-glowing lanterns. "Come on."

They proceeded to a clearing at the edge of the bog, where the ground was dry. There behind an alder clump was the long pile of damp wood Wizard had stacked with care, spiking the logs with the incense that had been guaranteed to smell either like gardenias or lilacs. The gypsy had been uncertain which, but Wizard didn't care as long as it was flowers. As a matter of fact, it was a rather piney scent that rose when Wizard fired the great heap. He fanned the flames to spread them and to make the smoke billow up.

"Don't listen too closely to my words," Coombs told Trail, "because my powers get weakened if too many humans get together on what I'm trying to do here. As a matter of fact, I can't even perfectly judge whether I can get this spirit to come back at all!"

"I won't say a word, or listen, Mr. Coombs. I'll just sit on this stump and have a cigar," Trail assured him.

Wizard wandered back and forth along the smoking barricade, casting the spell: "Whoever says these words to the dead shall be safe from all his enemies, visible or invisible. Nor can he be drowned by water nor burned in any fire nor can any judge pass upon him any unjust sentence."

The distant bright moon illuminated the shapes of the dark mountains behind Endless Quagmire and the ones rearing far off in the other direction beyond the valley. "When do things begin happening?" Trail asked.

"A word of caution," Wizard told him. "When you see them, don't go calling after them or in any way let them know we're here."

"I know," Trail said, puffing his cigar, jumpy.

"I command these ghosts to walk upon the earth once again. I forbid them to go into my house or barn or upon the highway. Father, Son, and Holy Ghost. Father, stand before me; Son, stand beside me; Holy Ghost, stand behind me. Whoever is stronger than these three, try now to attack me! Zoom, zoom, zoom."

Trail got up. "What's that?"

"It's not them, and you have to wait," Wizard said, irritated, worrying that something might have gone wrong, "for the message to get there."

"All right," Trail said.

"You aren't interested in a mastodon bone I found out here once, Mr. Trail, by any chance?"

"I don't know. What's it good for? And how am I going to see through all this smoke?"

"There they are," Wizard said. "Be quiet, or they'll be gone."

Through the screen of mingled fog and smoke, the girl was visible in the moonlight, her head veiled, her hair down around her shoulders; beside her the tiny fawn, collarless and with the shortened gilded horn fastened with nearly invisible straps to her forehead. Trail leaned forward, as close to the fire as he dared.

"By damn, you did it," he said, so clearly that Marn heard him.

Her skin gleamed pale in the strange light, like some pagan nymph returned. She thought she seemed unreal even to herself, glancing down through the cheesecloth disguise. Her breasts were tight, the nipples hard because of the chill; her small firm body, used to continual work, was well-proportioned. The fawn felt gay and wild, being a nocturnal animal and liking the dark. She sprang into the air, shaking her head at the annoyance fastened there, and bounded before the slowly moving girl. Wizard had instructed Marn to circle the field three times, always as if she were about to leave, so that he could seem to call her back. When Marn reached the far end, she could hear Wizard speaking his incantations again, and he threw more damp kindling on to build the smoke screen up. She heard Trail's praise as she turned and came toward the men again.

"I swear! You are a wizard."

Marn thought of how she'd wished in a daydream that she belonged rightly to the admiring young man. Then there was some confusion, and a new voice joined the others, muffled. Marn tried to recognize it, wondering if it might be Henry's. Wizard was declaring, "Only way to finish off a ghost is by a silver bullet. That's what'll do it."

"By damn, who'd want this ghost killed!" Trail laughed.

"And it doesn't have to be all silver," Marn's father said, severe. "Just a little will do."

The other voice said, soft and stifled, "Can't you make her stop for a moment? I'd like to look at her."

"No, I can't" said Wizard, "and don't make so much noise, either. You're late as it is, and that's why you got a special price."

Marn shivered and thought how she had only one more turn about the place and this year's ghost raising was over. Who knew what would be by next year at this time? Over on the Greenfield Road she could hear a dog barking and wondered whose it was. Back in the quagmire the mallard ducks were quaw-quawing because some danger approached their feeding spot. It might be the great owl with horns or some slinking weasel or sable. Somewhere a rabbit screamed faintly and hysterically as it was caught. And there was the sound that the alder leaves made as they moved continually even though there was no wind, and the occasional rasping together of the bare twigs of the dead trees that stood in water nearby.

Trail was saying, "Make her return, Wizard."

And her father protesting, "She's been three times around as agreed."

"You say there's no chance to see her later?" Trail asked. "I'll pay what fee you demand, Mr. Coombs."

"That girl's a ghost." Wizard's voice became high-pitched again. "And she's heading back to the other world. And a promise is a promise, too. A deal is a deal. And you stay right here where you swore you would!"

"I will, I swear. And I plan on coming back every year, too!"

Marn could hear Trail's laugh plainly, as she slipped into the bushes, the fawn on her heels, and across one of the moldering logs that bridged some quicksand. She was trembling with the chill, pulling off the veil, nervous. She had hung her dress on a tree snag and quickly got into it. The fawn leapt after, as she ran home over the familiar darkened paths where the moonlight accented the mist of the rolling fog. Her mind, anxious, was still on who the other party had been, and considering if it were Henry, as she hoped. At the barn, the fawn followed her in, and she undid the straps of the steer's horn and put the little animal back in with the foster-mother white goat and went to the house.

But her mother didn't even know another customer had come, though she'd kept her eyes open for one. "Who did he sound like that you can think of? Did he have a town or a country voice? Why's your father so slow in getting his business finished!" Mrs. Coombs went to the door to look into the night, before putting the unicorn's horn back on the closet shelf.

But when Wizard finally did appear, pleased with his increased profits, he gave neither of them any satisfaction. He said he couldn't reveal anything, as he'd made a compact, besides giving the man a special one-third-off rate because he'd come late and missed a part of the ghost-raising. The fellow had tied a great kerchief across his face and only his eyes showed dimly, and his hair was covered too, with a tight knit cap. He'd talked low and said his identity must be his own secret. He was just curious to see a country fable come true.

Of course, Wizard aggravated his wife by saying that he naturally knew who the man was, despite the attempted concealment, being as he'd viewed him already that evening in the mirror he kept in his pants pocket for that purpose and had been looking for him to come all along.

"Then tell," she demanded.

"No." He was setting the lanterns on the table and heading for the bedroom.

"Why! And how'd he make his way out there in the quag-mire with no one to show him the path? And where'd he tie his horse? Was he a big man, and how was he dressed? From a farm house or a town house?"

But Wizard held firm, and all that the two women could do was speculate with each other. In the morning, Marn broached the subject again while she and her mother were busy together in the kitchen. "You think that was Sheepman Blackburn's son?"

"Or Dutchman's Farmer?" Mrs. Coombs cried. "He's al-ways got a big red kerchief on him all the time like Wizard says this man was wearing. But where would either of those two get that much money? And I've noticed you aren't taking time off and going up on the mountain any more like you did a while back, Marn. I knew you were doing that. And did you have a quarrel? And any time you want to talk about it, you let me know. I'll always side with you, if your father makes any trouble about what you ever want to do. He's a good man, but excitable." And Mrs. Coombs smoothed back the stray wisps of hair that came loose from her bun.

Marn thought how she ought to say it to her mother, how things seemed to stand. But the words stuck in her mouth, and it was a predicament so clearly of Marn's own making, having nothing to do with her parents, that she could not speak of it to her mother in confidence. As the days went by, Marn began to get it in her mind that she ought to go up there on the mountain and confront Henry Blackburn. It might be that his attitude toward her would return to the old tender way, if he were aware that they had a mutual problem. Marn tried to think up a plausible excuse to visit the Sheepman's place openly. When the first week of November had passed, she was sure of the situation.

One morning she came awake from a half-dream as living as life, and there was a clear memory of it. She was back in the shepherd's hut with the young man and lay in the crook of his arm while rain stormed outside. The dog Tam was guarding the sheep, and the two people were in love. Marn was impressed with the fantasy, listening to the splashing of the rain outside and the beating of it on the Wizard's high roof overhead. She thought how she would tell her parents that now that winter was upon them, it was time to get yarn and knit some heavy socks for her father and herself and a sweater, too, for Mrs. Coombs. And the place to go was up on the bald to Mrs. Blackburn, where one could get undyed wool that the Sheepman saved back because it didn't meet market standards but was plenty good enough for his family; and he didn't charge much for it, either. Marn got out of bed determined, but when she was in the barn, she decided to wait a day because one of the horned cows had just dropped her calf. Marn knelt to rub it dry with a sack. It was a solid brown color and a heifer. She took a bucket of wheat bran to the kitchen and heated water and put in sorghum to make a mash for the old cow. She brought her warm water, too. When Wizard came to look, he said they would raise it, and he named it Aphrodite. He stood in his dripping slicker outside the stall, pleased.

He told his daughter, "The reason she came that plain brown color is because that was what I wanted, and I've been careful to hang an ordinary gunny sack on the wall before her. Now you take Dutchman's bull: the reason he's mixed black-and-white like that is that his men must have hung a spotted cloth before his dam's manger all the while she was carrying him. What a mother sees has a strong influence on her child. With a human being, if she breaks a dish while she's carrying a child, she might lose it. And she's got to watch about not looking at rabbits, or she might get a harelip baby. And not to look at snakes or owls, either. We took care that you would be well-born, girl!"

The next morning Marn brought up the subject of the yarn, and her parents made no objection to her going up to Blackburn's for it. Mrs. Coombs advised her to wear a stocking cap and the heaviest coat in the closet, though, because the rain had changed to sleet last night and there might even be snow by evening, at least on the mountaintop. "And while you're there," she told Marn, "ask Mrs. Blackburn if they've gathered any balsam needles. I'd like just enough for a small pillow."

"And don't pay much, girl, either," Wizard told her. "In fact, don't pay any cash at all. I'll make up a bundle of a few winter remedies they're bound to be needing anyway and you can just make it a trade."

"My land," Mrs. Coombs said. "You'd think we were the Scotchmen, not the Blackburns!"

It was mid-morning before Wizard was done rummaging here and there in his stores and had the package ready for Marn. She went to the barn to free the fawn and let it come along, because whether it rained or sleeted or snowed, the growing deer's heavy undercoat kept her comfortable; and besides, Marn wanted the small animal's company. Wizard's two black birds were confined in the barn these days much of the time. Venus knew how to get off the ground now, flapping her powerful, broad wings and soaring as far as the nearby mountaintops sometimes. She returned every time, wheeling and dropping down at Wizard's call. Still, he was afraid she might take a notion to migrate south, and the crow, too; and so he shut them up in the barn unless it was near feeding time. Then he felt it was safe to let them out and up for an hour, one eye on his small figure moving about the barnyard and swamp far below.

As Marn went into the barn, Venus scurried over to see if she had brought a tidbit. The only sound the buzzard ever made was a flapping of her wings, and an occasional hiss. The crow, however, craned his neck and uttered half-human noises that sounded like words, as he bowed in welcome to Marn. Then he hopped down into Odin's stall and pecked at the great goat's forelegs to make him rise. He stood beside the shaggy, mild beast, who leaned his head down to sniff in greeting. The crow liked the hot steaming breath, and stayed motionless and friendly as Marn and the deer went out the door.

Wizard handed her the bundle he'd made up, and said, "That young Mr. Trail's been at the house for the second time now pestering me about the venison his old man wants. I've promised him two. You keep your eye out for that herd because they'll be on their way down for the winter. Count the old ones for me: there ought to be about eight antlered bucks this season, if nothing's been bothering them, and I plan to take all but two out of them."

"All right, Father."

The trip up the steep mountainside was a five-mile one, and Marn hadn't gone the second mile when she did come upon the deer, white-tails, on a slope beside one of the streams that led down to Endless Quagmire. The fawn, who considered

Marn her mother, and took her cues from her, held motionless beside the girl, hidden by the bushes, startled by the little crowd of wild, strange animals. Marn counted eleven antlered males, but thought how she wouldn't tell her parent and would say that the herd must still be high up in the forest. She knew Wizard never shot a doe, and that he guarded the herd from hunters. But he baited them down into the lowlands in the winters, and coaxed them near his farmyard with salt boxes, and would neatly select with his gun the bucks he wished to drop, and would let Odin drag each in on the sled so the hides would not be harmed. The leader lowered his head now and gazed in Marn's direction, sensing some intruder. As long as the girl and fawn were unmoving, the white-tail buck could not distinguish them properly from the underbush and bordering trees. His dark, large eyes were far-sighted and placed at the sides of his head so that he could see a pursuer on his trail and know where to bound and weave to escape, rather than spot some prey standing before him. Marn thought how he might be her fawn's father, for all she knew, as she backed away quietly, followed by the baby deer. She knew there was nothing she could do to stop the progress of the herd in its inexorable movement down through the climax forest toward the winter marsh feed ground and the salt boxes below.

There was no path up the mountain, but Marn, without consciously thinking of it, took the same way she had gone all her life when she had business at Sheepman's place. In the past summer, of course, she had used it so steadily that she knew it by heart and saw it in her dreams. At the forest's ending at the top where the pastures began, Marn pushed through the bordering scrub; the laurel leaves, pinched with the cold, and the deciduous blackberries, stripped of their green, scratching at her hands. The bald was empty of any life, sheep or man, and the wind, which she hadn't felt down in the protecting forest, blew with constant force from the faraway mountain swells that stretched off and became the white sky. The fawn trotted close to Marn's side because of the bitterness of the blast, as the girl hurried across the bleak, stony landscape, heading for Sheepman Blackburn's long low stables and pens and his house beyond. She pulled the stocking cap down around her ears and tied the scarf tighter that the wind tried to rip away, passing by the small, half-concealed shepherd's hut. Up ahead were the thick-wooled animals, huddled in the lots in close-packed groups, appearing almost twice the size they were in the warm season, their winter-ready coats unsheared. In the distance, heads down and eating, with hay and straw scattered in the tufts of their rough red coats, were the pair of gigantic oxen.

The rambling, one-storied home that she approached was a combination of *T*'s and *L*'s, connected by covered passageways, as additional rooms had been made by Sheepman's forebears for their expanding families. Now but four people lived here and scraped a living from the wool and the women's quilting and the wintertime chairmaking of Sheepman's that offended his son so, and that Sheepman prided himself on. Smoke spiraled up from one of the log and clay chimneys. As Marn went up the rough path to knock, the heavy-furred shepherd dog, Tam, came bursting from the door barking, followed by Henry Blackburn, a mackinaw on his arm that he was pulling on. "Hello, Marn! I just looked out the window and saw you coming!"

"How are you, Henry?"

His air was vigorous, and he appeared delighted to see

her, his stubborn mouth in a wide grin, his sandy hair rough in the fierce gale. "Why don't you ever come up here any more? I miss you!" he cried.

Marn thought how she was wrong in the church and she would never be able to put Henry from her mind. He was so handsome and bold, his Scotch-green eyes bright! She said, "I'm here for some yarn from your mother."

"Didn't you want to see me just a little?" he laughed. "I've got all sorts of things to tell you."

But still he didn't touch her; and as she patted the baby deer, alarmed somewhat by the noisy Tam, Marn thought how Henry used to put his arm about her at once and call her Sweetheart and how things now differed from then. "My father sent some medicine in trade," she told him, handing him the parcel she held.

He put it by the pathside. "Don't go into the house yet. I want to show you the sheep, Marn."

"I'd rather go in by the fire." She put her cold hands in her pockets.

"In a minute. Come talk with me first."

"All right. And I need to speak to you about something, too, Henry."

"What is it?" He seemed excited, beating his hands together, and she followed him to a lean-to where the stone wall at the north stopped the wind. "First I want to talk to you, Marn. And tell you what you've meant to me, and that I'm sorry I lost my temper the night of the Fair and that I know your father played that trick on you. And if that's what's bothering you, it needn't. I know he made that supper up, Marn. And I've been waiting for the next time I saw you to tell you to forget it."

"That's not what it is I need to speak of," she said, urgent.

But his laughter was gone now and he was earnest. "I've been very fond of you, Marn, and I know you've liked me very much. I think I've taken advantage of you. I'm twenty-two, and five years older, and I didn't mean that to happen that time in the hut, either."

"I came up here about that, Henry."

But he paid no heed to her. "The point I want to make is that I'm sorry if I ever have been rude to you, Marn. I'm taking a new turn in my life." Henry frowned. "I've been down to see Katrin Willem yesterday. And I'm going to marry her."

"What do you mean?"

"And can you feature me running that Dutchman's farm someday when I'm old and gray, and taking over that big armchair in his kitchen and handling the hired men from there?"

"Katrin told me her father wants her to marry Sam Trail, Henry."

"Dutchman can't always have his way, Marn." Henry laughed, jumpy, and she saw the gold flecks in his greenish eyes. "And he'll have to go my way this time, I think. There's little else he can do."

"Mr. Willem doesn't like you," Marn told the young man, her gray eyes hard, her voice high. "He calls you poor and he wants his daughter to marry a rich man's son. You're nothing."

Henry flushed. "Maybe so, but I'm going to be the father of his grandchild and that ought to make him change his mind. Besides, I figure he'll like me fine when I remind him he's getting a hand free-for-nothing when he gets me for a son-in-law. He'll jump at that, Marn. And it's not like we'd been planning something behind his back. Katrin's afraid, and I want you to talk to her. She doesn't have anyone to turn to, Marn."

"Let her go to Nell," Marn said, scornful, "her sister-in-law to be."

"Nell says she won't speak to Katrin, because she can't stand her father. And Nell sent back that chiming clock Dutchman gave her, too. Nell won't even speak to me since she knows, and my family's in a fight. Katrin's the one to think of, Marn, and that's why I want you to help. She's not only afraid of her father when he hears, but of having a baby!"

Marn patted the fawn, who pushed against the girl for warmth. She said, bitter, "It's nice you bought Katrin that ruby ring at the Fair back there to wear on her left hand, so she's all ready."

Henry put his arm about Marn, coaxing. "Listen, Marn, I know how you feel because I was rather in love with you last summer, but that's all in the past and now we need you to be our friend."

Marn moved away from him. "Well, I was never in love with you, that is sure, Henry!"

"Come on, don't be that way. Did you ever see those silver candlesticks on Dutchman's sideboard? I'm going to buy more of those when I get to making money and set them all up and down that big table at Willem's, Marn. And I'd rather make money on mules than sheep any day, too."

"What makes you think you'll live there? Why not bring Katrin up on the mountain to shear the wool and learn to weave?" Marn mourned. "What'll become of the Wrestling Ram? And how will your father ever run this place without you?"

"The way I look at it," Henry told her, firm, "is that

Dutchman Willem wants my sister to marry him because he needs a woman to keep his kitchen and manage his house. Well, now he'll have his daughter to do that besides a son to take over when he gets old. That's a good bargain! And Nell will never marry him. Right now she's over at Randall Grim's schoolhouse scrubbing and sweeping for him."

"I wanted to see Nell," Marn said.

"She goes over there all the time. And Marn, we're going to tell Dutchman that we want to marry at Christmas, and properly, in the church."

"I promised I'd be home early today," Marn told him. "And I'm going to talk to your mother about the yarn now." The wind whistled around the corner and she looked at Henry. "I don't want to help you and Katrin, either." She walked away.

The red came in the man's face, and he shouted after her, "How was that ghost raising a few weeks ago that your father put on? One fellow I was talking with says he saw it last year and thinks it's a waitress from Greenfield and not some ghost girl at all! What about that?"

She turned, shivering. "No. My father always raises true ghosts from the dead, Henry, and I'm surprised at you. As a matter of fact, we even thought maybe you came this year! We should have known you'd never find that kind of money." She turned toward the house, feeling as if she were drowning, not listening to his shouted response to her words.

"Witch!" Henry went away from the girl in his fury and into the stables to hunt out the Wrestling Ram and vent himself in the exercise while he worked out his case.

Marn hurried to the house, bringing along the package the Wizard had made up. The fawn dashed, playful, ahead of her. Marn was considering how she needed to think on tangible, immediate things, like the feel of yarn and how she'd ask Mrs. Blackburn if she had an extra pair of the wood needles that Sheepman carved, to let her have with the yarn. The woman answered her knock, and Marn asked, "Can the baby deer come in with me?"

"I don't see why not." Mrs. Blackburn opened the door wide. "This place is getting fewer and fewer people on it, and we might as well have some animals in for company."

"I've come to trade," Marn said.

"Well, go stand over where it's warm while we do it, then."

Marn went to the woven rug by the crackling flames in the clay-and-log fireplace, where Sheepman, wizened and dried, sat brooding over the new turn of his rebellious son. Marn was succeeding in forcing from her mind her first dismay at Henry's news. She recalled one time last year when she'd found a starving vixen feeding her cubs and dragging a trap about on her forepaw. And there was the time she'd noticed a persistent mockingbird lay an egg in the same place every day for over a month while a coon came to thieve each time the one she'd covered with grass. Marn had heard of birds that laid eggs in other birds' nests and pierced the eggs they found there and broke them and carried them off. It was the way of life and its ramifications; and Marn thought how she had seen enough of the troubles that came to the wild, through man's agency and nature's own ways, to be able to face her own.

She put a hand, maternal, on the fawn's collar. She knew one thing for sure: she would bring her baby to full term and she would care for it. She would set her mind in the coming weeks on trying to find somebody to father it, and, if unsuccessful, would work out something else. She went to help

Mrs. Blackburn set out hot tea to have while they talked, and was concerned when a saucer slipped and broke, remembering Wizard's words after the brown cow birthed her new calf and how that might make a human mother lose her child.

Later, with her sacks of yarn and balsam, Marn took her leave, nodding to the absent-eyed Sheepman and shaking hands with Mrs. Blackburn, who patted the fawn and invited Marn, "You come back to visit when Nell's here and bring the beast with you."

"Thank you for the new-carved needles," Marn told her, going out into the falling snowflakes. The fawn trotted ahead into the whitening world. Marn thought how she believed in many of her father's superstitions, because who knew for sure? And she would be careful thereafter about looking at owls or snakes or rabbits or any of the dangers that roamed everywhere, like Satan in the Book of Job, who declared that he came *from going to and fro in the earth, and from walking up and down in it.*

*

*

5

*

The Dutchman's Kitchen

Mrs. Coombs claimed that Wizard's mirror had told him what was happening before almost anybody around the countryside had known. He had stamped into his house, the snow powdering off his worn-out canvas coat and melting in his bushy black hair. He pulled off his outer clothing and came to stand before the stove, while Mrs. Coombs shook up the fire to make it crackle. Wizard reached in his pants pocket for the mirror and turned back the black cloth that covered it.

He said, "Trouble."

"What kind?" his wife asked.

"I might tell you more when I study it out," he told her, "but it's going on over at Dutchman Willem's, and it's nothing puny like Stableman's trollopy wife taking up with that Farmer, either. It's more like the working of certain spells of mine cast in the past to keep that daughter of ours safe."

It was a fortnight since Marn had come down from the

mountains as the blizzard was starting. Wizard had asked her about the herd of white-tails he was waiting for. She told him she'd seen neither hide nor hair of any one. However, Wizard slipped out into the deep snow the very next morning before breakfast and surprised the lot of them, and selected and shot down two heavy-coated, sleek bucks for Sam Trail's father. They were two-year-olds, well-antlered and already quarreling with the herd leader, half again their size and rather ponderous. Wizard went to harness up Odin, and the great buck goat dug his cloven hooves in the drifts and leaned into the wide leather strap that went across his chest. Wizard had to tie a rope to the drag-sled and tug away at it, too, before the pair of them could get it moving. And it took Wizard all of a day to skin and dress the animals out and hang them and salt down the hides. As soon as he could find out which way the big storm was going, he planned to haul the venison into Greenfield and deliver it to old man Trail as promised. December was a week away, and the roads to Greenfield were sometimes impassable in the dead of winter to anyone not on a light-footed, muscled saddle horse.

Sam Trail's sorrel gelding was just that, and before Wizard could get started, not trusting the way yet, Sam was by again, needling him. "You swore you'd deliver that deer meat to my father's back door in the month of November." Trail stood just inside the Coombs' front door, the collar to his sheepswool coat turned up, unable to stay away for long these days from the attraction of the Wizard's place. "How about that? Let's get moving, Mr. Coombs."

"Take it easy. *Answer not a fool according to his folly,*" the Wizard said. "I'm just waiting for the weather to settle. That meat's prime and it's all wrapped in tow sacks and waiting to go. I don't want to get stuck on the road with it, is all. And I've even thought of throwing the antlers in if you think a rich man's got any use for them."

"My father'll like that. He'll hang them on the dining room wall near the chandeliers. You're sharp when it comes to pleasing customers."

"I've been doing that all my life, Mr. Trail. Some ways I'm like your father. He's made his wealth on satisfied people. When he sells a parcel of land, he'll leave a team of plowing horses tied to a tree on it. And when he sells a speed saddle mare, he outfits her with a proper saddle and bridle, or lets her foal go with her and gives her new shoes all around. Some ways we're alike."

Mrs. Coombs, over by the stove, had to snicker at that, but Mr. Trail said, "You've got a satisfied customer in me, all right." And he glanced at Marn, clicking the wood needles she'd got at Blackburn's, and half done with the second pair of socks by now.

"I have to think of the future, too," Wizard said. "You're more likely to come back to trade if I throw in some extras to boot like those antlers."

"Did you throw in any extras that night back there, Wizard?" Trail asked him.

"Why don't you stop harping on that, young man?" Wizard said, testy. "Now, I'm tanning those hides for buckskins if you know of anyone interested."

"I wouldn't mind if you wanted to make up both of them in buckskin lap robes for my buggy," Trail told him. "I'd like to return here as often as I can think up an excuse."

"Come take a look at the skins, then, and tell me ahead of time what you're prepared to pay." Wizard wanted to get Mr.

Trail away from the house in order to make two things clear: first, that his daughter wasn't available for sleeping with, and second, it had been some tart from Greenfield that night and not Marn.

Trail didn't believe either of Mr. Coombs' points, but behaved as if he did, affable and handing the little man a couple of cigars. Trail guaranteed, too, that he'd pay the exorbitant price put on the finished hides. He thanked Wizard and went to the house to say goodbye. Mrs. Coombs pressed upon him some of her sweet cakes that she'd whisked into the oven shortly after Trail arrived.

"And have a cup of tea with us before you go out in the cold, and what's the news anywhere about?" She pulled a chair out for him. "Sit."

He took it, smoothing down his blond hair from the part in the middle, hoping he appeared dashing and not at all confused, asking Marn over at her knitting, "Don't you want to hear? There's been an elopement!"

Marn brought her work to the table, knowing it would be about Henry and Katrin, thinking how Mr. Trail was available to be the father for her child, except that he was in another stratum of society than she, being a rich man's son, and that at present the young man was in the house hoping for something else from Marn and it wouldn't be marriage. She sighed. "Tell us about it then, Mr. Trail."

"Well, for one thing," he said, as Mrs. Coombs put the food and tea before him, "I let Henry Blackburn borrow one of my father's fast horses and my big-wheeled buggy, so he could go down to Willem's farm and get Katrin Willem and run away with her."

"My gracious," Mrs. Coombs said, stopping still in her

tracks. "I'd say that was nonsense if it didn't come from you, Mr. Trail."

"I thought they wanted a proper church wedding at Christmas," Marn said.

"Where did you hear that, girl?" her mother asked her.

"So they did," Sam said. And he told them, "The only thing I've learned in my life up to now is that a girl is a lot like some mules, and I don't know if she stays that way. If you can make certain mules think they first thought up what you want them to do, everything's fine. But if they get other ideas, you might as well go along. Now I told you at the Greenfield Fair that I was doing my best with Katrin Willem, Mrs. Coombs. But she had her own ideas. So I've given her up and all I'm doing is helping them get together. I might as well."

"My land, didn't Mr. Willem want them to marry in the church by the preacher?" Mrs. Coombs asked.

"Dutchman lost his temper," Trail said. "He's plagued with more women problems than any man he ever heard of. He swore by the name of Martin Luther that before his heifer would marry a never-do-well, he'd buy another stone from Sears and Roebuck and put Katrin under it himself."

"When did they go off?" Mrs. Coombs asked. "And in weather like this, with the roads deep in snow. And my husband saw that trouble coming in that mirror of his, too."

"As a matter of fact, Greenfield's where they are today," Trail said. "They're still using that horse and rig I lent them. They're hunting up the justice or preacher or whoever it takes to do it."

"I wouldn't have thought Katrin Willem was bold enough to go against what her father told her to do." The woman marveled at the scandal.

"Katrin says," Trail told her, "that when it's a past fact, her father will come around. Mr. Willem needs a woman to run his house, and Henry says he's getting a first-rate hand thrown in extra to boot."

When the young man got up to go, Mrs. Coombs was cordial with him. She had none of Wizard's worries about Marn and Sam Trail's interest in her. Mrs. Coombs had no desire to try to control fate, which seemed to her to be ruled by some divine or satanic preordination. "Whenever you're just passing by, drop in," she invited him.

"Well, thank you, I will!"

When the Wizard arrived for the noon meal, she told him what Trail had reported. "That's only the beginning," Wizard jeered at the news. "That boy's telling you what everybody knows by now. I'll guarantee Dutchman's daughter won't be let back on Willem's land. He's going to disinherit her. And she won't get back from Greenfield till tomorrow night, either, due to the condition of Greenfield Pike." He turned on Marn. "Remember when this young fellow was sweet on you a few months past? I've managed to turn him onto Willem's daughter to save your soul and body. What if you were in her place?"

"How will Dutchman Willem ever get along?" Mrs. Coombs cried. "How could he do that to his only child! And her a pretty, plump one like Katrin. Answer that."

"*A fool's mouth is his destruction,*" Wizard told her. "I know but I'll talk no more."

Then, two days later, Sam Trail was back with further reports for the women, sitting across the table from Marn while she sewed together the pieces she had knit, to make a long-sleeved sweater for her mother. Marn bent over the stitches, seeming to pay little heed to the visitor, while Mrs.

Coombs clucked over him and hung his natty sheepswool coat on a hook and set out a plate and the vinegar pie she'd prepared just in case, using fresh eggs and honey and new-turned cider she'd got at the store.

Trail lit a cigar, and loosened the stiff collar of his white shirt, and cut a huge piece out of the pie. He told them that what Wizard predicted had come true. The runaway pair had returned after a day's delay in Greenfield and a night spent at a hotel there. Dutchman was waiting at the steps of the kitchen, puffing at a meerschaum pipe, a shotgun in his hands. Trail had been doing mule business with Mr. Willem, and watched the whole disturbance from the kitchen window. Dutchman had made Henry sit in the yellow buggy, while Katrin could come past him up the stairs and into her room, and pack her clothes into a cracked wood-and-leather trunk that had been her mother's. And Mr. Willem let her take the bedding from her own room and her comb and hairpins and what was in her bureau. But he drew the line when his daughter asked, weeping, for her mother's silver candlesticks. And Mr. Willem waved his gun and shouted to Henry that he was to inform his sister, Nell Blackburn, that the proposal Dutchman had made to her was off for good and always, and he hoped someone married her sometime because he'd never! And Henry's Scotch temper got up, and he yelled back what wasn't true, that his sister was as good as wedded to someone else right now and had been leading Dutchman a merry piper's dance. And then Trail helped the crying Katrin haul her trunk to the buggy and strap it onto the carryall on the back. And off the two of them drove up to the top of Bald Mountain, where Mrs. Blackburn and Sheepman said that the couple might live as long as they liked in one of the cabin's many, roomy, built-on *T*'s, and they hoped it would be forever. Henry's parents weren't concerned over Willem's attitude regarding Katrin's inheritance, and thought that in time he'd put Katrin back in his will. They were thankful mainly that their son was staying, as they felt their sheep needed Henry much more than Willem's mules did. And they were sure, too, that while Willem would be able to replace his daughter's help in the kitchen with some woman of his many hired men, Sheepman, who grew smaller as he aged, and whose trembling, wiry hands were much better able to fit together chairs than assist some strong-minded ewe with her lamb, or dock the tails of a flock of young ones, or shear the whole lot of them twice a year, could never replace his son. He had no money to hire, and if he did, who would consent to come and live on his lonely bald, anyway?

Sam Trail had one more piece of information for Mrs. Coombs and Marn. Dutchman Willem had told the store-keeper up the road to noise it around that he would pay reasonable wages to a talented house and kitchen woman. Then, for the first time, Marn Coombs smiled with pleasure on Trail. He was nonplussed at first, and then leaned over the table when her mother's back was turned and whispered to Marn that if she would meet him halfway down the path to the meadow, he would make it more than worth her while. But all Marn would do was put down her work and go to get the kettle to refill his cup with hot tea, and take the knife to give him another helping of the pie. Trail sighed at the girl bending over him. As he got up to go later, she went to the door, too.

"Did you hear of anyone applying for that position open at Mr. Willem's?" she asked him.

Trail pulled from the pocket of his sheepswool coat a pink, paper-wrapped gift he'd brought along just in case the Wizard's daughter were even a little yielding. He pressed it into her hands. "Not the last I heard, Miss Combs. For Dutchman has such a reputation for driving his help, no one wants it. Are you sure you wouldn't like to take a very short walk?"

She shook her head and he left. Back at the table she unwrapped a pretty china-headed doll with real hair and dressed like a lady. Mrs. Coombs admired it and urged Marn to hide it from Wizard, who might think his daughter had put herself into debt to the young man from Greenfield if she accepted such a present. But Marn would not, and declared she was seventeen and would do as she pleased. She left the toy on the table, daring her father's wrath, because Marn intended to go over to Mr. Willem's at the first opportunity she got and ask if he would employ her.

As it happened, Wizard made up his mind early next morning that he would take a chance on the roads being passable and go on to Greenfield with the venison promised to Mr. Trail's father. Wizard loaded the bulging, frozen sacks into the cart and tossed the branching antlers on top of it all. He climbed up on the seat, swathed in sweaters and scarves, the newly knitted socks under his boots and a heavy cap on. He clucked and the pair of horned cows moved off slowly into the drifts, threatened by the long pole in Wizard's elbow crook.

Marn decided to tell Mrs. Coombs a part of the truth. She explained that she felt it was time she assumed some responsibility. "And it's not that I want to leave home, Mother. It's just that I ought to begin to pay back some of all you and Father have done for me and all he's spent on me in my life.

And it isn't as if I were going all the way to Greenfield to look for a position."

Mrs. Coombs protested a little. "It's like that raccoon cub over there coming back to his hollow with a chicken for his parents to eat. The only debt you owe Wizard and me is to care for your own children whenever they come. And besides, it'll be dull around here with nobody but your father and me. Now, are you sure you don't want to wait a year? It's not like we aren't making a living."

"I think I'll just go ask," Marn said. "Mr. Willem could have someone else already." She went to put on a wool smock over her everyday dress, her gray eyes bright. The smock had been handed down but was mended decently and would keep her warm. She brushed out her hair, looking in the small mirror, and then put it up carefully, pinning it neatly. The doll lay on the pillow on her bed. She went to get into her outdoor things.

"I guess the storm's laid," her mother said. "And I wish we had a horse, so you didn't have to walk. And I wonder if Wizard would mind if he knew you were going over there now? And I wonder if he does know? Do you think he'll remember I told him to bring back a tin of tea?" The woman stood in the door, not minding the wind, pushing her hair into its bun, her energetic voice following her daughter.

Marn walked fast. The ground was frozen, and where it was smooth, the going was easy. Where it was roughened, as she went through the Dutchman's orchards, from the wheels of rakes and the shares of plows, and there were some drifts, she stumbled sometimes. She met no one as she finally passed Willem's barns, and saw only some children of the hired people, at home from their school still because of the heavy snows, playing about one of the small cabins. There was no one at the house, either, for she stood inside the door and called repeatedly and got no reply. The kitchen was in confusion. Just outside, by the big door, was a heap of varied sizes of pumpkins, frozen and wasting. In the entry, cabbages were cast untidily along the wall. The hired men had made their own breakfast, and no one had come to clean up. Egg shells and bacon rinds and knives and spatulas and spoons littered the table beside the great black stove. Grease had spattered on the floor, where there were crumbs and debris from the supper the night before, too. About were unwashed kettles and skillets and platters and plates, and eating utensils and cups, removed from their places in the cupboards or their hooks upon the walls and ceiling, and telling the story of the master's dilemma. A bench had been overturned, and Marn went to straighten it. The reed cage of three cardinals still hung in the window, their seed gone and no water in their dish. They fluttered and twittered, their eyes on her. The room was cool and the breakfast coals were out.

Marn went to the shed in the yard and brought in wood, and shook the grate and laid a fresh fire. She pumped a kettle of water and put it on to heat. She hung her coat and stocking cap on a hook and set her boots under them. She put on a dirty apron she found dropped in a corner. She cleared the table and brushed the benches and lined them up properly. The big armchair had been pushed back from the table head, and she returned it to its place. She brought grain to the birds, and water, and swept the floor, and scraped the plates and pots, and cleaned them with soft yellow lye soap she found, and the water now hot.

She looked in the pantry and discovered a row of crocks,

some holding sausages seasoned with sage and laid down in fat, and others with pickles flavored with branches of dill and tiny black peppercorns, or with sauerkraut touched with garlic cloves. And there were shelves of canned tomatoes and beans put up in mason jars, and jellies and jams and preserves. And there was a line of jars of water-glassed eggs, against the winter season when the hens would almost cease their laying. One long shelf was reserved for nothing but the bread that was made weekly. Marn was looking for fresh meat, but saw none. She went into the yard, heading for the smoke-shack where Farmer had taken a ham leg down from a hook for her early in the fall when she'd come for the white goat. She called out to the children playing across the yard, that she had seen earlier.

"Where's Mr. Willem gone? Where's everybody?"

They answered that all of their fathers and their older brothers and most of their mothers were in the cornfield today, helping haul the stacked shocks in for a party to come soon, that the owner of the farm gave every year at this time for his hands and any of the neighbors, too, who liked music and a dance, in exchange for husking the year's crop of corn ears from the stalks during the fete.

"And they say anyone who finds a red ear gets a penny. Is that right?" a child called.

"And what's your name, Lady?" another cried.

"And who are you!"

Marn turned from them, for she was in a hurry, and unbarred the heavy shed door and found in the dark recesses a string of a dozen fresh-killed and cleaned rabbits from the dovecote nearby. And there were smoked slabs of half-hogs swung from the rafters, and quarters of steers, and plucked, pale-bodied geese, and ducks hanging from their skinny necks, and cloth sacks of tiny doves for pies.

She took half of the string of rabbits to the kitchen with her and disjointed them and got some of the sausage meat and lard to start them sizzling in the kettle over the noisy fire in the big stove. She looked for country wine and, finding none, added cider to the rabbit dish from a keg in the pantry. She began to cut up cabbages to boil, and then to peel the potatoes the way she remembered Mr. Willem liked. And she would take care not to skin the apples but just to get the core out, because that time in September Katrin Willem had told Marn and Schoolmaster Grim that her father liked his apples done in that particular fashion, and his potatoes in the other.

She set the table with the heavy white plates, unsure of the number but putting out plenty, and a spoon and knife across every plate, and a cup by it, too. She considered setting out the silver candlesticks, but decided it might be thought presumptuous. She pulled off the soiled apron and put it out of the way, and smoothed her smock and straightened it. She wondered if her hair looked all right, but was afraid to go into the house's interior to find a mirror. She replaced some of the pins and hoped it would do.

When the jack brayed outside and a wagon rumbled and voices were heard, Marn flushed. It was Dutchman himself who came stamping in to line up how he was going to handle the middle meal of the day this time. The scent of mules and barns and cold fields was on him, and the smoke of the long clay pipe he drew on as he glared about the kitchen, ignoring the girl. He wore a brown fur cap and mittens, and the bear-skin collar to his short coat was turned up. He kicked the snow from his boots on the entry floor. He stalked across the kitchen to the stove and, taking his pipe from his mouth with one mittened hand, lifted the kettle's lid with the other. He glanced sharp-eyed at the thick gravy bubbling about the browned meat.

"That should have been wine in there, Wizard's daughter, not cider. Eh?"

"I couldn't find it."

"Can you make a decent red wine?"

"If the grapes are dead ripe and I can have cane sugar, and if you'll let it stand a year in its keg, Mr. Willem."

"There's too many plates out on the table, eh?"

"I didn't know."

"I had a thrifty wife not long ago, Wizard's girl. Can you remember her? You used to come and trade with her."

Marn told him, "Mrs. Willem always gave me a chair when I was here, even when I was little."

She waited while the smoke from the pipe wreathed into the darkened rafters, hewn and squared by his grandfather out of the forest that had stood there once. He said, "I can't abide to see waste. Did you take a look at those pumpkins out there?"

"I can do pumpkins three ways." She spoke steadily. "I'd bring them in to thaw and then I'd make enough pies to last a week. And I'd put up more in mason jars to have all through the winter. And the rest I'd boil in sugar for pumpkin preserves, which are best if you use some ginger or forest roots I know for flavor, like sassafras."

Dutchman told her, "Get the meal out on the table. And you can be the mistress here for as long as I like your ways and no longer. Eh? And how old are you? Are you past twenty yet? And I pay properly, too, and bonus if deserving."

"Thank you, Mr. Willem." Marn hurried to get the heavy

bowl from the sideboard to hold the food simmering in the kettle.

"And tomorrow you'll ring the bell, too," the man declared, going to hang up his bearskin cap and coat. He pulled on the rope that went to the black bell in the dormer roof; iron on iron clanged and echoed, and there were distant shouts in answer. Dutchman returned to seat himself in the heavy chair that ruled the table. He knocked his pipe out in the beaten metal bowl that stood by his plate and was etched with Dutch figures of men and windmills and was very old. The man's round eyes appeared like porcelain, as hard and as blue. Dutchman was used to calculations and shrewd judgments, and today he was as pleased as at any time in his fifty-odd years. His muscled arms lay relaxed along the gnarled, thick, wood chair arms. Dutchman felt his justice and wisdom. He added, "And I'll tell the people hired here that you're to be called Miss Coombs while you're running this house and the women are to do as you decide. I'll have this place respectable, even though you are the child of a paltry Wizard. And you can sleep in the attic, not my daughter's bedroom."

Marn nodded, content. "All right, Mr. Willem."

Then just before the first of the hands, the Farmer, came clumping in, Dutchman ordered Marn, "And why not put those fancy candlesticks of my wife's on the table, too, sometime before this meal gets started and over and it's too late!"

The Farmer was stopped in his tracks at sight of Marn. His white teeth flashed. "Hey, little girl!"

"Now you sit, Farmer," Dutchman shouted. "And call her Miss Coombs, too. And when she's done with this noon dinner, you're to take her in the mule cart to that shack they live in and help her get her things back here by nightfall. I'm not about to put up with one more meal got together by the worth-less wives of the men I hire here." He glared at Stableman as he came in with the others on Farmer's heels.

When Marn had dished all the food out, and there was only the clatter of silverware on dishes and the noises of eating in the room, and she was ready to seat herself, she went to stand beside the man at the table's head. Her fingers at her sides worked nervously at the wool of her smock. "Mr. Willem."

He interrupted his meal to look up at her. "I like my coffee now and the men get theirs later." And when she'd brought the steaming pot and poured his cup, he sipped it noisily. "Eh? What now? Is it about the sum I'll pay?"

She whispered, "No, it's that I want to know if I can bring a fawn here."

"Speak up," he said. "A what?"

"A baby deer. I had her in your kitchen here once. I'm afraid my father might sell her if I leave her at home. And I promise she'll stay out of your way."

The Dutchman was prepared to deny her, but saw how the young girl's gray eyes were filling, and was reminded of his daughter just turned out from home now, and how easily Katrin had used to weep. "Then you can bring it, but don't think that means I'm an indulgent man, because I'm not. It's not in my blood to be easy."

"Thank you," she told him again. Marn felt how all was going her way, and she blessed whoever it was that was holy and divine and was helping her.

The little driving mare mules that Farmer hitched to the cart were bred from speed mares and not meant for heavy draft work. Their black coats glistened because of the daily grooming Dutchman insisted upon, and the cottonseed meal he mixed into their feed. There were pink and orange rosettes fastened on their oiled black leather bridles, for Willem liked decorations on everything, from his barn side where the gigantic white mule in the scarlet harness had been painted and was kept touched up every few years, to his tall blue bedroom bureau which had flowers and birds scrolled on the faces of the drawers. Farmer let the eager mule team go at a fast clip, hardly slackening as he wheeled off the road finally and up the lane that led to Wizard's shack. Coombs' pair of horned brown cows had just walked away from their wood yoke and were going where Wizard told them, to their stall, sure that he would follow with meadow hay and some sort of grain that he'd scrounged from somewhere.

"Hey there!" Farmer shouted after him. "Don't you want to know what's going on with your daughter?"

But Wizard Coombs waited until he had given his waiting cattle their feed and tended to what else was needing his attention in the little barn before he came to the house. His wife had already advised him where Marn had gone, and how she felt her responsibilities in life and was today applying for an opening Dutchman Willem had for a woman to keep his house. Wizard realized, as soon as he heard the hired man and the mule cart clattering up the lane, that his daughter had been accepted, and he would make no objection. Wizard had directed Mrs. Coombs, when he heard what was going on, "If she talks that valley man into taking her, you let her go and don't fight her. She's been restless lately, like Venus and that crow of mine that I had to lock in the barn in case they took a notion to migrate. They'd have flown back in spring, and maybe the girl will return, too, in time. I'll be glad to have her tampering hands off my traps, and I'll tell her that. And it's the truth, too, that we could use some cash around her. This is a family of free spenders been living in this shack."

"Well, I don't know," Mrs. Coombs had answered. "I'll have to think of something to liven things up, if she's living in another house. I wonder if I could find a parrot or some talking bird in Greenfield sometime."

"All I can say," he stated, "is I'll hope for some quiet and peace, maybe, if half the women hereabout leave my house."

"Well, I'll get that nice Mr. Trail to buy me one, not you," she threatened, "when he's passing by, bringing news."

"You think that young Trail comes here to see anyone but our daughter?" Wizard had said. "You think he'll come if she's gone? And who do you think put a spell on Mr. Trail to lust in the first place and so to bring over that fifty dollars spot cash to see a ghost walk in a meadow?"

"Wizard," she'd laughed, affectionate, "sometimes I think you feel responsible for the sun's rising and setting. You believe you spell it to do what it does naturally by itself. Gracious, all I'll credit you for is seeing your opportunity and taking advantage of it."

And so Wizard was friendly when he came into the house and even went so far as to go with Farmer out to the barn to pick up the fawn for Marn, and the white goat with the little horns, that she would return to Willem's now. The Farmer wanted to take a look at the buzzard and crow that had so many tales told about them. "Have you got some magic you'd like to sell me, too, Wizard?" he asked.

"It could be," Wizard returned, sly, "but first you ought to tell me what problems you want solved. Are you still lechering after that Queen-of-Sheba wife of Dutchman's Stableman? He bought another no-good talisman at the Greenfield Fair from me; he wouldn't pay for the expensive one I offered, and that's the reason she's still letting you come over when Stableman's out of the way."

"Is that the reason?" Farmer laughed, standing tall and ugly, no hat on his thick tow hair, his jacket open to the cold, and the cotton red kerchief knotted at his neck. "My trouble is I like them all. I even chased Miss Katrin Willem down when I got the chance."

"Have you ever been here before?" Wizard asked, uncertain to this day who the stranger was that had appeared suddenly in the foggy moonlight on that first Friday of October to see Marn in the meadow, and had increased Wizard's take that night so gratifyingly.

"No, for Dutchman Willem doesn't give any of us time off, except for church on Sunday. All he can think of is work, and right now it's corn. He's having a shindig on Thanksgiving like always, but not because he likes the music. It's to bribe us hands, and his neighbors as well, to husk all the shocks for him and get the ears safely into the bins. He even gives out pennies to the children to help. And does that crow there know any tricks?"

The black bird had flown to Wizard's shoulder, and Farmer put out a huge finger to touch its feathers. The crow reached down with its beak and clamped, vicelike, upon the member. Farmer drew back hastily and shook his hand "Ouch."

Wizard laughed and reached up to brush the crow from him. The bird flapped to the ground, squawking foolishly, delighted. It flew up and landed on the door to Odin's stall, where the little calf of the brown cow was lying, together with the shaggy, smelly beast. Wizard got some corn grains and tossed them to the crow, who caught each one and stored them back in his mouth to play with later.

"He can hold eleven," Wizard said, "without dropping one."

"Do you ever change your soul with his and travel about in his body?" Farmer wanted to know, towering beside the little man with the black shock of hair and the great scarf wrapped about his neck.

"How do you think I knew you'd never been here before in your life?" Wizard said, scorning the ignorant ways of the untutored. "I do that all the time. And there's another body I'm going to start using pretty soon when it's spring and she circles the mountains and gets higher than the crow ever thought of."

Up in the rafters the vulture was watching the two with a quick eye that in the sun was colored like a topaz, in love with the man whom she thought of as mother and friend, wary of the other who stamped and moved in unsubtle ways and could be a danger. "I don't fancy that kind of a bird," Farmer told Wizard. "I figure it's waiting for me to die."

"Venus is," Wizard said. "Now, there's some, like me, who never die and have no age reckoned by man. When that buzzard is eighty and thinking of passing on, I'll get a new buzzard from a stump somewhere. What sort of charm did you think I might interest you in, Farmer? You don't need one to stir women, it seems to me."

"Have you got one for the toothache, just in case? Or any fortune-telling cards I might buy?"

"I've got both in the house. The cards tell whether someone plans murder or suicide or is inclined to lunacy, so you can be sure of anyone you have doubts about. Also, the length of life, the number of children someone will have, and how often they will marry—or take up with someone, at any rate. And they aren't cheap."

"I'll take a pack, besides the toothache remedy."

"You aren't making a mistake." Wizard led the white goat, the fawn following.

They went to the house, where Marn and Mrs. Coombs were deciding what to pack and what to leave behind of the girl's belongings, putting in a nightgown and winter dresses, leaving the summer clothes and the ones too ragged for a prosperous farmer's house. Marn took the comb and brush and the mother-of-pearl mirror and the new china doll from Mr. Trail, which she wrapped carefully in a shawl so it wouldn't break. Farmer picked up the fawn and the goat and tied them to the back of the high seat. He threw in the bundles the women had ready. Then Wizard gave his daughter a hand up to the seat, where Farmer held the reins to the little mare mules. They stood waiting for the signal, wanting to gallop home to Dutchman's barn, which was twenty times the size of Wizard's, and where they didn't get offered shelled corn, but were fed a mixture of cracked grains and meal, ground by the windmills that turned the stone wheels one upon another.

"Stay away from that fellow there beside you, who's up to no good," Wizard told Marn. "And you be a credit to us, since you're so anxious to get away. And how much of a wage is Mr. Willem paying you, and what out of it do you figure to send us old folks?"

"He didn't say," Marn said. "But I'll put aside half for you, if that's all right."

Her mother came behind Wizard. "Send what you can spare, Marn. We don't need it."

"She's not going to have an expense in the world," Wizard objected. "You keep a third and bring the rest to us, girl."

"Well, I will, Father." Marn pulled the heavy rug over her knees, glad that there was to be no row about her going, and thankful to have a haven from her parents' keen eyes while she worked out what she would do. The fawn squeaked behind her and the goat bleated, uncertain.

"Buy yourself a proper dress when you get your money," Mrs. Coombs cried, as the cart started up. "Now that you're going out into the world, you don't have to advertise your poor beginnings. Spend plenty for it! When Mr. Trail comes by, I'll tell him of your new position. He'll visit you there, and you can tell him what kind of dress you want and give him the cash, and he can bring it from Greenfield sometime!" As Farmer drove off, Marn's mother was still calling after her, into the world that lay white-covered and the wind that had exhausted itself in the big storm just past.

Farmer patted Marn's knee. "Don't send them a penny, little girl. They've got no rights over you. Parents are always that way. And Dutchman won't give you overmuch anyway."

"I intend to send my father two-thirds of what I'm paid." Marn pushed his hand from her. "And you say Miss Coombs, like you're supposed to."

"I've had my eye on how pretty you are," Farmer said, "ever since you came leading that little cow last September. And do you want to stop at the store for a ginger beer or candy? I wouldn't mind to buy you whatever you'd want."

"No." She was firm.

But he persisted, used to the ways of womenkind, and *no* meaning *perhaps*, and *perhaps* meaning *yes*. "Then let's stop at the apple-storing house when we pass the orchard, and I'll show you the size of the harvest we put down in wheat straw in bins to keep them from freezing this winter. Or else, can I look at your hand and tell your fortune? I can say how long you'll live. And what's the name of that pet deer of yours? Has she got as fancy a name as your father gives his creatures? And does Dutchman know you plan to bring her? He won't allow you to keep her."

"She's got no name," Marn said, "except *come here* or *lie down* or *here's your supper.*"

"Wouldn't you like to know how many children you're going to bear and how often you'll take up with someone, little girl? I've got a pack of cards here that tell."

But Marn did not want to speak, and the man decided to bide his time. "Did that crow of your father's ever bite you, little girl?"

"I've known that crow since its mother hatched it years ago," she said, scornful. "And why would it bite me? And I think it's got more sense than some men have, too."

When the mules pulled up at Willem's house, Farmer untied the fawn so it could leap down, and handed Marn her bundles. He drove on to the barn to unhitch the eager mules and turn the white goat back with her old mates and begin to relate to the curious among the help the entire happenings of the past hours. Farmer would embellish only where he thought it would increase the interest. "And then the Wizard said he does get into that crow's body now and then! And the bird can speak, too. It told its master: *Farmer kissed the new Mrs.*

Henry Blackburn when she was Miss Willem. And that turkey vulture talks, but in a whisper: *Did Miss Willem run from you, Farmer?* Now is there anyone among you hands who'd like to know if they're inclined to lunacy or suicide!"

Back in the house, Marn was letting the fawn follow her up the strange stairs to the second floor and up another, steep and unrailed and turning sharply at the top into a tiny, bare-floored, slant-ceilinged attic room. A narrow bed, on which was thrown a feather-filled quilt, was beside the dormer window, where hung the black iron bell that called the people in to breakfast and the noon dinner and would announce fires and weddings and holiday festivals; it had rung when the baby Katrin had been birthed twenty-two years ago downstairs. There was a chest under the opposite dormer window, and Marn folded her clothes in it. She put her nightgown under the featherbed cover, and on the small square table that stood by the bed she laid her mirror. She put the china doll in the broad, low windowsill. She would ask Mr. Willem for a candlestick or lamp, and maybe a chair or stool. If there were books anywhere in the house below, perhaps he might let her look into them. She would see if there were an extra Bible she could use, and if there were none, with her first money ever earned that belonged only to her, she would tell the next hired hand that went to Greenfield to buy her one. She would keep it on the chest over there and read it every night here in this place of safety, her bitterness put from her.

She thought of where the Lord God had said, *I will save my flock, and they shall no more be a prey. I will cause the evil beasts to cease out of the land: and they shall dwell safely in the wilderness, and sleep in the woods. And I will make them and the places round about my hill a blessing; there shall*

*be showers of blessing. And they shall be safe, and none shall
make them afraid.*

Marn went back down the two flights of stairs, the fawn
pattering on her heels. On the ground floor, she stopped in at
Dutchman's bedroom to lay back the covers on the high four-
poster before dark would fall. The furniture was massive and
white or blue-painted and decorated in a way Marn had never
seen or heard of. On the bed a great, soiled, crocheted counter-
pane was spread, that Mrs. Willem had put there before she
was hurt and died in the bed, and had not since been washed.
On the tall bureau was the little clock Dutchman had sent
up to Nell Blackburn that chimed the hours and which had
been returned.

On a round table before the curtained windows was a
parchment-bound Lutheran Bible that Dutchman had never
looked into, but which seemed to him a talisman connecting
him with all his ancestors, who were not barbarians as were
Chinese or Moors or Catholics. The book had a tinted flower
and cross on its cover; it was not like the third-hand, torn-
and-crumple-sheeted edition of Wizard's that he pored over
along with his books on remedies and magic, as closely as
did his daughter Marn. She looked now at the outside of Mr.
Willem's Bible, but did not dare to open it. She thought how
she would take down the curtains and clean them, and the
bedspread, the first chance she got.

Now there was the coming feast in the offing to think of,
which needed to be prepared for. She looked through the pantry and all the cupboards and counted in her mind what sup-
plies were on hand and what might be needed. That night
Dutchman said that in the morning he'd send up the women
who were used to help Katrin in the house, and they would

take orders from Marn. "And be firm, Miss Coombs, because they're a slovenly lot. Eh? If I find that you are, as well, because of your youth and upbringing, off you'll go."

"Yes, Mr. Willem," Marn said, the candle she'd found in the pantry in her hand, before going up to the attic. She'd seen no other book or paper, not even the common Almanac about, and had decided not to ask her employer for a Bible, but to obtain one when her first wages were received.

Marn didn't have to, though, because someone came to bear her a gift of one that very week. The jackass wheezed out in the barnyard to announce the tall black mare clattering up, Schoolmaster on her back, the little golden spaniel dashing after. Randall Grim had learned from the children of Willem's hired men in the schoolroom, of Marn's new position and had come to congratulate her and at the same time try to figure out what virtue had made Dutchman want to hire her and not another. Schoolmaster respected Willem as the most businesslike, substantial man around. And because of Marn's overnight new place as mistress here, his attitude toward her had subtly changed.

Grim tied his mare's reins to one of the big iron rings provided on the dovecote fence, beyond which he could see the baby deer he had given the girl a while ago. The fawn sniffed tamely through the fence at him, and at her side brown rabbits rose on their hind legs, too, and banties clucked among the gray doves, looking to see if the man had brought kitchen leavings for them. Randall Grim thought how he'd doubted Marn Coombs goodness ever since the evening when he'd seen the daughter of the Wizard let everyone but herself be fooled by the food her father had tainted. He wondered whether the Dutchman had been bewitched by the girl. Schoolmaster considered himself a man of no small learning, and had hoped to make himself an influence in the Old Mountain country. In college he'd led the debate teams; and, just as he'd learned Plato and the philosophers, he'd educated himself in those wrestling tricks he'd employed back at the Greenfield Fair. By wile or openness, he intended to master all opposition, whether of spirit or body. Schoolmaster Grim had asked Nell Blackburn about Marn when she came to tidy up his schoolhouse or cabin. Nell said Marn was her friend, and she was disappointed that Marn hadn't married her brother Henry instead of Willem's daughter, Katrin. Nell had reported only good of Wizard's daughter.

Schoolmaster pulled a brown paper package out of his coat pocket as he came to knock at the door. He ran his long fingers through his curly brown hair, his dark eyes conciliatory, his voice low. "I haven't seen you since the Greenfield Fair, Miss Coombs!"

"I can't shake hands because I've got flour all over me," she told him. "We're in a hurry around here."

"Did you hear about the big crowd gathered last week in Greenfield?" he asked her, grinning.

Marn frowned. "I feel that now I'll have some money of my own, I wish to pay you the seven dollars cash you gave my father for that fawn of mine, Mr. Grim."

"Forget it," he said, as he followed her through the entry, his dog at his heels. "Can't you see I'm trying to entertain you with a story? This crowd had seen the announcements HE IS COMING and then HE IS HERE, and no one was sure who HE was. But they all paid up and filled the hall; and the bell rang and the curtain went up, and there was a sign saying HE IS GONE! And I've got a present here for you, Miss Coombs."

In the kitchen the scents of the coming feast filled the air. Two women were at the far end of the room. One was washing and cutting up Rambo apples from the bushel at her side for the apple butter that would be used as a sauce with the pair of hogs, each weighing a quarter of a ton, that were to be roasted outside for a whole long day. The other's apron was stained with blood from the fresh-killed fowl laid on the table before her that she was boning and cleaning. Grim waved at them and they nodded back. He put the package on the table.

"Open it, why don't you?"

She wiped her hands on a towel and took it, hesitant. "Why did you bring it to me, Mr. Grim?"

"Because you were always quoting Scriptures every time you opened your mouth, it seemed to me."

Marn was delighted. The Bible was ordinary, with a black cardboard cover, but it was new and the leaves were untouched; and Marn couldn't wait to put it on her chest in the attic and open it under the candle flicker. She thought of how Randall Grim might ask someone like herself to marry and go off to his cabin. He had nice manners and a great education. And maybe she ought to think of ways to make him want her for a wife. "You could write your name in here that it's to me, and I'd like that, Mr. Grim."

"I will." He took the Bible to a corner chair, the spaniel crouching beside him, nose on silky paws, honey-colored eyes trailing Marn.

While he got out his pencil and wrote, Marn rolled the

dough for the meat pies. "I can't sit and visit, because we'll never be done," she said.

Grim gazed into the book that he was leafing through now. He'd just remarked to the Wizard's daughter that he hadn't seen her since the Greenfield Fair, and sometimes it almost seemed to him that that was the truth, so visionlike was the memory of that night when he'd left his cabin on a sudden impulse and arrived late at the Wizard Coombs' smoky meadow. He looked up at her now and asked quickly, "Miss Coombs, do you think Mr. Willem would mind if I came to this party he's throwing? I've husked corn before."

"You ask him," Marn said. "He's a strong-minded man and I doubt anyone could guess his feelings or thoughts."

"Well, I'd like to come over," Schoolmaster said. "And how's that deer I gave you? I thought Wizard might sell her again to somebody else."

"No," Marn told him. "My father wouldn't take money for what was rightfully mine. And as soon as I can, I want to pay you back for her. I'm keeping her in that dovecote with those rabbits and roosters until I think up a better place. If she's a bother, Mr. Willem might change his mind about letting me keep her here. And on this place everyone has to think how if they don't measure up, off they'll go!" One of the women from the other end of the room brought over a dish of boned fowl, and Marn began laying the pieces of meat in the soft dough she'd lined the long black pans with.

She was thinking how she liked having a kitchen that she could run, even if she was just hired to handle it for a while. And she thought how ever since she was grown and fifteen and Wizard had made her be the ghost girl and she'd started

opening more traps than ever on his animals and had been
in trouble with him, she'd wanted to be in a place where
another wasn't directing her every move. All the past summer,
Marn had yearned to go up on the mountain and shear the
sheep and make quilts with the Blackburn women and be
Henry's wife. That was the way she'd thought to escape.
She'd never dreamed of taking over a great valley house on
a prosperous farm down here. And she felt how she was
capable and made for it and would out-think Mr. Willem
whatever he might desire, so he would keep her on as long as
she could hide her coming child. And by then she hoped to
have someone like this Schoolmaster to help her.

And Marn was remembering that even on her birthday,
just before that moment of love with Henry Blackburn, when
she'd said *no and no,* it was only when her lover told her
clearly over the howl of the storm and the shriek of the wild
dogs outside that he'd wed her, and she believed him, that
she'd given in to Henry. She had thought even in that split
instant of the future. Marn wondered if women all over the
world did that. They bribed the man with themselves, and,
even if lost in desire, their thoughts moved ahead, onto the
kitchens and the decorated, blue-painted poster beds and the
bureaus and on their need to somewhat master their own fate.

She went over to the curly-headed man ruffling through
the thin pages of the book. He showed her where he had put
her name and his and the date. "That's two gifts I've given
you," he said softly.

Marn felt how she was beginning to like him and how she
would try to charm Grim. She counted all that had come to her
since her birthday and the pearl-handled mirror. She had her
fawn, the pretty china doll the other day, and now a Bible.

But then she was startled and worried because the man in the corner began revealing a secret about the red oxen of Sheepman Blackburn up on Bald Mountain. Nell had brought the new Mrs. Henry Blackburn over to Grim's schoolhouse with her to visit, because Katrin was bored with the dullness of the Sheepman's home and couldn't decide how to furnish or decorate, if at all, the part of it that had been given to herself and Henry when they married. Katrin had revealed to Schoolmaster in a whisper the Blackburn family secret.

"I don't want to know it!" Marn protested.

"If she told me, how can it be a secret any more?" Randall Grim asked. "Katrin says Sheepman warned her not to tell, but she can't hold back anything. It's all about how he grew those great red steers to twice the size of most by feeding them table scrapings and milk and eggs and even meat."

Marn said, "You ought not to ever spread a secret, Mr. Grim!"

"Sheepman Blackburn trained them from baby calves to eat food most people would never dream a hoofed animal would want, Miss Coombs."

Marn listened to the soft, persuasive voice going on and on. She thought of how, if she'd gone to live up there where Katrin now was and had the secret told to her, she'd have locked it in herself. It was like her father saying he would not reveal his magic spells, for they would lose their power if he did. Secrets were made to be kept. And Marn was, at just that moment, beginning to realize that she had come upon a secret of her own.

Schoolmaster continued talking, telling one of his jokes. "And those women appear pretty cruel over at that table. I notice they're beating the eggs and stoning the cherries and whipping the cream and mashing the potatoes!" He snapped his fingers at his dog.

Marn had recalled the stifled, muted voice out in the meadow back there, when the second customer had come to view the raising of the ghost and the unicorn. Marn knew suddenly that Mr. Grim had brought her the Bible today as an offering against his guilt about that. It was the dark and light of life, the false and true, the wrong and right. Henry Blackburn had lied to the world about the shepherd dog, Tam, saying that Tam had not looked out for the sheep; Henry's pride would always overcome truth. And the Schoolmaster had declared that he had not seen Marn since the Fair, and he would stick by that untruth; Randall Grim had hidden himself that night from Sam Trail and the Wizard, devious and ashamed, because he professed to be involved in the overcoming of wickedness and the championing of good.

Out in the dovecote was the fawn, Marn thought, with great, protruding, nocturnal eyes, the black-brown irises shaped very like the amber, oval ones of the Wizard's buck, Odin, but expanded so that the pupils were a slit because she was a night and he was a day animal. The baby deer, like her fellow white-tails that had come down from the mountain for the winter, and like the jack in the barn and the Schoolmaster's mare outside, could see equally well in all directions, though nowhere sharply and in depth. The rabbits' round eyes were nocturnal, too, but not so much as the deer's, because that species fed in day as well as night. The banty rooster was quick and alert for insects and small moving worms that he sighted closely with a single eye and then struck at almost blindly. In the perches of the cote over the banties were soft-feathered ringneck doves, the orange-red membranes of their eyes glitter-

ing crimson when the sun shone into them. The crow's eyes
were set forward, rather like a human's, so the bird looked
directly at his master or what prey he might be pursuing. The
eyes of the buzzard, Venus, were a dusky olive-yellow with
gold lights in them and an outer rim of gray. When Venus
saw a movement in the sky, she would tilt her head on a side
and watch it, and a human could look there and the sky seemed
empty. Marn was thinking how no one knew for sure when
the truth was there and when not. It depended on the nature
of the viewer what he did or did not see.

And then the subject was changed because the husband
of one of the hired women across the room came hustling in
to tell everyone that the Stableman had taken a potshot at the
Farmer, and the Farmer had disarmed him and knocked him
down and out. And then Farmer had saddled up two mules
and told the Stableman's beautiful wife to get up on one, and
he had shouted back to the other hands to tell Stableman when
he woke up that his wife had said *perhaps* meant *yes* in her
case and there 'was no telling if they would ever come back!

"They've gone away full speed!" The hired hand waved
his big-knuckled hands. "And devil only knows what'll take
place when Dutchman Willem gets in from the corn and finds
the best Farmer he ever had gone off with the trashiest though
the comeliest heifer on this place!"

*

*

6

*

The Wild Swan

MARN WAS putting together a plum kuchen the particular way Mr. Willem liked. It was dawn on Sunday, and the fragrant large kitchen, lit by oil lamps, was quiet except for her movements and the occasional twitter of the caged cardinals on their perches in the window. Mr. Willem had told Marn that the recipe was in the drawer under the towels, and she had found it among others written out in Bertha Willem's flowery scrawl. It took a lot of butter and sugar and eggs, but it would keep for days, and was not served out to the hands but put aside for his plate and the suppers that he took alone. Marn would serve him from the stove at the Master's Chair, and then go into the house to dust or light the lamps or turn down his bed. Later, when she cleared after him and did whatever must be done in preparation for breakfast, she would get tea and supper for herself.

Now she was kneading the ingredients on a floured board

so that the butter would melt and blend. She pressed the dough into a pan and began to lay upon it rows of the plums that had been put up in the season past. She crumbled the streusel on top, made of butter and sugar and flour, and put it in the oven of the big iron stove where the fire sparked. It was the hour when she had used to be out in the swamp turning free some of the creatures trapped there, and she thought of that, wondering what fluttered or waited silently in the large white flakes of the falling snow. Despite her new feeling of freedom, Marn was homesick. She had never in her life been away from her room in the Wizard's shack, and now for these many nights she had slept in the attic above, that was small and strange. She thought how she would ask Mr. Willem at break-fast if, after the service in the church that morning, she could go with her mother to her home, giving the excuse that there was something she needed, a dress or a pair of shoes.

The Dutchman didn't mind. He told her to stay until mid-afternoon if she wanted, and he'd send someone with a cart to drive her back, so she needn't hurry. In the pale morning light the hired men were shuffling in to the benches along the table. After the morning chores and breakfast on Sundays, they were customarily let off to do as they pleased for the rest of the morning. In the afternoon, they were expected to work, and today Dutchman had said they would butcher two out of the hog herd that had been gathered in when the last storm broke, under the barn in the low-ceilinged area where no man could walk upright. He ordered that the beasts would be scalded and cleaned, but left with the great heads on. On Monday they would be roasted outside all day long for the husking feast that night. Dutchman looked down the line of workers, as Marn set his dish of hot plum kuchen and a cup of coffee before him. He declared that he hoped to be back from Greenfield by nightfall.

"And I'll scour the town till I find them! I'll hunt out that young Sam Trail to help me. He knows every inch of the low-down part of Greenfield." He turned to Marn, demanding, "Anything you need in town I can get? Eh? Speak up."

She shook her head, startled at his attention. "No, thank you." Marn felt the vague nausea rising in her as it did sometimes in the mornings lately. She knew it was because of the coming child, and wondered if anyone noticed her visits to the blue-painted and decorated privy, waiting for it to pass.

The Stableman was pale, and glanced sidelong at Mr. Willem. "I ought to go with you!"

But Dutchman hit his clenched fist on the table and said no. "You're like a bull in a pantry and you'll bumble things! All I want is my Farmer back, and if I bring your woman, too, it'll be on your promise herewith that you'll take her back peaceably. If you won't and want to fight, I'll leave her in that town."

"I don't mind," Stableman said, "to make that promise."

Dutchman pounded the table again. *"A woman that's busy looking into a glass is too busy to look after a house,* they say. And that's the trouble with every wife or girl on this place who's got any measure of looks at all. Not one of them's worth her keep." He looked over at the Wizard's daughter who was feeling the illness in her, standing at the stove. "Except that one, maybe. And don't let me see you ever with a mirror in hand, Miss Coombs."

Marn rode in the slat-sided, mule-drawn wagon that had benches built along the sides, with the others of Dutchman's hired people who were church-goers. The snowfall had stopped for a while; the earth lay cleanly covered, seemingly pure. It was the second Sunday of Advent, and the preacher wanted everyone prepared for His birthday after two more Sundays. "It is the hour for all of us to rise from the sleep of sin and indifference. Now is the season for longing, the time to prepare ourselves, so we need not fear when the Judgment is at hand." The minister was a traveling one, and liked to stir his captive audience that became restive under his fiery eye and his psalms. *"Oh Lord, let not my enemies laugh at me, for none of them that wait on Thee shall be confounded!"*

Marn was sitting between two of the wives of the Dutchman's men; one was old and muttered her prayers audibly, not heeding the preacher. Marn's eyes went seeking her mother, but Mrs. Coombs didn't always come. She saw Henry Blackburn with his wife Katrin and the rest of the Blackburns, and Schoolmaster, too, beside Nell, in a back row. Homesick, Marn began thinking of Hebe and the brown calf Aphrodite and the gray game rooster and the speckled small one and the squirrel, all of whom ran free about Wizard's yard. And the great pair of turkeys that roosted outside the Coombs' kitchen door every night and knew Marn's voice and touch. She missed the growing young vulture, Venus, who responded to her emotionally, dipping her head and rushing about when she saw Marn. And the old crow of her father's, too. And Marn wondered who ever petted the wild white swan now. She thought of the doves in the kitchen that her mother let fly free with the finches, and how at Willem's farm the doves lived in the yard cote and were quite wild. Marn would hear them out there, reminding her of home. One would begin to coo and the others would join in: "Coo-crrrrrrooooo, coo!"

The man was speaking out of the Epistle to the Romans.

"It is high time to awake out of sleep. Let us walk honestly; not in revelry, and in chambering and wantonness, not in jealousy. Put on the Lord, and make not provision for the flesh, to fulfill the lusts thereof. Now I want to talk to you Old Mountain sinners about that, too!"

The sermon lasted more than an hour before the man turned loose his flock. "Let your minds be purified. And *Dominus Vobiscum,* too!" The preacher came down to stand at the door and shake everyone's hand as they went out into the sunless day, where their breath steamed. In the entry, warmed by a small stove, the Blackburn family and School-master Grim were talking with farmers of the countryside and neighbors about a new trouble with the sheep; it wasn't dog marauders this time, for no baying was ever heard. The Blackburns thought rather that some human thief was at work. Two or three sheep would disappear at a time and no trace be left. Henry waved his hands, speaking of it, and Sheepman shrugged, looking smaller and more defeated than ever.

"If it weren't for young Henry I'd get out of sheep," he sighed. "If my son and Katrin ever leave home, I'll give the flock up. I lock my bullocks in the shed, and they're too big for man or beast to bother. And no one would try to attack or steal a chair I'm making, either!"

Henry told the neighbors, "All I've got to count on nowadays to guard the sheep at night is that new fighting ram. My wife's ruining our dog Tam, by letting him in to protect her own self from the robbers, as if I'm not able to do that!" Henry's ire was up.

"I'm afraid all the time," Katrin cried. "And that's the truth." She saw Marn hurrying out the door and waved, but the Wizard's daughter paid her no heed.

Schoolmaster and Nell were shaking hands with the preacher, and Grim was doing most of the talking. "I'm very fond of the Apostle Paul myself and admired your sermonizing on the Epistle. I wouldn't mind to give you some of my own opinions. I like the stand he takes on marriage and divorce and widows and widowers and virgins, and that if you can get some power over your own will, then it's just as well if you live alone. I favor Saint Paul."

"Not I." Nell Blackburn said, restless. Nell felt she had done what she could to trap Randall Grim into marriage and all he wanted was someone to scrub his floors. "Have you got a wife?" she asked the preacher.

"I'm one of those people on fire, Miss Blackburn," he told her, "with the gospel word. I'm waiting for that fire to die down some before I get interested in anything else."

Marn was going quickly down the churchyard path, heading for her home on the other side of the Greenfield Road.

Halfway there, she heard steps far behind her, and Katrin's shout, "Marn, wait for me!" Katrin caught up, panting, bundled in her heavy coat of brown bear fur that had been her mother's. Her reddish-blonde hair was in a long braid, and her blue eyes were bright, her smooth cheeks red. She kissed Marn and cried, "I've missed you, and there's so much to tell! Why didn't you stop in the church? Didn't you see me wave? Why don't you ever come up on the mountain to visit? I'm lonesome. And I can't come to Papa's, because he said I wasn't ever to set foot on our farm again. And Randall told me you're having a husking feast tomorrow and he's been invited, and I wish Henry and I could come! And how is my Papa? That's what I'm going to your house about now."

"I wondered if marriage would settle you down, Katrin,"

Marn said, beginning to wish nowadays that Henry and Katrin would grow content with each other, and that the danger of their coming down to Dutchman's and taking the kitchen from Marn were past.

"I love marriage," Katrin ran on, "but I don't like having a baby or being up there with only the sheep. I miss the commotion of the farm and I miss Papa. Henry told me to put up curtains and a cloth on the table and to hang a new mirror on the wall. He gave me money to buy them. And he said I must sit at the loom and wheel and learn to weave and make up wool, and then I must make a rug for the floor and a spread for the bed. And I told Henry I didn't think I could ever learn!"

"After a while you'll be happy," Marn told her. "It's because you're homesick. I'm that way now. Mr. Willem told me I could go home for a visit today. I can stay till the afternoon."

"Aren't you afraid of Papa, Marn? I couldn't believe it when Randall told me you were going to work for Papa. Isn't he mean to you? How do you get along? Tell me everything, Marn!" Katrin was feeling the bite of jealousy in her. Marn knew she was. Katrin was like the ringneck dove chicks, that when they became fully as large as their parents still pleaded, wings whirring and outspread, to be cared for. Even when the hen dove went ahead and laid another pair of eggs, and the parents were busy keeping them warm, still the adolescent doves would beg, not liking to give up their dependence. Marn tried to change the subject. "Why are you coming to our house?"

"It's a secret." Katrin glanced sidelong at her friend. "I told Henry I forgot to take my redbirds from home, and that

I'm going to your place to ask your mother for another cage of them. But that's not the real reason I'm going there."

"I don't like hearing secrets," Marn said. "It makes trouble always. Down in the valley, they're telling how you revealed your father-in-law's secret about his famous red oxen and how they got so great."

"I've already told this particular secret to Nell," Katrin said, intense, "and that's why she's staying at the church and isn't here with me now. She's keeping Henry busy, while I'm going to see your father. I want a charm from Wizard, Marn."

"What kind of charm?" Marn asked, wary.

Katrin said, "Henry might be surprised if it works, too. And that's the secret."

"What kind? And why is it a secret!"

But Katrin only kept chattering on about all she was missing because she'd left her father's home. "I heard how Farmer ran away with that woman! And how Stableman shot at him. Do you think Farmer has gone forever, and will he marry the Stableman's wife? And did Farmer try to run after you in the barn, Marn, when you first came?"

"Katrin, tell me what charm you want from my father," Marn persisted.

And from the clapboard house of the Coombs, just ahead, came a nasal, unfamiliar voice. "Billy likes Alice. Hello, old girl. Billy likes Alice!"

"Who's that, Marn?" Katrin said.

"Who's Billy?" Marn wanted to know.

Mrs. Coombs opened the door to welcome them. "Someone called Alice had him before he came to me, girls." She hugged Marn and then pushed her hair back into the bun where it never stayed and shook hands with Katrin. "It's nice to see you, Miss Willem. I mean Mrs. Blackburn. You still look like a child to me, with that braid down your back and your pretty looks. How do you like wedded life and your new relations?"

"Is that Billy?" Katrin asked.

A ragged-feathered green parrot came waddling along the floor, cocking its crested head at the visitors. Mrs. Coombs took Katrin's coat and told her, "Billy's always as pleased as I am at company."

Marn was pulling off her boots and hanging her things on the pegs behind the door. The house seemed smaller than she remembered, and more cluttered and dusty. The windows were still full of tame dove and wild bird cages, and along the wall and behind the stove were hampers, each with some animal, captive or willing, in it. A red-shouldered hawk with a string dangling from its leg peered from a broomstick perch near the door.

Mrs. Coombs asked Marn, "How is your work at that big house?" She hustled about, heating water for some tea; the green bird, feathers ruffled, always at her heels, fluttering out of the way if she turned too quickly. "Are you homesick yet, girl? Because you will be."

"Not I," Marn said.

"Just wait," Mrs. Coombs told her. "I can still remember how I was when I first came to the Old Mountain country, before I got used to it being my home."

"I'm as homesick as I can be, Mrs. Coombs," Katrin said.

"I'm not." Marn denied it, her eyes on the raccoon cub, not in his cage any more and asleep for the moment under a corner chair, and content, as if he lay along a tree limb somewhere outside his home hollow.

Her mother said, "After you're over being homesick, you'll dream about this place, girl. Even when you get old, you'll see the house and the swamp as clear as today in your sleep, because you were raised here and it's built into your mind."

"I dream all the time about Papa," Katrin said. "And even when he roars in the dream and hits me and shouts at Henry, still I'm not afraid and I want to go home."

"You will in time, Mrs. Blackburn. Your father loves you, I'm sure. He's just angry with you now because you eloped."

"Where's the Wizard?" Katrin asked. "I have to see him. And I want another cageful of birds, too, Mrs. Coombs. Do you have any more cardinals?"

"No, but how about some little black-hooded juncos, instead? They're not flashy, but they're as friendly as you could want."

"Would you sell me that parrot, Mrs. Coombs?"

"Gracious, no!" Mrs. Coombs said. "I'd as soon sell one of you girls to someone. Billy's a gift from a friend of mine." She looked down at the bird, who returned her gaze, tipping its head on one side.

"Hello, old girl," the parrot said. "Billy likes Alice."

"I thought I'd just let him keep saying Alice," Mrs. Coombs said. "I don't mind the name, and I'm not going to teach or try to unteach anything he does. If Billy wants to fetch and carry teaspoons and bread crusts about the room, I don't mind. Wizard says I ought to break him of doing that. Wizard likes a beast or bird to pay attention, and I'm not that way." She looked at the hawk perched over the door. "You wouldn't want the hawk, would you, Mrs. Blackburn?"

"No, and where is your husband?"

"That hawk won't stay in a cage," Mrs. Coombs told

Katrin. "He'd sulk until he starved if you set him in a cage and closed the door. And he's not easy to feed, either. You have to take him out-of-doors and throw his food, and he catches it in mid-air. And he wants to come back into the house when he's finished and go to sleep."

"How much are the juncos?" Katrin asked. "I'll take them, Mrs. Coombs. But what I really came for is to talk with Mr. Coombs. It's a secret from my husband, too."

"Katrin wants a charm, but she won't tell what kind," Marn said, hoping the Wizard was off somewhere and unavailable.

"Your father's out in the barnyard, Marn," Mrs. Coombs said. "But seeing as Mrs. Blackburn arrived with you and how maybe she'd be wanting to buy something, I figure he'll be in at any minute, and that's why I'm laying him a place at the table along with ours." She clattered the spoons and knives down and began to sort them out. "Go get the teapot, girl."

And sure enough, just as the three were sitting down, Wizard Coombs did come stamping in. "You here for medicine, Mrs. Blackburn?" He took his chair, nodding at his daughter, because it seemed to him as if Marn had just gone out the door a little while ago. "Venus and the crow tagged along and are out on the porch if you want to say hello," he told Marn.

"Thanks, Father," Marn sighed, thinking how easily both her parents accepted her return, and how it was only to her that the time seemed long, since she was young; and then, too, it was she who had had the new experience. Marn even thought how her mother had found variety and comfort in Billy, in a way replacing Marn with the bird, bent upon her own interests.

"Can you make the charm or lay the kind of spell, Wizard," Katrin was saying, "that will make my Papa want me living in his house again so badly he won't mind if my husband comes too?"

"You can't think up a more difficult job for me," Wizard told her, "because of the stubborn nature of your father, and the dillydally nature of yourself. If it were the other way around, it'd be easy."

"Posh," Mrs. Coombs said to her husband, and she handed a spoon down to the parrot, who took it in his beak and paraded up and down so everyone might see his trick and praise him, "if Dutchman and his daughter were the other way around, there'd be no trouble in the first place."

Wizard ignored the interruption. "If you've got enough money, of course. And then, too, I'll need some article, clothing or jewels, that your husband bought particularly for you, Mrs. Blackburn. It's got to be of importance to you both."

Katrin twisted the gold circle on her finger, reluctant. "Henry never gave me a thing but this ruby ring, back there at the Greenfield Fair. All my clothes I've always had."

"I noticed that pretty ring when you first came in," Mrs. Coombs said. "And I figured maybe it came from that rich Mr. Sam Trail when he wanted to use up all his money on you at the Fair. He's a free spender and the one that gave me this parrot. He bought Billy in Greenfield the day after our daughter left us and brought him right out."

Katrin frowned. "Henry would see it was gone right away and ask what had happened to it."

"Doesn't your husband know you're here?" Wizard demanded.

"Henry doesn't believe in you or your powers," Marn told her father, cold.

"The Sheepman's son thinks she's here after that cage of juncos," Mrs. Coombs said.

"Henry would be angry if he knew," Katrin mourned. "And he has a terrible temper, too!"

"Cut your hand up a little, then, Mrs. Blackburn!" Wizard scorned the weakling child of Dutchman Willem. "Go and mash it a bit and tell him you've put the ring away and will slip it back on when the finger heals. And when the spell is all over, you can have the ring back. I won't keep it, just the money."

"How does the charm work?" Katrin asked, still turning the circle about upon her finger.

"You want me to lose my powers?" The Wizard was scathing with his customer. "And hand over the ruby ring and fifteen dollars."

"I don't have that much." Tears started to well in Katrin's blue eyes.

"How much have you got?"

"Ten, and it's to buy curtains and things. And I haven't even paid for the birds and cage. And Henry thinks I'm here for them!"

"No matter," Wizard said. "I'll have the gewgaw for earnest, and you can bring the remaining five and a dollar for the birds when you come to claim it, after the spell's worked and it's all over."

"What if it doesn't work, Father?" Marn said, knowing that all her own plans would go askew now as her father's magic was set into action. She took some pieces of biscuit and jam to the door and handed them out to the black birds waiting there for Wizard. The crow exclaimed hoarsely and snatched his and flew off, while the buzzard accepted her portion quietly and waited while the girl stroked her feathers; then she walked away to examine the treat.

When Marn returned to the table, Katrin was asking, "Is it a sure charm?" and tugging the circle with the glass stone from her plump finger and laying it on the table. Katrin took a handkerchief from her pocket and removed the wadded bills from it and put them beside the ring.

Wizard reached across and folded the money carefully, and put it in his pocket, and picked up the ring. "No spell is positive. There are too many factors involved. And this trifle is worth about four bits, too. It's the meaning it has for husband and wife that can help now. That's the only reason it's needed." Wizard felt how the tears Mrs. Blackburn shed were too easy; he hoped to stir her if she had to give up something dear and had to make up an alibi that wasn't simple to explain her ring's absence to her husband. Too, Wizard wanted to drive Katrin toward Dutchman, who was probably missing his daughter by now. He said, "All you have to do is stay away from your Papa, who has forgotten you for sure, Mrs. Blackburn. He's wiped you from his mind." The man stumbled over the parrot on the floor, as he got up and went to pull on his coat.

The bird fluffed his feathers to straighten them, and cried, "Hello, old girl," and hurried to his mistress' shoes.

Wizard grumbled, addressing himself to Katrin again. "And I could add that the spells I lay are no hoax. Ask my daughter here, who was sweet on your husband a while back. I employed the opposite of this charm then, because I was hoping to save her for a better fate." He slammed the door as he left.

Marn thought how there was nothing now to do but wait for the enchantment to get under way. Just as her skillful father had made Henry cease loving Marn, so he would make Katrin's Papa want her again. Then Katrin would come back to the Willem farm, and Henry with her; and that would be the end to Marn running the great kitchen and house, and living in the small warm attic room with the Bible on the chest and Sam Trail's doll in the window and the wavery-glassed mirror on the table. Abruptly, Marn wanted to be back there, and wished the cart were just pulling up outside to return her. Mrs. Coombs was saying soothing words to the pale and set-faced Katrin. The baby raccoon awoke and came over to the table for his usual cup of warm tea and sugar and milk. There came the noise of jingling bells and wheels and a horse approaching down the lane. Katrin took out her handkerchief and blew her nose.

Mrs. Coombs said, "There, there," and went to the door. She cried, "Why, it's that nice Mr. Trail again!"

The young man was tying up the fast sorrel gelding, who stamped the ground and champed his bit, hitched to a black, shining sleigh. Trail waved at Mrs. Coombs, shouting, "I just bought this rig in Greenfield, and I'm giving it its first run." He came to the door, diffident, his fancy leather cap in his hand, his eyes going past the other women and onto Marn, whom Trail dreamed of, asleep or awake, every now and then since he'd watched the pale-bodied girl circling the meadow, followed by the tiny fawn with the horn strapped to its forehead. He cried, "I came over from the church to see if I could escort the ladies wherever they'd like to go!"

And once again in his life, Trail was dazzled by the warmth of the smile of the Wizard's daughter, and once again he thought it was directed to himself, not knowing it was for what he did for her. Marn said, "I'd be glad if you could take me back to Mr. Willem's, after I've given you some tea and cake, Mr. Trail." And she got up to go to the stove and cupboard to get some for him.

"How's that little china-headed doll I gave you, Miss Coombs?" He grinned and then looked past her at the distraught Katrin. "Is she crying? What's the matter, Katrin?"

But Dutchman's daughter shook her head and would not reply. She was getting up the courage to go to where the knife was. And while Mrs. Coombs was handing Billy a broken biscuit to march about with and clearing Wizard's place, and Marn was setting the table for Trail, Katrin finally crossed the room and cut her left hand 'along the fingers. Dumbly, she stood looking at the blood flowing in a steady stream onto the side table.

Trail leaped from his seat. "Did you do that on purpose, Katrin?"

Mrs. Coombs brought a towel, and they made the young wife sit on a stool and lean her head on her lap until she felt better. Mrs. Coombs got a bottle of mullen leaves in oil and slipped them on the hand, and bound it with a piece of sheeting she stripped, and then knotted it. She scolded Katrin, "And you with a baby coming."

Katrin was sullen. "How can you tell that?"

"What do you think using a knife on yourself could do to your child," Mrs. Coombs cried. "Gracious, you have to think about things like that."

Marn had stood aside and watched the others while they

tended Katrin, and she told her now, scorning her ways, "Well, Henry won't ask you where the ruby ring is right away, anyhow."

Katrin sighed and looked up at Marn, and said what she'd been wanting to ever since Wizard had loosed his words less than an hour ago, about Marn and Henry being sweet on each other and how he'd broken the romance up. She said, "What did Nell tell me about you coming up the mountain all the summer long after my Henry!"

Marn flushed. "Don't talk like that."

Katrin whispered, "And more, too, Marn!"

Mrs. Coombs said, "The past is past, Mrs. Blackburn, and better let it rest. And Mr. Trail, why don't you let me cut a piece of this jelly cake for you."

"That's the first thing around here that I've understood," Trail said, "since Katrin cut herself there."

But then Katrin couldn't let the matter rest, and she came after Mrs. Coombs while the woman got a tattered sweater to button about the reed cage of lisping slate-and-white juncos. Katrin's lip began to tremble. "Mrs. Coombs, I'm afraid about everything, and my mother's dead and can't advise me, and Papa's written me out of his will, and my husband's too hasty, and Nell hates him, and she says she'll marry the first man she finds to get away. And what if I'm left all alone up there on the mountain next summer when I have my baby?"

"There, there. Don't cross so many bridges ahead of time," Mrs. Coombs advised.

While Sam Trail finished, and Katrin got her bear-fur coat from the nail, Marn found what she was looking for in the cupboard of her room: some old smocks that she would take back with her. She would be going into her fourth month

soon, and before long would need to disguise herself as much
as she could. And she thought, as she made the bundle up,
how every night she would pray to some divine One to break
the Wizard's new spell.

As she came from the bedroom, Sam Trail was picking up
Katrin's sweater-swathed bird cage, and Mrs. Coombs was
being cheerful. "You ought to try to enjoy life more as it comes,
Mrs. Blackburn."

"I agree with her all the way, Katrin," Sam cried.

Katrin was still pale and anxious. "I'll tell the Blackburns
that the accident made me late." She held her left arm inside
the coat because the sleeve wouldn't go over the bulky bandage.
Katrin asked Mrs. Coombs, "Do you think your husband's
charm will take?"

The woman came to tuck some cake wrapped in a napkin
in Katrin's pocket. "Are you sure you wouldn't like that little
raccoon besides those birds? I'll give him to you free for
nothing, Katrin. He's just learned to open the closet door and
he'd keep you busy."

But Katrin didn't want consolation, only a battle; and as
the sleigh slid down the path behind the fast gelding, one of
the girls on either side of Trail, a heavy robe over the knees of
all three and the bird cage at Katrin's feet, the young wife
leaned forward and told Marn, "And I wish it were anybody
but you caring for my Papa!"

Trail said, "I can't think of one thing worries me more than
squabbling pullets. Would either of you like to talk about
the sheep thieves that everyone else is talking about? And
how they work silently and in the dead of night and leave no
trace, not a print of foot or paw?"

Then Katrin had to lean across once more and say finally,

"You wanted Henry, and now do you want Papa, too?"

Marn narrowed her eyes and shrugged, and made herself not say a word. When they came to the church, Trail delivered Katrin and the birds to the Blackburn family, who were still in the church entry, by the hot stove, having cheese and bread with the itinerate preacher and hearing of the world past the mountains. Nell was hanging on the man's every word and didn't pay attention to Katrin's return or her bandage. Henry didn't notice it, either, not until late that afternoon. And then he made little of it. It was a good many days, too, before he happened to discover that his wife was wearing no ring.

As Trail and Marn slid over the country roads behind the galloping horse in the spanking new sleigh, Marn decided to let the pleasure of the moment rule her. She thought of what her mother had told Katrin about letting the past rest and enjoying life the way it was and not crossing so many bridges ahead of time. The shining steel runners slipped over the crust of snow, so the gelding ran as though he drew a weightless thing. Marn felt the man's desire for her, and when he put his arm about her shoulders, she let him, though she knew she was making problems for the future, and that the rich Mr. Trail undoubtedly misunderstood her yielding to the simple embrace.

In the Willem barnyard, the butchering for the husking party was taking place, the two scalded carcasses hanging from the wood scaffolding. The men were scraping and cleaning, and had already set in the kitchen a crock containing the hearts and livers and kidneys The latter would be sliced and braised in butter and onions and served for breakfast, and the dishpan of blood they caught, which Marn was expected to season and boil and make into the dark country pudding that

Dutchman favored. Marn looked away from the scene as they passed by, because blood on the earth at butchering time marked a child some way, it was said.

Trail let his gelding prance practically right up to the Willem kitchen door. He leaped down to help Marn descend from the sleigh's seat, her bundle in her hand. She said, "Thank you, Mr. Trail."

"Why not call me Sam?" he urged.

"I'd rather not," she sighed.

But he winked and said as she went in, "Every pearl has its price. And I'll be back for the party tomorrow night, Marn Coombs!"

The evening came and went, and night came on, and finally Dutchman arrived with his Farmer. They were both a little tipsy, because they'd stopped in at Wizard's and bought a quart mason jar of peach brandy. They'd left the Stableman's pretty wife out in the cart with the two riding mules tied behind, while they talked with Wizard about a present Dutchman wanted to bring back for Marn. Willem told Marn's father that she was a hard worker and he'd raise Marn's pay come spring if she stayed that way. Wizard said that the gift Marn would appreciate more than baubles or sweets would be one of her old pets that she missed nowadays. He told Dutchman that his daughter had been almost as fond of Jupiter, the swan, as she was of that fawn that hung about Marn all the time. Wizard said he needed the swan, though, and doubted he'd part with him at any price. Actually, Wizard Coombs wanted to get rid of the big white bird; he'd heard that the Sheriff from Greenfield had hired some new deputies and they'd be out one of these days, looking for hidden stills or any kind of misdemeanor that would bring fine-money into their office till.

He told Dutchman, "However, I'll make you a special price of five dollars. I was asking ten."

"Done," said Dutchman Willem, and unscrewed the lid and took another sip of brandy from the jar. "What's its name again?"

"Jupiter. That's after a god in a book I have, who turned into a swan."

Mrs. Coombs, as usual, interrupted him. "Next Wizard'll tell about how it bred a woman and she laid an egg."

The Farmer asked, "Who sat on it?"

And Mrs. Coombs said, "That's what I thought of when I first heard the tale, but Wizard claims his book doesn't go into that."

Dutchman and Farmer reined up outside Stableman's cabin, where a light was burning, and waited while the chilled woman went up the path. The door swung open, and as they drove on to the Master's house, the old noisy argument was beginning, Stableman shouting at his wife to get over to the fireplace where it was warm and she yelling that she'd as soon do as she pleased. Their voices became muffled as the door slammed upon the night.

In the Willem kitchen, the two men found Marn seated with her knitting by the black stove, not knowing if she were expected to have dinner prepared for her employer's return. She'd made a thick stew, using the hearts of the butchered hogs, and was keeping it simmering. Mr. Willem set the struggling Jupiter down in the entry, his legs and wings bound with strips of sacking. The bird hissed and made hoarse sounds of mingled fear and anger, his great eye gleaming yellow in the vague glow of the kitchen lamp. Marn came to see.

"Where'd he come from, Mr. Willem? How did you ever get him?"

"I talked your father into giving him up, which he didn't want to, Miss Coombs. I couldn't think of what to bring you back from Greenfield, as soon as I found those two runaways, to show you I like the way you work and that I expect you to keep it up. Eh?"

Marn smelled the rank brandy on them and felt an edge of fright, since she was alone and female and young. But she spoke boldly, "Thank you then. I'm glad to have him for mine."

"Wizard told me his name, but I forget it now. Eh?"

"He's called Jupiter," Marn said. "I'll take him to the dovecote. It's too warm for him in here."

"I'll do it for you, little girl," the Farmer said thickly. "Did you know one of those whistling swans had an egg by a woman once? I never heard of that before. They should have put it in a side show at the Greenfield Fair."

Marn was slipping into a coat, and lifting the heavy swan up in her arms. She was taking him out into the darkness, and at the door to the cote was unbinding the strips that held his legs and wings. He walked quietly into the pen. She thought how she was glad Jupiter had never had his wings cut, and how the first chance she got she'd let him fly up free. She'd tell Mr. Willem that he'd escaped by chance. When she returned to the kitchen, she saw that, still in their boots and heavy coats, the two men had found the food on the back of the stove and brought it to the table, Dutchman in the Master's Chair, his brown bearskin collar up, the Farmer on the bench at his right. The brandy jar between them was almost empty, and they were talking of this and that and never noticed Marn as she slipped by and up to her attic.

The next day tables were set up in the loft of the great white barn out of boards laid across sawhorses and covered with whatever tablecloths or bedsheets the hired women could get together, because Dutchman refused to spare any of his house linens to be ruined. All day long people marched up and down the broad staircase which Dutchman's father had set into one end of the huge barn when he built it long ago. The Old Mountain country people thought that stairway a strange idea. They'd never heard, either, of anyone keeping batteries of big chickens fattening for slaughter in a barn loft like Willem did, mostly Rocks and no games or banties at all. And he'd use little windmills to grind his grain. And in the yard of the black-and-white spotted bull, he'd hung a stump on a chain for the animal to play with, so he stayed even-tempered and never got feisty. At one end of the loft now was a great pile of rustling cornstalks. All the rest of the loft, save the clearing for the people around the cornstalks, was filled, towering to the high rafter beams with the sweet-odored hay crops of the year, clover and timothy and meadow grass and alfalfa.

That night, when the ears of corn were pulled off, the remaining stalks would be used for bedding the animals and for stuffing the mattresses of the hired people. Dutchman had directed his men to bring all their household chairs and benches and stools from the cabins to the barn and up the staircase and set them in the loft. And he said that if there weren't enough seats to go around, his own people were to remember that neighbors came first. They'd set up a little coal-oil heater and strung some lanterns on a rope in the open area.

Certain of Willem's men had been deputized to keep an eye on the latter, for if they fell and broke and their contents spilled, the barn would flame up in an instant like summer-dry kindling. Stacks of bushel baskets and heaps of gunny sacks waited for the harvest of corn ears that would be emptied into the tall cribs outside the barn.

By late afternoon one of the makeshift tables was crowded with the cold meat pies Marn had made of boned fowl, the dough fragrant with sage; and apple-butter sauce; and sweet cakes full of raisins and cut-up, dried fruit and spices. On another table would be served one of the two hogs that had been tended since dawn by Farmer over an outside fire in an old pit of stones and clay. Farmer turned them now and then judiciously with a five-tined pitchfork; he doused them with a rag mop dipped in a rich dark sauce made in the past summer of tomatoes, hot and sweet peppers, and a heavy hand's worth of seasonings. The Farmer would see to it that when one hog had been consumed, another would be brought to take its place. The hired women were carrying up the wide barn steps the food each specialized in: pies of dried farm fruits—plums, apples, peaches—with sour-milk crusts; and pans of mince cobblers, full of finely chopped beef mixed with suet and pepper and cider and sorghum molasses and chopped apples. They set out puddings of bread and eggs and milk, and there were jellies and marmalades and preserves, and pickles of grated cabbages or crab apples or watermelon rind or gherkins.

Mr. Willem gave Marn the keys to a cellar room, so she could let in the hands, who were to take two kegs of new hard cider to set out, as he'd instructed. Dutchman told Marn that next year he hoped to start some grape wine that she was to prepare in the fashion she knew of, as all Bertha Willem's was gone and he missed it in the cooking and with his supper, and had to get along on cheap fruit brandy that he picked up here and there and didn't like much. By morning the year's corn crop would be shucked and in the bins. Dutchman jingled the pennies in his pocket that would reward the children who found the scarce red ears. The older people played their own games sometimes, the men exacting higher rewards, disappearing with the women of their choice for a while down to the barn alley below the loft, where the warm beasts were stalled, their breath coming and going, even and fragrant.

The party was to begin just after sundown, when the milking and feeding were finished. Neighbors had been invited to come as soon as their own chores were done. Everyone looked forward to the change in routine, the entertainment. One of Willem's men could play a flute he owned and another a guitar that had come long ago from across the sea. An old man knew how to dance the way sailors danced when they were off in ships on alien oceans.

Dutchman Willem went into his bedroom to change into fresh clothes, and Marn ran to the attic to put on a dark, long-sleeved dress she'd made the winter past. It fit her form tightly but was becoming, and she wore a clean blue apron over it. Marn felt the prestige of her position, and wished to appear mature and a credit to Mr. Willem. She was to supervise the eating tables and see that all were well fed and knew the variety of food and drink available.

Schoolmaster Grim and young Trail arrived after things had gotten under way. The moon was in its last quarter and shed no light at all. The brown jackass wheezed in welcome to their horses from his stall, as they came into the barn. Schoolmaster unsaddled his mare and hung her feed bag about her ears and told the blond spaniel to lie nearby. Trail, meanwhile, had got one of Willem's men to unhitch his horse from the new black sleigh and feed it for him. Trail was in a hurry; he could hear the music piping and see the flickering of the lit lanterns and the master's shadow looming on the wall of the stairwell above. Willem was at the head of the wide steps and told Trail to put out the cigar he held in his hand.

"You want to burn down what I've built up, boy!" Dutchman shouted, and clapped Trail on the back. "Aren't all my pipes safe on the kitchen sideboard?"

The young man said, "It's not that I don't know better, Mr. Willem. The music overcame me. By damn, where's the peach brandy? I've been to visit Mrs. Coombs and she says you bought a supply yesterday."

"I bought enough to last me and my Farmer for one night," Dutchman told him over the whistle of the flute. "But here behind the chicken batteries is another private source." And he took Trail's arm. He got out the lightning and twisted the cork and handed the bottle over. "And take it easy, too. There's a long night ahead, boy, and you're here to husk corn!"

One of the wives was singing in a high contralto to the flute tune:

> Nearer my God to thee, nearer to thee,
> No more this face I see, nearer to thee!

And then the guitar was strumming, and other women joined in as the voice followed the next melody:

> Oh hush my love, you'll break my heart,
> Nor let me hear you cry;
> For best of friends will have to part
> And so must you and I!

Trail looked past everyone to the tables where Marn presided, watching out for the small stove behind her, and slicing the pork, and handing out plates, urging the people to help themselves. In her dark dress she appeared pale and older than her seventeen years. "I figure your housekeeper's a pearl among swine," Trail told Willem. "And I've got a question involving money that I'd like to put to you before the evening's over."

"Ask me now," Dutchman cried loudly. "Money's one thing I'll talk about any time." And he clinked the pennies in his pocket.

"I'd rather wait," Trail said and pulled his comb out and ran it through his blond hair on each side of the part in the middle. He straightened his snappy checked jacket. He felt the warmth of the liquor he'd just swallowed and counted on it to help his courage to ask to buy the favor of time with the housekeeper from her employer. Sam Trail, who had all manner of boldness when it came to jumping his gelding across a formidable stream, or riding into the coldest storm, gazed baffled at the strong-minded small woman across the barn loft. In the lamp's dim glow he seemed to see the image of her form as it had been that night when he'd been behind the smoke barricade and had laughed at the Wizard and thought it would be easy to gain the attentions of his daughter.

Trail told Dutchman, baffled, "I don't have the gall yet. When I do I'll come and put it to you. Now, I might as well pull some corn."

A few hours later, Dutchman sent the hired people's children home, his pennies now transferred to their pockets; at the stairhead was a basketful of red ears that would be used to decorate the parlor of the big house. Willem took a look at the work and figured it would be finished by not much past midnight. The flute player was red-faced and busy, and the wiry old hired man was cackling while he leapt about and danced the hornpipe. There was so much noise that few people noticed when a small-sized brawl began in one area.

Randall Grim had started it. He'd kept busy for the first few hours on the corn, as he felt since he'd practically invited himself he ought to pay his way properly. While he'd worked, silent, his companions sang loudly, laughed easily, and told every joke they could remember, from schoolchild to tavern. They filled his cup with cider along with theirs whenever the pitcher was passed, but Schoolmaster drank little. Now and again he looked across the people to the table where the Wizard's daughter was. All that he'd ever believed in and stood for was denied in Marn Coombs. And yet, here he sat, enchanted. He'd never had much trouble in denying women since he'd got through his twenties, and yet this one stirred him. When he'd brought her the Bible and written in it, he'd felt like some petitioner. She'd seemed to want to charm him there in Dutchman's kitchen for a while, and he'd decided then what he meant to do tonight. And that was why he'd wanted to be invited.

Slowly, as if moved by a power outside himself, he stood and dropped the ear he held in his hand in the sack on the floor and went over to Marn. He spoke to her in his insidious voice in the dim light of the coal-oil lanterns swinging from the rope. He put his hand on hers, feeling how he wanted to save the innocent girl from the hard life she would lead here. She pulled away, frowning. Randall Grim thought how, though Marn was out of and reared by an evil fellow, there was a peculiar mixture of softness and strength in her. Grim toyed with the medal in his pocket that he'd carried ever since he'd won it wrestling at the Greenfield Fair and made a name for himself and bested all who stood against him. When he'd first come to the countryside, he'd tracked a pack of killer dogs down, and he felt he'd do that again to dog or dragon, first chance he got. Schoolmaster enjoyed and hoped always to succeed in destroying evil. Dutchman Willem had declared before all that he was well pleased with his housekeeper, Miss Coombs, and her ways. And Randall Grim, fiddling as he did constantly with notions of right and wrong, felt that he tipped the balance when he gave the daughter of a Wizard a Bible, which was the beginning of the long way he intended to lead her. There was triumph in it; and he decided, while Marn filled a glass with hard cider for him, that he would reveal some of his thoughts to her.

He repeated what he'd stated a moment ago, in his soft voice, the words of King Lemuel in the Bible. "*A virtuous woman who can find,* Miss Coombs. *For her price is far above rubies!*"

Marn laughed at him. "I have heard also that *The eyes of man are never satisfied,* Mr. Grim. There's a text to preach, too, if that's what you're about to do."

"Hello, Marn Coombs!" And Trail was coming over, and Schoolmaster didn't like his bold, flushed look at all, and how he put his arm about the girl, and how she slipped away, but looking as if not displeased, and went to give someone else a piece of cold dove pie and a helping of black currant jam to go with it.

"You're drunk," Grim told Sam Trail.

"What I'm trying to do, Mr. Grim," Trail said, staggering

slightly, "is to get my courage up to ask someone something. Did you ever have that problem?"

"Never," Schoolmaster said, as Marn came back. "And I'd not admit it if I had."

"Why don't you let him alone, Mr. Grim," Marn said. "Mr. Trail's feeling too much lightning is all."

"Where'd he get anything stronger than cider?" Schoolmaster asked. "That's all I see. Is he hiding it in his coat pockets?" And he jabbed at Trail under his checkered jacket with his fist in the soft high part in front where his ribs parted, aiming accurately.

The young man grunted and buckled. "Say, don't do that!" And looked suddenly a little white.

But Schoolmaster's heat was in him, and needing to be rid of the unwanted party, he said, "Stand up. Are you a man or a boy?"

Trail saw, in his slow and addled brain, what Grim had in mind, and he pulled at his jacket to unbutton it and get it off and cast it on the floor. He felt he was a man of no courage. He'd had the same problem back at the Greenfield Fair, when he was clean sober and Dutchman's daughter had egged him on to fight. Then, too, he had wanted nothing less than a wrestling match. Now his body and tongue were disobedient, and he tried to stand steadily and say clearly, "Better look before I leap on you, Mr. Grim!"

The hot voice of Schoolmaster and the loud garbled speech of Trail over the sound of the music had drawn the attention of others, who paused to look at the pair and decide if it were worth dropping their tasks and pleasures and coming for a closer view.

Marn called to them, "It's not anything except Mr. Grim

isn't drunk and Mr. Trail is!" She felt the anger move in her.

Schoolmaster didn't bother to pull off his sweater, even, and said, "Speak up. I have that same problem with my pupils." And he caught the young man under the jaw, in the neck, with a sharp careful thrust, so Trail gasped and sighed as he went down in a heap. Schoolmaster turned to Marn, running his fingers through his brown curly hair, his dark eyes bright.

She asked, "Why did you do that with no cause, Mr. Grim?"

He told her, "Not only drunk but fainthearted, and I didn't like the way he put his arm about you."

But Marn knelt over Sam Trail and said, "Are you hurt?"

The onlookers, from where they were, had decided it was nothing and paid no further heed, already beginning to sing to the guitar:

Oh, I'm a wandering gambler, I gamble all around,
Whenever I meet a deck of cards I lay my money
down, oh!

Trail rose slowly to a knee, and with Marn's help got to his feet. He clutched the girl's arm, his face close to hers, and cried out so anyone could hear, "All I wanted was to buy your time from Dutchman! That's what I came over here for tonight."

When Grim put a hand out in rage against him, Marn said, "Let him go, now." She picked up Trail's coat and gave it to him.

Schoolmaster watched the young man stumble off, his checked jacket dragging from his hand, heading for the stairway where Dutchman ruled, going past him without a word and down the broad steps to find his horse and new sleigh below. Grim's desire was burning more now than before, because of the scuffle, which was about Marn; and he said in his soft way, "Oh, don't you understand that I want to save you from all this?"

"What do you mean, Mr. Grim?"

And he told her, "I hadn't meant to say it so plainly or so soon. I've been thinking a long while on you and your case, and what I'd like to do is to save your soul."

Marn's voice was hard. "I think you mean the same as Mr. Trail!"

Schoolmaster's face darkened and he said, "I'm speaking of marriage, then, since you will have it said straight out, Miss Coombs."

"Have you been thinking on my case ever since that Friday in the meadow back there when you hid your face from the world, and my father gave you a special rate?"

Grim dropped his eyes and felt how the anger of humiliation drove all other feelings from him. "That was a false thing to do," he said, "passing off ghosts on folks."

"I doubt anyone who came was fooled," she said, "and that's my father's trade, dealing in gullibility."

"Are you a witch, then, Marn Coombs?" And his soft voice came higher-pitched now.

But she put her shoulders back and said good evening, and walked away from him and everybody. She heard Grim's rough call after her to return, and she thought how she was finished with the notion that she'd ever go off to that learned man's cabin and let him raise a child of hers to his ways. She'd sooner go into Endless Quagmire in the spring and bear it alone and raise it like a wild animal's cub. As soon as she got her first pay, she'd cancel her debt with Randall Grim for buying the fawn from Wizard, and then she'd be done with him.

At the stairhead she nodded at her employer. "Goodnight,

Mr. Willem." Dutchman grunted when he saw her go, busy tying up another full sack of corn ears, not needing Marn any more for the night. The hired women, too, would go to their cabins without any cleaning up. The debris of the party would be taken care of in the morning, and Marn must be up at dawn. She walked slowly to the house, past the rows of beehives, thinking that when the weather warmed she would rake the walks the way Dutchman's wife had once done neatly every morning, so that people looking at them would know that order prevailed in that particular household. Marn was up in her attic, turning back her featherbed, when she remembered a thing she'd wanted to do.

She came down the stairs in the empty house and pulled on her boots and a coat and went out in the snow to the dovecote. There she opened the gate and felt her way in the almost utter darkness. The deer rose and squeaked and came to nuzzle her, sleepy. Marn sensed where the swan was, more than seeing him. She groped in the corner where he usually was. He didn't strike but hissed slightly and then was still as she touched his feathers.

"Jupiter," she whispered.

She put her hands about the long wiry neck to make a collar to lead him out of the opened narrow gate. He stamped heavily along, padding awkwardly beside her, earthbound. When she had him on the pathway she told him, "Now fly."

And he did, after a while. At first he stood still in the darkness, lit only by a few stars. Then he spread his seven-foot-broad wings and beat them slowly, unhurried and unfrightened; he moved flapping along the road to the barn. Marn could scarcely make out his huge body rising finally, but she heard the noise and the rushing air. It seemed he was completely gone, until there came a faraway hoarse yelp as he reached the horizon. Marn thought of how the Whistling Swan had had to sit at the Fair with Wizard's gilded crown for a collar, and how he'd lived confined in a tiny pen, accepting a bowl of bread and milk from her. It seemed the great white bird was partly Marn's self, and his delight and satisfaction hers.

She went back, her mind turning onto the scuffle earlier between the two men, and her ever-present problem that appeared to remain a riddle. She wished she had the power to look into a mirror of the future where the answer, sad or not, lay. She opened the attic window before getting into bed, and it seemed there was a certain change of tenor in the noises from the people at the barn. The laughter and the flute's piping ceased in a sudden stillness that might simply mean some new entertainment was taking place. And then the people's voices began to rise again, and after awhile she thought she heard the guitar softly.

In the morning Marn learned what had happened. She wondered if Wizard had seen the accident in his mirror before Sheepman Blackburn, weakening and fumbling, had slipped and fallen up on the mountaintop where he had gone out into the early night, believing he'd heard a sheep thief after the flock. He'd been found dead at a rocky cliff's foot by his son, who swore vengeance. And now Henry Blackburn was lord over Bald Mountain, people said, and a herd of sheep and three women.

7

The Footprints of Venus

MARN WAS watching the fawn running one morning in the fresh snow; she set the empty bucket by the gate of the dovecote and went to the fence to wait for the little deer to be done. It was some time after the husking party and Christmas was a day away. Dutchman Willem had passed out the fall wages and bonuses to his hands a few mornings ago at breakfast, and Marn had immediately sent Mr. Grim the seven dollars she figured she owed him for buying the fawn for her that time. She planned to give what was left of her pay to her parents the first chance she got. The older children of Dutchman's hands had taken the money for the Schoolmaster with them to the school; and when they returned they reported to Marn that, as of that very morning, school was out and most had passed and Randall Grim would not be teaching there any longer. He was leaving these parts soon, and a new teacher would come as soon as one could be found after the holidays. The children were jubilant.

Marn waited while the young animal played her favorite game: the fawn would walk away from Marn, high-stepping and slow, and then snort suddenly and begin making prancing, collected, high bounds, all four feet gathered under her at the peak of each, until she reached the farthest end of the field, stopping there and wheeling and returning at full speed in extended leaps until she reached Marn's side. She would halt there and toss her head and squeak, and be off again as before, going in a mincing, bouncing gait as she went away, and returning in a rush. The adolescent deer would pant open-mouthed, and continue the sport as if she could never have enough. She would vary the course, looking for obstacles, a small stream or storm-fallen branch to hurdle. She was long-legged and delicate, and confident that Marn would stay where she left her.

She appeared as wild as any of the mistrusting white-tails around Marn's father's swamp in this season, who fled like shadows if they heard the step of man or scented his spoor. They feared with reason, and around the earth it was the plague of lonely mankind that all wild fauna ran from him. If one did not, man as a rule, startled, struck it down. Marn felt it was a consolation and reprieve for her kind when this one creature leaped over a pasture stream and galloped full tilt to her side. Isaiah said, in every Bible printed all over her land, that the *leopard shall lie down with the kid; and the calf and the young lion and the fatling together and the cow and the bear shall feed; their young ones shall lie down together. They shall not hurt nor destroy in all my holy mountain.*

The deer followed Marn back to the cote, going through the gate, docile, and lying under the dove nest boxes where the rabbits were and it was sheltered and Marn had set out hay and ear corn for her.

As Marn was returning to the house, Sam Trail came riding up Dutchman's snow-packed road with a string of mares to leave with the Willem pedigreed ass. About an hour later he came knocking at the kitchen door. Marn hadn't seen Sam Trail since the night of the corn-husking feast, and she thought his hesitancy and his frown as he stood there stamping the snow from his boots were due to embarrassment about his behavior then.

"Come on in, Mr. Trail. Have you been to see my mother lately?" she said. "I've got a favor to ask of you."

"As a matter of fact," he said, "I stopped in on the way here. I've taken a fancy to her sugar cake and her steady talk. And then I wanted to check on those white-tail lap-robe skins, too, that Wizard is making up for me."

"Do you think you could drop off my pay to my parents when you pass their place on your road home. I've been looking for a way to get it there."

"All right, and now do you want to know why, before I go back to Greenfield, I'm riding to the top of the mountain to see Henry Blackburn!" Trail frowned again.

"Is anything wrong?"

"It is and it isn't," Trail told her.

When Marn had heard, back there on the morning after the husking party, about Sheepman Blackburn's death, she'd known at once that Wizard's spell was broken and that Katrin would never come down from the mountain and back to Dutchman's house to live. By the Sheepman's will. Henry Blackburn was to be responsible for the care and content of the Blackburn women, and besides, the ownership of the

Blackburn house and stables and animals, the pastures and forests upon Bald Mountain were in Henry's hands; he would be his own master. And his wife, Katrin, might as well resign herself to being the youngest of the women on the place, and bear her baby with no more complaints.

Marn told Sam Trail to seat himself in Dutchman's big chair at the head of the long table, and she put hot coffee and breakfast leavings before him. "One thing," he said, "is Henry put those giant red oxen, Irish and Brown, up for sale. And the minute my father heard of it, he bought them. And Henry's price wasn't a low one. I'm riding up there now to bring the beasts down."

"I'm glad to hear your father's taking them," Marn said. "I thought Henry might set that pair at hard work right away and cut their feed and stop shining up their coats and horns."

"So did my old man," Sam said. "And he says that'd ruin their earning power right away. He figures to put them behind a stockade on our farm as a permanent exhibit and make a charge. I told your mother, and she said in some ways my father's just like the Wizard in finding ways to talk people out of their money, Miss Coombs." Trail pushed his coffee cup back. "And speaking of the Wizard, he came into your house just as I was leaving and told me to warn Mr. Willem about some trouble that might to be coming his way."

Marn was wary. "I wish my father wouldn't do that."

"Wizard says last night he took out that mirror that lives in a little black sack in his pocket. And in it he saw something going on: a barn burning. And he figures since Dutchman's got a new-filled barn and a lot of enemies among his neighbors and his hired hands because of it, he ought to be careful."

"Did you tell Mr. Willem yet?" Marn asked.

"He only snorted and said with all the barns in the Old Mountain countryside just filled with hay and corn crops, he hadn't a doubt one of them would catch fire pretty soon and prove Wizard's magical talents."

"I wish you hadn't told him, Mr. Trail," Marn sighed.

"When are you going to call me Sam?" the young man asked, and then remembered that seemingly Marn Coombs never would and he might as well give up the case. He sighed and looked at the young woman in her tidy dress and apron, her flaxen hair bound up into a bun like her mother wore. "What did you ever do with that little doll, Miss Coombs?"

"I put it in my window," she told him. "I've got a nice room here. If you'll wait a moment, I'll run get that money for my parents."

When she returned, Trail was by the door, his brows knitted again, hesitating. He took the packet she gave him and put it in the inside pocket of his coat. "I had one more thing to say to you."

Marn told him, "If it's about what happened on the husking night, I've never paid any heed to it. And the children say Randall Grim's leaving these parts, and so there's an end to that."

"What's bothering me," Trail said, "is that Schoolmaster's stirring trouble. He doesn't spend time in his own cabin, but in visiting about and speaking his mind."

"About what?"

"About your father mostly: Wizard Coombs. And he drops it in the middle of his talk on here and there, that buzzard tracks have been seen in the snow where the Blackburn sheep have been disappearing. And sometimes he says crow."

"People have always whispered about Wizard, Mr. Trail,"

Marn shrugged, putting it from her, "since I was old enough to hear it. And it means nothing."

"Schoolmaster himself says he's only making sport, but the last time I heard him was in the store on Greenfield Pike, and Willem's Stableman was there. I didn't see Stableman laugh when he claimed Wizard's charms weren't holding his wandering wife."

"It'll pass," Marn said. "Seeing a bird's footprints is silly; if it were a man's, it would be different. Promise you won't forget to leave my pay with my mother. Tomorrow's Christmas and I'd like them to have it."

"I won't," Trail swore.

Now it was true that Schoolmaster was spending his last days in the countryside traveling around, for when Trail arrived at the snow-deep bald on top of the mountain to pick up the oxen, Randall Grim's tall black mare and his shaggy bay, steamy-breathed in the brittle cold, stamped where they were hitched to the rail outside. Trail tied his gelding beside them and went into the Blackburn cabin. Since Sheepman's death, Henry and Katrin had moved into the main part of the house. Schoolmaster, the floor beneath him a damp pool where the snow from his boots melted, was speaking in his soft way to the three Blackburn women and Henry. He snapped his fingers at the blond spaniel beside him, whose long silky-haired tail was still, and who held Grim's wool cap between his forepaws, and who kept growling over at Blackburn's big shepherd, Tam, lying at Katrin's feet, his heavy coat sleek now because of the attention his master's wife gave him these days.

Schoolmaster was saying, "There might be crows spending the winter here, but every buzzard anyone heard of has gone south long ago." Grim looked up at Sam Trail. "Are you one that believes in black magic and that a man can travel in the body of a bird? Do you know that Mr. Willem's Farmer thinks Wizard Coombs shoots down white-tail deer by firing a ball of hair and not a shell? Do you think it's healthy for a countryside to have that kind of a man in its midst!"

"I wondered why the lap robes for my buggy that Mr. Coombs is tanning for me have no tear in them. So that's it!' But Trail's grin faded as he looked around at the people sitting silently and listening, even the formerly gay and irrepressible Katrin, no ring on her hand that was in the folds of her dress.

Mrs. Blackburn was sewing in a corner, and Nell, ever interested in any bachelor that came, hurried to the kitchen for tea and cheese and bread to put before Mr. Trail. Nell Blackburn had given up Randall Grim long before she knew he was leaving his employment at the school and cared little for him now. She thought his talk was idle and silly; she refused to take him seriously. When Nell came back into the room, pushing the pins in that held the braids of gray-streaked brown around her head, she said, scornful, "How about the true part, Mr. Grim, like Wizard coaxing wild birds down from the sky and trees by making their own calls? And squeaking like the rats to lure them into his traps. Marn told Henry and me about it."

"When did Marn tell you that?" Katrin said, quick.

"Long ago sometime," Henry told his wife, aware by now of Katrin's jealousy of the past. His hazel eyes were bright. "Maybe my father was a wizard, too, or how could he ever have grown those red oxen so tall and kept the secret from everyone? Do you think you can keep them that way, Sam?"

"My old man's going to baby Irish and Brown," Trail said, "and give them the best of everything."

"What I can't abide about Wizard Coombs," Grim told everyone, unable to let the subject go ever since the Wizard's daughter had turned his offer of marriage down so abruptly and easily and in his balked desire, now feeling a fury about her, "is his pride. He's got no humility. *A man's pride shall bring him low: but he that is of a lowly spirit shall obtain honour,* said Solomon!"

"Well," Henry said to Trail, "I've got a lot of plans for that small fortune your father paid me for the bullocks. I might do some fancying up of this house and the sheep sheds. I could even paint a great white curly-horned Dorset ram on some shack's side."

"I'd like that," Katrin said, "since I can never go and see Papa's white mule on our barn anymore."

It had even incensed Randall Grim when the Wizard's daughter, on the day school let out, had had the grit to send him back some cash he'd spent one time for that illegal fawn she had for a pet. He muttered to his dog what he'd said once a while ago, from Exodus, *Thou shalt not suffer a witch to live,* when he'd first heard about a Wizard here in the western mountains of North Carolina.

"It's not going to satisfy me to shoot a vulture or crow, Schoolmaster," Henry said. "What gets my Scotch temper up is a real sheep thief or two after my stock. That's what I'm after!" The young man's sandy hair stood up roughly and he waved his hand in emphasis.

"What do you think I'm referring to?" Schoolmaster growled softly, patting his dog.

Trail felt an edge of worry when he heard Grim muttering on witches and wizards, for he felt that there might be danger in this man who was something of a fanatic and had strength and cunning in his body and mind. He said, "It's time I started the oxen down, Henry. Where do you keep all those furbelows, like their red horn tassels and that big mahogany yoke? Can you come along and show me?"

"Let's go," Henry said. "It'll take you the rest of the day to get them to Greenfield, not being used to you and also being the most single-minded beasts I ever knew."

As soon as they were outside and alone in the snow, Trail asked the Sheepman's son, "Would you like me to tell the Sheriff to come out and take a look around? It's past his territory, up on this mountain, but he's a friend of mine and he'd be glad to bring a couple of deputies and come. They're used to trailing thieves and might get your sheep back for you."

Henry was delighted. "I'll even throw in a jar of that special polish my dad used on those cattle's horns, Sam, to get an extra shine when he took them to the Fair."

When Trail finally got the red oxen started on the white-drifted, uneven pathway down, he had a time with them. The pair of animals weren't used to the feisty gelding Trail rode and kept wheeling to try to get at him with their horns. And Trail was so occupied in handling the unruly beasts, who missed their former master's tapping signals with a little buggy whip and his soft encouragements, and were bewildered by the new coaxing voice from the man on the fast sorrel, that he forgot completely about stopping at Coombs' place and leaving Marn's packet of money. He was all the way to his father's house outside of Greenfield before he remembered. He decided that delivery could wait until his return in less than a week, still during the holiday season, when he would be picking up the mares that had been served at Dutchman's. It would be just about New Years, and maybe Marn Coombs would be in a festive mood and wouldn't mind spending some time visiting with Trail and he would get somewhere for a change. He would tuck a gift for her in his pocket, hopeful, a long blue silk scarf he'd picked out with care. Sam Trail had no way of knowing that Marn would be in a predicament, and he planned to stop in to visit with Mrs. Coombs on the way to Willem's.

During the following few days Trail had a busy time in the town of Greenfield. It was the celebration season, and he and two companions got drunk and went riding, as they liked to do every once in a while, up the marble steps of the county courthouse in Greenfield, Trail on his racing gelding, and through the wide doors. Trail's father, who had trusted him since the age of fourteen to handle any of the strings of mares or mules he turned over to him, or to gently break his young wild horses to ride, didn't reprove Trail about his reckless escapades, waiting for them to pass. In the courthouse hall, Sam Trail had even done some shouting about raising ghost girls, which he recalled vaguely. When the new county deputies leaned over the balcony and called down about their fines, Trail had tossed on the floor enough bills to pay for himself and his companions, plus five dollars to boot for the Sheriff.

Trail had taken that opportunity to inform the deputies about there being a sheep thief or two back in the countryside, and how he'd like to see the Sheriff do a little investigating. The deputies had called down that a trip out there was already planned within the week, and the Sheriff was

taking two of them with him for a surprise visit to Wizard
Coombs regarding swans and fawns that he kept against the
law. Trail, who was feeling good, shouted up to the men on
the balcony that he didn't know about swans, but the only
fawn he knew of belonged to Dutchman Willem's housekeeper, and hands off! And Trail flung down some more bills
on the marble floor for them as he and his friends went cantering out of the hallway and charging down the slippery courthouse steps.

Sam Trail was surprised then one early morning, a couple
of days before New Years, to see, as he went at a slow gallop
down the road toward Old Mountain country, his gelding
splashing the slush behind and over Trail's boots because a
thaw had made the road muddy and the fog was a thick curtain, approaching on foot out of the mist, clad in a heavy coat
and boots, a woman with a beautiful face and, Trail knew,
a figure to match, whom he recognized as the wife of the
Stableman from Dutchman Willem's farm. Sam waved, and
the woman nodded at him, as he reined up alongside and
tipped his cap.

"You're that rich Mr. Trail. I know you," she said.

"If I weren't due somewhere, I'd give you a ride behind
me back to Greenfield, because that's where I suppose you're
going," Trail said, awkward.

"That's right, and I hope not to be followed this time,"
Stableman's wife told him. "Some folks are in a state back
there, and I picked this early morning time to leave. You
couldn't change your mind about where you're headed?" And
she smiled like a sunrise on Trail.

The young man stirred, embarrassed, in his saddle, feeling
how unhandy he always must be with women. He turned his

cap in his hand, and the gelding under him was jumpy. "No."

"I thought not, and I don't mind the long walk, as long as I'm out from under that untidy cabin and that mite of a man!" Her dark large eyes burned. "You'll find trouble brewing at Mr. Willem's, though I doubt he knows of it. Are you interested? I'd tell you about it for a sum."

Trail reached in his pocket quickly and gave her a handsome bill so there would be no haggling and she would say it at once. He was afraid that the pleasant Mrs. Coombs might be in trouble because of her husband's trade. Trail was surprised at how he enjoyed his visits to that small confused house where he was welcomed, at least by the woman, for himself and not for the money his father had. "Has it to do with the Schoolmaster that's leaving?"

She folded the cash and slipped it within her coat, into the low collar of her dress. "Him and others, though he's the leader. All men need, after you've stirred them up a little, is someone to follow! And Stableman's in the middle, too, and all in a lather because Wizard's charms to hold me never worked. He claims even if they were cheap ones, they should have helped. He can't see that it's himself and his ranting, and never a nice word, that lost me long ago."

"Don't talk about your husband. Tell me about Randall Grim!"

"The Schoolmaster had his shotgun with him last night when he was down at our cabin. He comes there every night or so. He says all he's ever wanted since he came here has been to rid this countryside of evilness. That's his business in the world. And he never thinks of self and his satisfactions— though I'll say I've seen a look down in his eyes so I know I could get him for my own if I ever wanted." She shrugged, graceful. "The Schoolmaster says he's been paid his wages for the semester in full and is leaving, and on his way out he intends to track down the sheep stealer."

"Who does he say the thief might be?"

"He says be the footprints of a bird called Venus, or man called Wizard, or of a dog or dragon."

"Does Dutchman Willem know? Or his housekeeper, the Wizard's daughter? Or the Blackburns? Or Wizard himself, what they're planning?"

"I've said all I know to you. I might stay in Greenfield a while when I get there. I've had offers. I might let you know where I am, Mr. Trail." And Stableman's wife nodded, friendly, and started away down the road, walking into the wet moving mist so that as the young man watched her she seemed, like an apparition, to disappear before his eyes.

Trail sighed and wished what he often did, that the skill he was known for with his father's mares could be transferred to his handling of the women he admired. He got a cigar from the coat pocket where the silk scarf lay wrapped in tissue and ribbon, lit it, and continued to canter along on his fog-shrouded way toward the Coombs. If Sam Trail had known how Marn Coombs felt at that moment, he most likely wouldn't have stopped by at her parents' house, but have taken the cutoff before he reached it and hurried straight to Dutchman's.

For Marn was considering leaving the Old Mountain country, too, because of an incident two nights before that she'd been worrying on ever since. She had gone up to her attic room and lit the candles and turned back the bed and got into her nightdress with long sleeves, and taken the Bible with Randall Grim's inscription in it from the chest to the bed with her. The candles flickered on the pages as she settled back against the down pillow. And then she heard the master of the farm calling from two staircases below. He had never before disturbed her in the night, and she thought how he might have fallen or hurt himself somehow, or that something dangerous might be happening, and she dropped the book and ran down quickly.

He had retreated to his bedroom and bellowed out to her from there that she should come in. Barefooted, she stood in the doorway, frowning. "Are you all right, Mr. Willem?"

"And you come in here."

She shook her head. "I thought something had gone wrong."

The oil lamp burned steadily. Dutchman was smoking his long meerschaum pipe, and Marn saw his eyes like blue porcelain gleaming upon her; so she felt a new thing pierce in her, like fear or the hypnotism that she'd seen sometimes in an animal that wouldn't run because a lantern shone in its eyes or Wizard had given its own mate's cry and the animal wasn't sure what it had heard.

Dutchman got up heavily from the side of the big bed and came to where she stood, half-leaning on the door frame. "You know I saved you from that young Sam Trail a couple of times? He keeps trying to get up the courage to ask me for you. Did the Wizard ever have that problem? Eh? You're comely, and you know I'm lonely here, don't you, child?"

"Don't do anything," Marn whispered, not knowing how to move.

"I won't," he said. "You just come sit beside me in here for a little while and talk to me. It's one of your duties. Eh?" The smoke wreathed around them as he took her hand and led her in. The four-poster, white-painted bed loomed, and behind it, in the shadow, the tall blue bureau with the chiming clock on it that Nell Blackburn had sent back, and on a round table the parchment Bible with the flower and cross on its cover. Willem sat on the edge of the bed, still holding Marn's hand, and she stood before him.

"What is it?"

"I need a wife at night." He sounded impatient. "Stop standing there like a child." He let Marn's hand go and pointed to the pillowed chair beside the bed. "Sit!"

She obeyed, and he puffed his pipe and gazed into the room's corner, absent.

"I don't want to discuss it," she said and thought if there were some way she could handle this new event.

He turned, as if he'd forgot the girl's presence, and reached for her soft arm and held it in his heavy grip. He spoke loudly. "I wouldn't marry one like you. But I'd like you to live in here and not up in that little room. I'd like you to move your clothes down. I went up there to look this evening while you were in the kitchen. And I thought it seemed cold. I want you to do what I say. Eh?"

"You mustn't talk so, Mr. Willem." Marn tried to stop his words.

"I won't get you with child, Miss Coombs," he said. "I'd be careful of that."

And it came to Marn that there was nothing else for her to say, and she told him, "I am already, Mr. Willem."

That didn't stop Dutchman a bit, though, and his sharp eyes turned on her and he said quietly, "I thought as much on mornings once and again, when I'd see you somewhat ill. And I'll propose something else now. You do as bid, and when that yard-child comes along, I'll claim it for mine by some wench here and keep your name clear. They say a bargain's a bargain, and I'll be glad to abide by that. Eh?"

She stood up steadily and said clearly, "Can I think about this, Mr. Willem?"

"Eh? What is it you have to consider? What else can you do?"

"I have to think, though," she said, "if you please."

"How much time do you need?"

"I'll let you know. Don't push me."

And when he saw her pale look, he sighed and said roughly, "Go on then. Go along!"

She slipped from his presence and ran up the stairs. At the top, in the attic, she thought she wished there were a lock on the door. But then she knew that the house's master would not come up on his own, but would wait for her to come down to him. It was a trap, and he had sprung it, and she was in it. Marn knew for sure that she would now have to leave this haven place, which was no longer safe. And she had no notion where to go. She sat on her cot's edge late into the night; the candles sputtered and guttered and no answers came. She held the Bible unopened, knowing the words inside and how sometime she would turn to them. But now the riddle's solution was up to her. When the flames went out at last, so that the wavery-glassed, mother-of-pearl mirror gave back only the dark sky, Marn went to sit in the low, chilly window ledge where the china-headed doll was.

Outside it seemed she saw flickerings along the winter paths to the barn and the Stableman's cabin that might be lanterns moving. She thought perhaps some mare or brood milk cow was having trouble birthing its young. How could Marn, occupied with her own problem, imagine that imputations against herself as well as her father were being made out there? How could she know that a battle had waged in Stableman's hut earlier, the wife scoffing at spells, saying find one to make her husband handsome and bold and she'd be welded to him soon enough!

How could the girl, upset by her newest trouble, or the restless Dutchman, shifting and turning in his tall poster bed downstairs, imagine the goings-on out there in the December air, how others had come to Stableman's cabin with complaints about Wizard Coombs, in which they mingled the truth with hearsay, forgot the Wizard's readiness with soothing, healing forest and meadow herbs, and recollected only his incantations, his sly eye, and his offhanded way with all who dealt with him. By the middle of the night, those present were a few of Willem's more worthless and lazy hands, as well as the old couple Dutchman hired, who were hardworking and honest, but truly did feel that Wizard flew about when he pleased in the bodies of his black birds, at times using the clever small crow and again the wide-winged, soaring, giant-clawed, young vulture called Venus, and that their foot-tracks in the snow where the sheep were disappearing and where Sheepman Blackburn had slid and met his death was significant. And sure enough, of course, in the middle of the group Randall Grim and his shotgun. The latter was talking about iniquity in the community, and wasn't above using Bible words.

"The character *of the fathers* will be visited *upon the children unto the third and fourth generation,* and that's the truth." Schoolmaster ran his fingers through his brown curls, alert. He was remembering how when the witch girl, playing ghost, had circled the meadow that time, he'd asked her father to make her stop a moment so he could look upon her, and he'd been refused. He wondered if the Wizard's daughter went around now and spread it that he'd asked her to marry and been refused. Looking back, he couldn't conceive of why he'd ever lost his head and done that, and maybe there was truly witchcraft in it! Grim felt his control over the small mob that were building their hysteria the way a pack of sheep-killing dogs did, that had no interest in the satisfaction of hunger, only in the passionate act of killing itself.

Nothing unusual took place in the countryside, at least on the surface, in the next two days. The weather prepared to change itself: the air pressure fluctuated, and the few snow-flakes that fell were large and wet. The people felt an unease; those with heavy tempers were unreliable, those who had had a grief fell into a deeper melancholy, sunny-tempered folks became withdrawn, ones with old wounds or broken bones felt twinges and aches. Stableman's wife dallied about until the proper moment to put on her boots and coat and leave. Dutch-man waited, leashing his impatience, for his housekeeper to speak. And for Marn herself, all continued to seem black while she examined possibilities; she never raised her eyes to meet another's as she moved about the house or fed the tableful of men or the master in the great kitchen.

And that was the position Marn Coombs was in while Sam Trail in the early morning went cantering on his chestnut sorrel gelding down Greenfield Road through the thick fog, smoking his cigar and thundering over the little bridge that spanned the confluence of the waters that came down from the ancient Carolina mountains, heading for Wizard Coombs' shack.

8

The Silver Candlestick

THE STAGE was set and the people moved into their places and took their parts. None could control himself. Because of what had happened to each when he was very small and as he grew into adolescence, and because of what each had taken up without knowing it as his prejudices and beliefs and desires, he behaved as he did. On the top of the mountain towering over the treacherous quagmire, mist wreathed like a net about the Blackburn cabin. In the dawns, the heat of the approaching sun, warming areas that the night had cooled, would make the fog, which had settled into the swamps below, restless. And then sometimes, if a wind tide happened to be sucked downward and to stir through it, the white stuff formed into columns that staggered in the air like directionless ghosts.

Some of Dutchman Willem's men had been absent at the long table that morning but he paid little heed, used to it that when the weather changed, as it just had in the unseasonable

233

thaw, various of the wives and those of the hired men who were lazier or perhaps more aged, refused to leave their beds or firesides. Today, as it happened, they weren't in their valley cabins at all, though, but on the mountain in Henry Blackburn's, summoned there because of a new development around dawn that had put the young man in a righteous temper. Henry had the support of his wife now in all that went on, but not his sister Nell, who listened from the kitchen, incredulous but holding her tongue. His old mother, carding in the corner, had no interest at all in her vehement son's crusade, but dwelled in daydreams of the past where Sheepman Blackburn still was and she wished she were.

Henry had been wakeful in the night, listening to the creaking of the old roof here and there as the load of winter snow, melting, shifted and slid to the ground. The big dog Tam had been restless, as always, and paced out of the dark room and down the hall and back. Henry objected every now and then to the shepherd dog being confined to the house instead of guarding the sheep, but Katrin burst into such tears, as she was used to employ with her Papa in emergencies, that Henry let the matter rest. Katrin claimed that she was afraid all the time when Henry was away, and if he were present she still needed the dog to give warning when the thief or thieves after the sheep decided to attack humans for a change.

Katrin was awake beside him, worrying as she sometimes did nowadays about her ring. She'd kept the bandage on over the cut far after the time when it healed, and now was beginning to feel that she'd have to retrieve the ring soon somehow from the Wizard. She was aware that Henry's wrath against her would be great if he found his wife had engaged in magic regarding his future. Katrin had never had an opportunity to keep her part of the bargain with Wizard Coombs and had not come down to pay the remaining five dollars she owed on the spell he was to put on Dutchman so he would ask Henry and Katrin to come home, besides a dollar for that cage of juncos Mrs. Coombs let Katrin take on credit. Of course, then the spell had been broken because of what Wizard Coombs claimed privately was due to the conjunction of Saturn and the moon, which was just in the dark then, as well as the cheapness of Katrin's red-glass ring; and Henry's father, out after sheep stealers, had slipped on the rocks above a cliff and breathed his last before anyone got to him.

Henry, turning about on the bed, spoke finally, when dawn came, to his wife. "Are you awake?"

She said yes, and he began to say that he was happy she was his and that the baby would come in the summer, and that he was glad he was master of the mountain though sorry to lose his dad with whom he'd disagreed so much. Henry began to talk about the Greenfield Fair the past fall, as he started to make love to Katrin. He said that when he'd given her the ruby ring and put it on her left hand, where it remained until she reached her Papa's and she transferred it to the right, that that was when he first knew he loved her and wanted to marry! He groped for Katrin's left hand, which she tried to slip under her heavy hips. Henry thought she was playing at first, but when he put his hand on the finger and found the ring was gone, he raised his voice and asked his wife for a fast explanation.

Katrin could not lie and say it was somewhere else, and she broke down and began to weep stormily. Henry slapped her then and said she must talk. And so she did, and she added, after confessing her transaction with Wizard and how she'd

pledged the ring for money still owed, that she'd been listening with interest to the conversations in the cabin lately when
people of the countryside had visited there, among others
her Papa's Stableman and the Schoolmaster. She'd heard
Randall say that he'd got it into his head for some reason that
it was time to run wizards out of the country. And then
Randall had grumbled out, so Katrin saw Nell Blackburn go
pale and drop the saucer she was drying in the kitchen doorway, that the Bible backed him up and that Wizards' daughters
were born-and-bred witches.

Katrin whispered, while Henry held her soft shoulder
with his vise-like hand so a bruised spot showed there later,
that she didn't like Marn Coombs any more, whom she'd once
called her best friend. She knew, and Henry needn't ask her
how because wild demons couldn't drag it from her, that Marn
had tried, using wiles and enchantments, to win Henry away
from Katrin! And she wept to Henry, who became further
enraged since his wife was such a silly, that she hated it
that Wizard's charm had not only failed to return her and
Henry to her Papa's, but had backfired disastrously, and now
Henry, being master, would never leave his sheep farm. Katrin
couldn't bear it that Marn Coombs, who had run after Henry,
was boss of her Papa's house nowadays, and seemingly was
well liked and would remain forever and a year!

Henry rose suddenly from the bed and left his wife,
stumbling to the chair where his clothes were laid. He dressed
swiftly and let the dog Tam out with him, not even hearing
his wife's protests, and was gone into the deep fog of the
early light, plunging down the mountainside, his boots sliding
in the melting snow, to bring together a flock of men who

would not only gain vengeance for his dad's death by taking the law into their hands and hanging a sheep thief, but would give him the chance to defend the new Blackburn wife from anyone who took advantage of her innocence; he intended to put the ruby ring back on Katrin's finger in a hurry!

And so, very soon he was rapping on Stableman's cabin door and Stableman was hurrying out, not noticing that his wife began at once to pull on her boots and heavy coat. Stableman, by Henry's orders, scuttled over to Schoolmaster's cabin on Old Mountain. Grim, ready for traveling in his homeknit blue sweater and tight cap, was loading his mares, lock, stock, and barrel. Stableman notified him that the Sheepman's son was on fire and wanting to move fast. Schoolmaster told Stableman to get up on the smaller mare, and the two rode steadily through the heavy mists, down the ox paths of one mountain and up those of another until they reached Henry Blackburn's.

There in the center of the dozen others that Henry had called together from the countryside was the small old fellow from Willem's, cackling. "How many times have I watched that crow in years past, knowing what was going on, and nobody to listen but my old woman!"

And Schoolmaster reported what Stableman actually hadn't noticed but didn't deny: "As we passed that cliff just now I can say that you'd better count your sheep this morning, Blackburn. My spaniel went right to them, and even in all that fog I could make them out in the crust of the thawing snow: a buzzard's tracks, which is a sign of a wizard nearby who is able to conceal his own footprints through learned, nefarious knowledge. And let's get a move on, too!"

"I'm finally in a hurry," Henry replied, while Nell listened to the lot of them, aghast, "due to my wife being truly taken in and robbed even of objects of value."

The whole troop, trailed by Randall Grim's two travel-ready mares and his small, silky, barking dog, who knew a chase was under way, went storming down the mist-blanketed mountain. When they reached Wizard's house, having left Schoolmaster's horses tied on Greenfield Road, the door was locked, for Mrs. Coombs had seen them emerging from the thick fog and crossing the misty clearing. They hammered on the door and shouted that they intended to hang a wizard and later take care of a witch! Mrs. Coombs yelled back through the keyhole what for? And Henry Blackburn declared that she must open at once or he would knock the door in, and that his wife's red ring was not where it belonged and what did she know about that?

"All I can tell you," she replied, "is the business transacted that day between my husband and Katrin Blackburn took place in front of me, and I'll guarantee it was legitimate."

"Where's the Wizard?" Schoolmaster said in his low clear voice.

"Nobody's here," Mrs. Coombs cried. "And Mrs. Blackburn's old enough to be a wife and trade as she pleases, and not all spells work every time."

Behind her in the house there was no song from any of the birds or chatter from any small animal; they seemed to be holding their breath and listening. A nasal, inquiring voice at her feet said softly under the door crack to those outside, "Billy likes Alice. Craaaaawk!"

"Who's that?" Henry said and pounded on the door again.

"And Wizard's gone off to Greenfield," she stated, "and might not be back till tomorrow at the soonest!"

"It's open or we break it down," Randall Grim said; and so Mrs. Coombs picked up Billy to protect him from any trampling feet and turned the key.

"Schoolmaster!" Mrs. Coombs said, as he walked in after Henry Blackburn, "have you lost your mind?" But he just stood there holding one of his double-barreled shotguns, so she knew he'd never be a bit of help.

The gathered people waited on the small porch while Henry said his say and Grim backed him up. "First, I've come to reclaim the ring, which will absolve my wife's debt!" Henry's voice was loud and shook, and he glared, and the gold lights glittered in his hazel eyes; so that the woman got afraid, and went into the bedroom where Wizard had a drawer for such things, and hunted out the trifle and gave it to Henry. He put it in his pocket and then he roared again, and the others came to stand behind him, that he'd kill Mrs. Coombs if he didn't get the information, and where was the Wizard?

"He's in the barn then, feeding the brown cows, before taking them out to work today," she sighed.

At which the herd of them streaked off, yelping. And Mrs. Coombs, with Billy waddling after, went to watch from the house door, knocking on wood, knowing Wizard was aware of the hunters since he always knew what was going on. The people were trying the big door of the rickety barn, firmly barred on the inside, the latch hidden. Mrs. Coombs, in the middle of the nightmare, was reliving the same scene many years past, when Wizard had been hounded out of another countryside. Marn had been a child in arms then, and they had had to come to Old Mountain country without scrap or penny to their name, only the knowledge of herbs and charms in Wizard's head to make their living by. In Mrs. Coombs' opinion, no one had been the worse for it. It was just too bad that now and then somebody who seemed harmless and friendly struck a spark to a group of people, the way those men out there now were doing to the pile of corn shucks under the barn side; and the human beings, just like that dry wood, kindled and then flamed.

The shouts were muted in the heavy mist that rolled about the clearing, telling the man inside with the beasts to come out because they had a rope that halted magic-makers. And then they yelled louder as the barn upper-storey door swung open, and from it the crow fluttered and the great black turkey vulture, Venus, flapped, making their way toward the dead trees of the quagmire. The old duffer from Willem's exclaimed that one of them was the Wizard for sure! And at the same moment that Randall Grim was taking aim and firing on them, the little man with the shock of black hair, a red scarf about his neck and wearing no coat, only a ragged sweater because of the thaw, swung down on a rope from a small loft shutter on another side of the barn. The huge, twisted-horned, yellow goat, Odin, leaped to the ground after without hesitating, stumbling on the high manure heap piled there, scrambling to his feet. And the pair were fleeing side by side into the blanket of fog upon the swamp.

Randall Grim called out that he'd never missed a shot on bird or beast before but he'd just wasted two shells. Everyone could see that but a single black feather was drifting down, and that the birds had disappeared. He ordered the eager blond spaniel, "Hurry! Start tracking."

Mrs. Coombs waited until the flock of men were all headed

for the shifting mist of the quagmire before running to the barn to rescue the cows. She knew where the latch was to lift the heavy bar inside, and she swung open the door. The cows were recalcitrant, not wanting to leave their breakfast, their lungs not yet stung by the smoke that was filling the interior as the flames licked up the walls and found the packed hay in the loft over them.

Finally, as she was tugging at the wide leather collar about the neck of the little belled Hebe, she heard the pounding hoofs of Sam Trail's gelding racing up the lane. Trail had seen the billowing smoke from the road and tossed his half-finished cigar from him, digging his heels into his horse's flanks so that it swung into its racing stride. He'd noticed, as he left Green-field Road, the mares of Schoolmaster Grim, tied to a tree, the tall and the little one, loaded down with panniers full of strapped, imitation-leather suitcases and bundles and bags, and his other shotgun on top. In the Wizard's yard, Sam Trail dropped the reins and leaped off and ran to the barn. Red forked flames were spurting from the roof at one end, and smoke was pouring from the wide loft opening from which the crow and buzzard had flown, as the hay caught and smouldered before bursting into fire.

Trail glimpsed the last of the running men and shouted, "What's going on!"

"Get Aphrodite, Mr. Trail!" she yelled, "and I'll get the old cow."

He hurried to obey, coughing, the smoke almost too thick for him to see the pen where the calf was. Mrs. Coombs followed to lead out the last of the brown beasts by the chain about its horns. "Where are the birds?" Trail gasped, as he lifted up the heavy baby cow.

"They left with Mr. Coombs," she told him, over the noise of the flames and the bawling of the cows in the yard, worried at the change in their routine and the smell of singed fur. "And Odin too."

They stood and gazed at the doomed building, which was fast becoming a shell that would collapse when the loft floor fell through and the inside of the barn became a great red cinder. Trail said, "There's no wind to speak of and the house is safe. How did it catch, and what's happening, and who are those men, and have the Sheriff and his deputies been here, and is that why everyone's running?"

Mrs. Coombs, her hair strands scraggling and the color gone from her face, patted the calf by her. "Thank you for saving Aphrodite, Mr. Trail. I thought I'd lose one of the beasts, anyway."

There was the sound of another beam falling, and a crackling as more hot timbers caught and blazed up. The two people went back near the porch of the house where the heat was not too strong, while Mrs. Coombs told Trail in a rambling fashion something of what had gone on. "Try to stick to the point, if you can," he asked.

"I'd just like to add," she said, "that this isn't the first time Mr. Coombs and I have had this particular problem with mankind. And it's usually caused by someone like that nice Schoolmaster. Would you ever think a man who knows all about how to train children would lead a pack of grown men on a shilly-shally affair like this?"

"Wasn't Henry Blackburn right at his side?" Trail asked. "And aren't you afraid they'll catch your husband and hang him? Or Mr. Grim will shoot him?"

"Mr. Blackburn's got the state of his household more than the world on his mind. It just happened that today they both came up together. Mr. Coombs is pretty safe out there. With the fog like this and him knowing his way about, I'm worried more for the rest of them." She gazed, resigned, as the barn crumbled and fell in and its remains blazed high for the moment, consuming finally the winter supply of hay and corn and Wizard's dried herbs and such, as well as various tools and odds and ends they'd had since the beginning of time and were used to. The woman looked at Trail, frowning. "Why would the Sheriff and his deputies be coming to see Wizard today, Mr. Trail?"

"I asked them to come."

She was reproachful. "Now why would you do that to Mr. Coombs? He doesn't like surprises. He'd like to be warned."

"I saw trouble when I first heard sheep thief and the Wizard's name being linked. I thought they'd have been here by now. Which reminds me of why I happened to come by, besides being hungry and wanting some of your tea in the middle of the morning by a small fire. I didn't figure on one that size."

"Since you can't do any good, but might get mixed up and hurt if you went into Endless Quagmire right now, come on in the house," Mrs. Coombs said, "and tell me why you're here, and anything else you can think of interesting. When it cools off out there, I'll try to study out what to do."

And so Trail pulled out the packet of Marn's pay and settled at his place at the table. "As far as rebuilding, I'll be glad to help out with money. And here's your daughter's."

"Now that's nice of her." She put it on the mantel where

Wizard Coombs kept his books. And then, though her hands trembled and were blackened, and her skirt was burned in a section, she shook the grate and put on the kettle.

Trail said, "Do you think that was the barn your husband saw burning in that mirror of his last week when he told me to warn Mr. Willem to watch out?"

Mrs. Coombs gave the parrot a piece of cutlery to parade with about the place. "One of Wizard's problems with his predictions is that there's so much guesswork involved, Mr. Trail. Land, I've told him he ought not to be so free in telling them to people."

Trail watched the swaggering Billy. "Is that bird I brought you a success?"

"Yes, except I figured he'd make conversation," Mrs. Coombs said, "and he just keeps saying over and over what somebody somewhere told him once to say. I don't mind, but you take those two tame birds of Wizard's, I can talk with them. They speak in their own tongue and me in mine, but we understand. I like Billy and I'm glad to have him around to celebrate the New Years with us since Marn's working out, but he's not bright."

While they talked back and forth with each other, their minds were on what was going on outside the small kitchen windows. There, as Mrs. Coombs hoped, Wizard was still safe. He and the big yellow goat led the yapping spaniel and the men, some silent and furious, others noisy and cursing, over the terrain, much of it bog and quicksand, with certain paths that were continuous that no one but Wizard knew, because he had made them and traveled them often, over bridges of fallen trees and dead roots. Once when Schoolmaster's spaniel, agile and swift, caught up with Wizard, Odin wheeled, abrupt, and rolled him over in the mud with his great crooked horns, and held him there, half-suffocating, before galloping after his master. Randall Grim aimed and shot once, believing he'd caught up with his victim, and was baffled when the noise echoed dully and the old man of Willem's shouted that it was but a shade of a man that he'd fired on.

Overhead, in nearby trees, the crow followed Coombs' progress, silent and staying hidden. Only once had he called out, when the goat butted the little long-haired dog, and then he shouted hoarsely in encouragement, "Hey, hey!" Above the swamp, the heavens cleared as the fog descended the mountain. The bald where the Blackburns lived became clothed in clear sunlight. Over Endless Quagmire, her feathers iridescent and shining in the yellow light, the vulture Venus soared, wheeling and circling, her dusky topaz eye so sharp and far-seeing that she knew at all moments where the Wizard, whom she thought of as closest of all creatures to her, ducked and scurried.

The dense vapor in the quagmire behaved as it did because of the recent weather change, and though the mountainside was slowly becoming free of mist, it would be afternoon before the low valley was. Repeatedly, it seemed to Schoolmaster, in the lead, the white stuff formed a wavering man with a wisping, trailing scarf. And then Grim thought, as he stumbled and fell headlong into the edge of a deep bog, that it must be a shade, because a man out there would have been drowned and trapped in the sucking mud. The others clearly saw the Wizard's ghost girl and reported it later, her white form solid and shaped, and some beast ran after that could be the long-and-golden-horned unicorn.

One time Wizard Coombs felt a spark of fear, for he broke through one of the rotting bridges into quicksand. But he spoke commandingly to Odin, who thought of him just as Venus did, and the animal returned to stand elbow-deep in the mud, his long side whiskers and beard dripping, while Wizard threw his red scarf about the horns and the thick shaggy neck of the strong-scented animal, and pulled himself safe.

In later years, Randall Grim, in cities outside, told his scarce-believed tale; and though his passion in time abated, his sorrow never did. For Wizard, knowing his problem was the keen-nosed dog and not the bumbling men, led the spaniel squarely over a well-concealed iron predator trap set for weasels and martin, who robbed nests of the wild wood ducks and mallards and widgeon of the swamp. It snapped, and the dog was wounded and struggling. Randall Grim heard him just ahead yelping, and saw the movements in the mist, and thought at last the spaniel had got the Wizard down and held him by his tattered sweater. Grim raised his shotgun and emptied the barrels and killed his own beloved companion. And then it seemed to him a reality that Coombs had been indeed under the dog and had melted away just after turning the bullet. Nothing ever afterwards changed that opinion of Schoolmaster Grim's. And he felt an increased need to lay his hands now on his prey in retaliation.

Wizard Coombs' plan was to keep circling until he tired his pursuers. No man could help him now, he felt, only the useful fog and his skill upon his own territory. And so he was surprised when he heard loud hollas, and horses descending Bald Mountain and approaching the edge of the quagmire. He decided to see if it meant more pursuers or valid assistance, and advanced cautiously. He recognized the Sheriff's voice, a familiar one, not unfriendly. Trusting to luck, he headed for it, through the near-impenetrable moving mist that cleared as the ground became drier.

The two deputies were yelling, "Hands off the Wizard, you men, or off to jail you all go. And let's not see anyone slipping away. The party's over! And let's see the shotgun we heard fired a few minutes ago. And any other guns, and quickly!"

Wizard Coombs, followed by the muddy, amber-eyed, enormous, shaggy goat, himself disheveled and dripping, came out of the swamp and up to the Sheriff, complaining, high-voiced, "I had an idea, if the fog lasted long enough, to drown the whole pack of them in time. And then I'd spend the rest of my life charging fees to show people their ghosts!"

The Sheriff was dry. "I heard you got rid of your illegal fawn and swan. Is that true?"

"Take a look," Wizard said, "any time. And what are you doing here? How do you know about this chase?"

"We've been talking to old Mrs. Blackburn and young Sheepman's wife, too, who told us a story about some charm you sold her that was no good and she got cheated. And they said young Sheepman's temper was up and he'd collected a whole fancy gang from the countryside to back him while he took over the law for himself. I told you this would happen some day, Coombs. Your business is a touchy one."

"Well, before that gang gets here, I'm heading back to my barn to see if my wife had the luck to put out the fire they started. I saw a barn burn down in one of my gadgets a week ago, and I'm hoping it wasn't my own."

The Sheriff shrugged. "It's your own fault, Coombs, if it has. You ought to be more careful about casting spells!"

Wizard sighed, tired out. "All I want is for you to net that trigger-happy bunch and send them home. I look on them all as future customers. You just tell them I'm not hanging this time. I'll face the future as it comes." And Wizard Coombs slipped into the fog again.

Within the next few minutes, the Sheriff collected four out of the pack: Henry Blackburn and those of Willem's men who were close on his heels, all muddy, red-faced, panting. Others would get away, the most clever managing to make it clear back to their cabins on Dutchman's place without being spotted by the alert deputies. Some of the more awkward or unlucky would be picked up one by one, as they groped and scrambled, bewildered, out of the treacherous area later.

The deputies mocked Blackburn on two counts: first for letting a little woman like his pretty wife, Katrin, bulldoze him into keeping his shepherd dog Tam in, so that the whole sheep flock was unguarded all of every night long, while Henry kept his wife warm. The deputies laughed at that, and said the sheep had been sliding off the same dangerous rock cliff where Sheepman Blackburn fell, and Henry ought to tend to business and fence it off. And a little bunch of baaing woollies had been sighted about ten miles from Blackburn's cabin the other way, and why didn't he set out after them, and they'd describe the place? And secondly, they railed at young Blackburn for being taken in by a noisy troublemaker like Schoolmaster Randall Grim, whom they were looking forward to having a talk with also!

While they were making game of Henry, back behind a great hollow snag was silent Randall Grim, still shocked by the sudden death of his little dog, who lay back there in the claws of that trap and done in by his best-beloved master. He was further shocked, in this moment of horror and unreality, to hear the guffaws and ribbing of Henry by the delighted deputies. Taking his chances on the dangers of the swamp rather than the humiliation of ridicule as well as questioning, Grim turned and headed for the Greenfield Road. The way was the one he'd taken that time when he'd come to the meadow to see Marn Coombs and fallen for her. He went roundabout the Wizard's shack now, and had no opportunity to observe whether the barn had burned fully or not. He was almost regretting the past hours, especially since the adventure had had no successful conclusion, but had become a comedy, a fiasco. He reached his mares scratched and bruised, his brown curly hair wet and grimy from when he had fallen that time full-length in the bog; his gun was lost and also his knit cap; his high-neck sweater was torn. He was glad to mount and start on his journey toward Greenfield.

The reason no one in Wizard's shack saw Schoolmaster stumble along the foggy far cover of trees and reach the pike and retrieve his mares was that Mrs. Coombs and Sam Trail at that moment were rushing to the edge of the clearing where Wizard was approaching, limping, his hand for support in the long hairs of Odin's back. The crow, noisy now, was fluttering just ahead of the pair, squawking and silly, while the vulture, in response to Wizard's call, had come down and was hopping along nearby, picking up sticks to carry a while and ducking her head whenever Coombs looked at her.

"Did the Sheriff finally get to you?" Trail called. "I asked him to get a move on!"

"Are you the one who sent him? I wondered how he got

there. And what for? To make trouble for me, Mr. Trail?" Wizard was rather shrill, fired up.

"Those were my very words, Wizard," his wife put in, "but Mr. Trail heard folks calling you sheep thief and saying hanging and told the Sheriff to investigate. I thought you always knew everything going on, and here's something right under your own nose and all about you and you never knew it." She laughed at him, indulgent.

Wizard growled, looking over at the coals where his barn had stood. The brown cows and calf had wandered into the woods where the other fowl, the wild turkeys and chickens and the pet squirrel, had fled when the flames grew high. "How'll I stand the loss!"

"My gracious," Mrs. Coombs cried, "let me get some dry sweaters and socks and shirts, and give you some hot tea before we figure on that."

"I'll help you out, Mr. Coombs," Trail said swiftly, feeling the soft package in his pocket where the scarf for Marn lay in its tissue and ribbon. "That's what money's for. I'll turn over whatever you need, and you can pay it back in different ways."

"If you're speaking of my daughter, Mr. Trail," Wizard told him, cutting, "I'm not in any way interested."

Mrs. Coombs soothed her husband. "Marn sent her pay by Mr. Trail. I put it up on the mantel. That ought to make you feel better."

Wizard looked at his wife. "She got it a week ago. Why the delay? And did she send half or two-thirds like she promised?"

"It's my fault, as I could explain if I had a chance," Trail told him.

"Don't bother." Wizard ignored the young man, as he went past him and up the steps of the house, leaving the three curiosity-minded creatures, the yellow buck and the two birds, to investigate the interesting changes in their home yard. Before Coombs went in, he turned, his rumpled shock of hair upright, his deep-set eyes dark and shadowed. "Next time you see our daughter, you tell her for me that if she wants to come back home, it's all right with me and I'll take care of her. Tell her that stands whatever trouble she's in, too!"

"I happen to be going over to Willem's right now," Trail said, as he and Mrs. Coombs followed Wizard into the kitchen, where the birds were beginning to chirp and twitter and the young raccoon came out from behind his chair to be petted "to pick up some mares. I'm sure to see Miss Coombs, and I'll give her the message."

"I didn't like the way those fiddle-faddle men talked witch," Mrs. Coombs sighed.

"You needn't worry," Trail told her. "That Sheriff's strong-minded about law breakers." And he asked Wizard Coombs, "Do you want a cigar?"

But Wizard wouldn't answer, scrubbing at the sink, splashing the water, while Mrs. Coombs chattered on about this and that to bring her husband to a more cheerful mood. And so Sam Trail lit one for himself and left a couple on the table and was striding out to the gelding, eager because he had all kinds of things to tell Marn Coombs, and mounting into the saddle. Mrs. Coombs' steady voice followed him down the mist-dim road, lost after a while as the distance between them increased. "And ask our daughter how that swan is that her father sold Mr. Willem for a present for her!"

But then Sam Trail was taken aback when he arrived at the Willem kitchen door, where the fog, although not as thick and damp as in the swamp area, still like a huge beast prowled; it withdrew to sit on quiet haunches and watch the valley house a while before it would go away. Marn let Trail in, and he began to give her the news of how he'd forgot to leave her money off and it had been delayed a week and he was sorry. And how he'd met Stableman's wife on the road and she'd been the first to warn him of the trouble beginning to take place. Marn paid no heed at all. "Why aren't you listening to me?" he demanded.

She frowned, "What did you say, Mr. Trail?"

"That Schoolmaster Grim and Henry Blackburn led a mob of men down from the bald and burned your father's barn and tried to catch him in the quagmire and hang him!"

"I'm sorry," she said. "I don't understand." And she was weeping then, the great tears, which she didn't know were there, coming down as she walked back and forth.

Trail said, "What's wrong, Marn Coombs? Tell me right out."

And she said, "Mr. Willem says I must come down from my room in the attic to live below here with him."

"Say you will not," Trail advised, matter-of-fact.

She shook her head. "I have to go somewhere, and I don't know where or how, and there's nothing I can think of to do."

"Dutchman Willem can't make you do anything."

"And I don't want to bother you with it, either, Mr. Trail."

The man felt a desperation in him to stop the steady strong tears, and said, "Come with me then, to my father's farm."

"No. For I don't want to live that way, and I don't know

why I'm telling you this, either. It's none of your affair. And there's nothing you can do."

Trail pulled the tissue-and-ribboned gift from his pocket and tore it open, and the long blue silk fluttered as he shoved it at her. "I picked that out for you," he said loudly, and surprised himself by declaring abruptly, "And I'll marry you, too!"

She looked at the scarf, bewildered. "I couldn't do that. This is my own worry and nobody else's."

"If you'll have me," Trail said, elated by the logical turn events had taken, for once not feeling awkward and as though he had to smooth his hair and prepare his appearance, at ease with this small woman in the fragrant clean room.

"I'm the Wizard's daughter and you're a rich man's son, and I won't. But thank you for asking me," Marn sighed.

"My mother will like the way you run a house," he said. "And my father, the way you've been brought up to handle animals."

"I'm sorry," she said. "But I'm in trouble, too. Mr. Willem knows, and that's part of his bargain, that he'd take and care for a child of mine. And I won't let one go to him."

Trail told her, pleased, "We'll raise it the way your father did his birds and goat, and you with your wild deer out there, so it will think I'm its parent the way they do!"

"No." And the blue scarf rippled in her hands in the dim light from the kitchen windows. There the red cardinals watched from their perches; their door was open nowadays, so they flew about the room and returned to the cage when they liked.

"You might as well," the young man said, "for I'll never find one like you, and I have a hard time getting my way with women I admire, and I'd appreciate it."

"I won't have much to bring with me," she said.

"Then you've decided you'll come! We'll need the swan, too; your mother asked after him."

"I turned Jupiter free as soon as I could," she said. "I've just got the fawn."

"The unicorn," Trail corrected her, and bent to kiss Marn's mouth, where she stood studying still. "Now what?"

"I like Mr. Willem," she told him, "and whatever will he do, Mr. Trail?"

"Could you call me Sam now, Marn?"

And they heard him then, the master of the farm stamping up the graveled walk, looking for a cup of coffee. Marn frowned. "How are we going to say it to him, Sam?" And she took Trail's hand.

"What's this? Eh!" Dutchman roared when he saw them standing there like two innocents in the middle of his kitchen.

"I'm going to marry your housekeeper," Trail said, firm, "and right away, too."

Dutchman shouted at that. "She's not ready for marriage, and I'm making a bargain with her right now. If you want Miss Coombs, you'd better wait a year at least."

"No," Trail said, "and I plan to spend everything I've got on her and whoever it turns out to be."

"I'm getting your coffee now, Mr. Willem," Marn said. "And I promise not to leave until I find a woman to take over here that suits you."

"There's not such a one in this countryside," the master said, and breathed heavily as he settled in his great chair at the table's head. He sipped on the hot coffee Marn brought for the two of them. He accepted the warm, morning-baked plum kuchen that fell apart before his knife and fork.

"I've got one in mind," Marn said, thoughtful, "and I'll go see if she's willing, which she might be now."

Dutchman sighed. "I don't like having you leave here, Wizard's daughter. It's been the nearest to the way it was when Bertha was alive and keeping my house. All but in that fashion I told you of the night before last, when I bid you move down from that small room and come live with me."

Marn stood at his chair side where his strong arms lay along the wood arms. "I'm sorry I couldn't."

They paused there in a half-dream, the three of them, thinking on how their lives were suddenly changing from what they had been only briefly before. And then Trail began telling what he knew of the incidents of the morning, and how the Sheriff had arrived, and now there would be no more talk, in the open at least, regarding wizards and witches. Dutchman was astonished that he had known nothing of it. Farmer had mentioned to him the secret meetings, but made game of them, saying it was the hired hands who were of no account or had scores to settle, like Stableman, who composed them. Farmer had thought it would blow over just as soon as the Wrestling Schoolmaster quitted these parts.

Trail told Marn, "I've a message from your father to come home any time you want and it's all right with him. And he said that stood for whatever problems you had bothering you, too."

"Was Father hurt any way?" asked Marn. "Is the barn truly gone, and are Hebe and Aphrodite safe?"

And hoofbeats were outside, the law arriving: the Sheriff and his deputies, wanting to advise Dutchman to get after his men, so they'd think next time they got invited to follow some leaders. The Sheriff reported, too, that enough money had been collected from the pair who had run the show to rebuild Wizard Coombs' barn, and the money was in Wizard's hands, too. "Your father said to tell you he's satisfied about the whole thing and wants to know when you're coming home," the Sheriff told Marn. "He said to say he knew what your trouble was and didn't mind at all."

Marn flushed. "Thank you then. I've got no troubles." And stood close to Sam Trail.

Dutchman was curt. "I'll ride my men on this, I assure you. Eh? And I'll say, too, that the fine I'm levying on that Stableman of mine, who's been running about instead of working, is that his wife is to be banned from this place! And if he stays himself, he's got to get one less pretty and not so lecherous." And Willem accepted the long white clay pipe Marn brought him, filled as he liked, with tobacco packed not too tightly or loosely. He lit it and began to speak again, but was interrupted.

For another visitor was arriving, disheveled and distraught, her long braids undone from the pins, now lost, that had held it in a circle about her head. Her hair was tangled and her bare arms were scratched. She gasped on seeing the Sheriff, "Marn there's in danger! I got lost in the fog coming down from the mountain, and I've been all morning getting here. I was afraid I'd be too late!"

"It appears that this countryside is made up of your friends as well as enemies, Miss Coombs," the Sheriff said.

A deputy added, "We wondered why we didn't see you up at your brother's cabin this morning, Miss Blackburn."

Nell sighed, "Then she's all right," and went over close to Marn and whispered, "Can you tell me how our Henry, feeling as he did about you in the summertime, could this winter name you a witch?"

"Two reasons, Nell," Marn said softly. "The Blackburn temper and his love for Katrin, too. It's all mixed up, and it doesn't matter. Come and sit here at the table and have coffee and Mr. Willem's favorite plum cake. I'm just about to put some out for the Sheriff and his men and Sam."

The smoke from Dutchman's pipe hung fragrant over the table as he looked up at Nell Blackburn, rosy-faced because she'd found Marn unharmed and because of the effort of her long journey on foot. "Seat her by me, Miss Coombs," he directed.

Marn drew out the chair to his right and Nell took it, while the others found places down the table, knowing how untidy she must appear in this well-ordered kitchen, her dress torn and her hair about her shoulders. Her hazel Scotch eyes were bright, and to the Dutchman she seemed vulnerable and not at all severe the way she'd used to be, as she smiled at him. "Thank you."

"If Miss Blackburn doesn't mind hearing about her brother," the Sheriff said, as he began to eat, "I'd like to finish what I started to say about fining the ringleaders, when she came in. We'll have to be on the road in a few minutes."

"You mean you took Henry's money away?" Nell said. "It's only his due. I don't feel sorry for my brother."

"It was a great amount, too," the Sheriff said. "And Blackburn claimed it all came from the sale of two red oxen, which we know isn't the truth."

"Sheriff," Trail said, "my father wanted those beasts, and he handed Mr. Blackburn the first price he named for them."

"Well," a deputy said, "it's enough to rebuild half of a small barn."

"And as for that teacher," the Sheriff grinned, "we apprehended him down the Greenfield Pike and stripped him of pretty near all the wages paid him a few days ago by the County Board."

"He had it in a saddlebag strapped to his tall black horse," a deputy said, "and told us to take every last cent if we liked. He said he was done with deciding wrong from right for the rest of his days and missed his spaniel, too."

"We'll keep an eye on him, Mr. Willem," the Sheriff said, getting to his feet, the deputies following suit, "if he stays around Greenfield. He had company that looked like she was leaving Old Mountain country, too: a woman riding side-wise on the panniers of a little shaggy bay mare. I've seen her before, that good-looking, trollopy one that ran away with your Farmer a while ago, and you brought back here."

"That saves me from throwing her off the place," Dutchman said, as the men left. "And who can tell, maybe that talkative Schoolmaster will get on with Stableman's wife. You never can tell about a woman, which way she'll go. Eh?" And his eyes fell, condemning, on Marn.

"Mr. Willem," Marn said, bold, stopping beside Sam Trail's chair, so he reached for her hand and held it and that gave her courage, "the one I was thinking of asking if she wanted this position was Nell Blackburn here!"

"Marn's marrying me," Sam Trail told Nell. "And this is a good time to name conditions with Mr. Willem, too."

Dutchman drew on his pipe a last time and knocked it out in the aged silver bowl with the Dutch figures scrolled into it that was before his plate. "Well, Miss Blackburn? I'm not speaking of marriage this day, but of business. Eh?" And his shrewd blue eyes narrowed. "I'll pay what you ask that's fair. And bonus when earned."

Nell looked at him, and Mr. Willem seemed an easier man than she'd ever dreamed before. She wondered if it were because she'd grown to dislike Randall Grim so quickly, or because bachelors were rare in the countryside, or because she'd begun to fight with her lordly brother and couldn't bear the home cabin any more. But she said, "Can I sit outside and sew on the porch after supper and do no work at all then if I like?"

"Every evening, if you've a mind," Dutchman told her.

"And if my Ma wants to come down, can I bring her, for she's old and depends on me and Henry wants her to work all the time? Katrin will have her hands full when the baby comes, and forget to bring Ma her tea at the hours she likes it."

"I don't mind a house full," Willem said. "What I can't abide is an empty one."

"And if I want to spin and weave and take the prize at the yearly Fair in Greenfield?"

"You're welcome," he said, short.

"Then I'll take the position," Nell laughed. To herself she was trying out the name Nell Willem and not minding it a bit.

"There's nothing to hold us here any more," Sam Trail cried to Marn. "Go and pack your things, and we'll load them on one of that string of mares. I'll take your fawn on the saddle with me or it can follow behind. I want to take you home!"

"I might as well start to work right now," Nell said. "I'll clear the table, and you forget about everything but your new life, Marn."

Dutchman, while his freshly hired housekeeper took over, leaned back in his chair, brooding, looking at the Wizard's daughter standing by young Trail, clasping a long blue soft scarf in one hand. He asked, "Is there something around this house that you'd like for a wedding gift, Miss Coombs? I've never known your likes and dislikes, although you know mine. And all I ever gave you was that big white bird, and I watched you turn it loose just a little time after I made it your own."

"No," she said. "It's been gift enough that I've been a respected woman here working in your kitchen. I never felt that way before."

But the Dutchman thumped on his chair arms, emphatic, raising his voice. "I insist! Whatever it is."

She looked about the room. "Then could I have one of those silver candlesticks that were Mrs. Willem's? They mean the way I've been treated here to me."

"Take them both! Eh?" Dutchman ordered her.

"No," Marn said, "one is enough, and sometime you might want the other for your daughter Katrin."

Marn went over to the sideboard and took the well-polished stick, and it gleamed and the blue silk trembled as she ran light-footed from the room. She went up the two flights of stairs to pack her few possessions before she would ride away and become Mrs. Sam Trail and live in a big house on a farm full of mares and mules, where her fawn would feel at home, and she could have any animal or pet she pleased. Marn thought of the words that were in the huge book Mr. Willem owned, below in the bedroom, that he didn't even know were there for anyone to read: *My beloved spoke and said unto me, Rise up and come away. The flowers appear on the earth; the time of the singing of birds is come.*